Cal pretended for an instant that the toddler nestled against him was his child, and that Emma was his wife.

"That's the sweetest thing I've ever seen," Emma whispered, tears shimmering in her eyes. "That little toddler is so trusting, leaning against you on the picnic bench that way."

"Maybe the kid just knows a good guy when she sees one," Cal said.

Emma turned toward him then, her lips curved upward. When his lips touched hers again, she welcomed him with a soft moan, and he tumbled deeply into the kiss. *She's the one,* he thought, deepening the kiss.

But that was ridiculous. He and Emma were becoming good friends, and they were sexually attracted, but otherwise, they had little to nothing in common. Right now, though, he couldn't remember why that mattered....

Dear Reader,

Summer is a time for backyard barbecues and fun family gatherings. But with all the running around you'll be doing, don't forget to make time for yourself. And there's no better way to escape than with a Special Edition novel. Each month we offer six brand-new romances about people just like you—trying to find the perfect balance between life, career, family, romance....

To start, pick up *Hunter's Woman* by bestselling author Lindsay McKenna. Continuing her riveting MORGAN'S MERCENARIES: THE HUNTERS series, she pairs a strong-willed THAT SPECIAL WOMAN! with the ruggedly handsome soldier who loved her once—and is determined to win her back!

Every woman longs to be noticed for her true beauty—and the heroine of Joan Elliott Pickart's latest book, *The Irresistible Mr. Sinclair,* is no different; this novel features another wonderful hero in the author's exciting cross-line miniseries with Silhouette Desire, THE BACHELOR BET. And for those hankering to return to the beloved Western land that Myrna Temte takes us to in her HEARTS OF WYOMING series, don't miss *The Gal Who Took the West.*

And it's family that brings the next three couples together—a baby on the way in *Penny Parker's Pregnant!* by Stella Bagwell, the next installment in her TWINS ON THE DOORSTEP series that began in Silhouette Romance and will return there in January 2000; adorable twins in Robin Lee Hatcher's *Taking Care of the Twins;* and a millionaire's heir-to-be in talented new author Teresa Carpenter's *The Baby Due Date.*

I hope you enjoy these six emotional must-reads written *by* women like you, *for* women like you!

Sincerely,

Karen Taylor Richman
Senior Editor

Please address questions and book requests to:
Silhouette Reader Service
U.S.: 3010 Walden Ave., P.O. Box 1325, Buffalo, NY 14269
Canadian: P.O. Box 609, Fort Erie, Ont. L2A 5X3

MYRNA TEMTE

THE GAL WHO TOOK THE WEST

Silhouette®

SPECIAL EDITION®

Published by Silhouette Books
America's Publisher of Contemporary Romance

To the Elf Princess. May her spirit and confidence live forever.

My thanks for help with research goes to: Debra Sims, Douglas, Wyoming; Mr. Jeronimo Villalta, for information about Harley-Davidson motorcycles; and for medical information to Susie Ready, B.S.N., and Jolene Haskins, A.R.P.N., both of Sacred Heart Medical Center, Spokane, Washington. Any mistakes are my own.

 SILHOUETTE BOOKS

ISBN 0-373-24257-3

THE GAL WHO TOOK THE WEST

Copyright © 1999 by Myrna Temte

Visit us at www.romance.net

Printed in U.S.A.

Books by Myrna Temte

Silhouette Special Edition

Wendy Wyoming #483
Powder River Reunion #572
The Last Good Man Alive #643
*For Pete's Sake #739
*Silent Sam's Salvation #745
*Heartbreak Hank #751
The Forever Night #816
Room for Annie #861
A Lawman for Kelly #1075
†Pale Rider #1124
**A Father's Vow #1172
†Urban Cowboy #1181
†Wrangler #1238
†The Gal Who Took the West #1257

*Cowboy Country
**Montana Mavericks: Return to Whitehorn
†Hearts of Wyoming

Silhouette Books

Montana Mavericks
Sleeping with the Enemy

MYRNA TEMTE

grew up in Montana and attended college in Wyoming, where she met and married her husband. Marriage didn't necessarily mean settling down for the Temtes—they have lived in six different states, including Washington, where they currently reside. "Moving so much is difficult," the author says, "but it is also wonderful stimulation for a writer."

Though always a "readaholic," Myrna never dreamed of becoming an author. But while spending time at home to care for her first child, she began to seek an outlet from the neverending duties of housekeeping and child rearing. She started reading romances and soon became hooked, both as a reader and a writer. Now Myrna appreciates the best of all possible worlds—a loving family and a challenging career that lets her set her own hours and turn her imagination loose.

McBride Family Tree

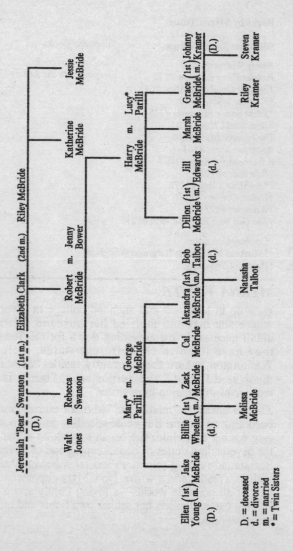

Chapter One

"**S**ure is dead around here, boss," Sylvia Benson groused, settling her wide rump onto a bar stool. "I swear I thought that shift would never end."

Cal McBride gave the tired waitress a sympathetic smile, fixed her a weak whiskey ditch and set it in front of her on the bar. "Wednesdays are always quiet, Syl."

She took a swallow from her drink and wrinkled her nose at him, then muttered, "Serve sissy drinks like that and it'll be dead here all the time."

Cal chuckled and shook his head. In the ten years he'd owned Cal's Place, the best—and often the only—bar and restaurant in Sunshine Gap, Wyoming, he and Sylvia had worked out a friendly bickering routine. He'd inherited her from the previous owner, and while she was loud, nosy and occasionally crude, the customers loved her.

She was also loyal, dependable and a skilled waitress. She didn't take much guff off of anyone, but her heart was as big as Yellowstone National Park. Cal intended to keep her on his staff forever if possible. In a town as small as Sunshine Gap, good help was harder to find than customers on a Wednesday.

Sylvia lit up, inhaled a drag and blew out a stream of smoke, then took another swig from her drink and banged the glass back down on the bar. "I'm tellin' you, Cal, we need some *action* in this town, or we're all gonna die of boredom."

"Once those movie folks start showing up, we'll have more business than we can handle."

"You *hope*," Sylvia said.

"You're hoping for the same thing, aren't you?"

"Yeah, me and everybody else. But you'd better *really* hope those folks don't cause any trouble. There's still lots of grumbling about bringing so many Californians here."

"Last I heard, their money spends as good as anybody else's," Cal said.

Sylvia propped her chin on the heel of one hand and scrunched up her face as if she were giving his remarks serious consideration. Before she could get out an appropriately pithy response, however, the roar of a motorcycle engine ripped through the momentary silence. Cal exchanged a surprised glance with her, then dried his hands and stepped from behind the bar to check it out.

He opened the front door and watched a big, chrome-studded bike make an illegal U-turn at the end of the block and come back toward the bar. A small, secret part of him envied the rider for the freedom the gleaming, red-and-black Harley-Davidson motorcycle represented. He shoved that part back down inside himself where it belonged.

He had too many commitments in Sunshine Gap even to dream about taking off on a bike like that. He wouldn't mind getting a closer look at it, though. A guy didn't see many motorcycles this far from the interstate. The Gap was more of a pickup and horse trailer kind of town.

The bike slowed, its engine noise dropping to a throaty grumble when the driver turned into a space barely five feet from Cal's door. With a flick of a wrist, the driver silenced the engine. The stranger rocked the bike back onto its kickstand, then swung his right leg over the saddle and stood upright.

He was a short, wiry little fella, and he wore black leather chaps over a pair of jeans, hiking boots, black leather gloves and a matching jacket that looked at least two sizes too big for him. The pool-playing cowboys joined Cal in the doorway, watching with interest while the driver pulled off the neon-red helmet covering his entire head.

To Cal's surprise, a delicate, decidedly feminine face emerged. The woman had big blue eyes, a slightly square chin and the cheekbones of a fashion model. Setting the helmet on the seat, she yanked down the jacket's zipper and fanned the open sides, revealing a skin-hugging tank top as red as her helmet.

The top obviously left no room for a bra, not that she needed one by any stretch of the imagination—and man, oh, man, were they all ever imagining. She reached up toward the back of her head, yanked out some kind of a clip and a sun-streaked light-brown ponytail fell past her shoulders. Her hair was mashed from the helmet, but Cal figured it ought to be real pretty when it was combed.

Then she peeled off her jacket and draped it over the handlebars. Her arms were tanned and slender, but with muscles as well defined as an Olympic athlete's. Cal barely had time to wonder about that when she leaned down to poke around in a storage compartment behind the seat. Her jeans pulled tight across her backside, delineating every curve and indentation for her fascinated audience.

"Damn," Ronnie Black breathed in Cal's left ear, stretching the word into two syllables.

Joe Wright gave a low whistle in Cal's right ear, then drawled, "Oh, honey."

"Honey?" Cal snorted. "That's trouble on two legs, boys."

Ronnie leaned closer to Cal, his gaze trained on the

woman's sweetly rounded bottom. "Bet they're great legs, though."

As if to confirm Cal's assessment, however, the woman straightened up, shot them an irritated glance and propped her fists on her hips. "What're you bozos looking at? Haven't you ever seen a woman before?"

Cal wished she hadn't done that. He really did. Most guys with half a brain would run like hell from a woman with a temper. Unfortunately he wasn't one of them.

Call him a fool, but he'd always found a woman with a temper…exciting. Challenging. Alluring. He shifted his weight to his right leg and tugged at the bottom of his vest, but it didn't stop the message his libido sent to his body. Even now, right here on Main Street in front of God and everybody, he could feel himself getting excited.

It didn't matter. This woman might be the stuff of late-night fantasies, but he was well past the age when he might have acted on that sort of foolishness. Every time he tended bar, he heard story after story about love gone wrong, and most of them started with some idiot who didn't know when to keep his pants zipped. That was just sex, of course.

And love? Well, it sure hadn't brought much happiness to anyone he knew. After seeing all of the tears and anguish falling in love had caused in his own family, Cal wanted no part of it. Oh, he was sick and tired of living like a monk and being the odd man out at every social gathering in Sunshine Gap.

He'd always wanted kids of his own, too, and he had great respect for the institution of marriage. But he was far too practical to make the same mistakes everyone else did. A smart man married someone who fit into his life-style and made him feel comfortable, not someone who stirred things up like…well, like some sexy, hot-tempered babe.

Which was exactly why Cal intended to marry his best friend Sandy Bishop on August twenty-fourth. She was sweet, pretty and intelligent, exactly the kind of woman he was supposed to marry. She shared his opinion about love, and neither of them had to pretend otherwise.

Keeping all of that firmly in mind, Cal shoved Ronnie and Joe back into the bar and smiled at the woman. "Beg your pardon, ma'am. Come on in. Your first drink is on the house."

She raised her chin. Though she was at least eight inches shorter than he was, she still managed to give the impression of looking down her nose at him. "Is this your...establishment?"

"Yes, ma'am." He raised one hand, indicating the sign mounted on the building. "Name's Cal McBride. Welcome to Sunshine Gap."

Offering him neither her hand nor her name, she gave him a surprisingly regal nod. "Thank you."

Taking her sweet time about it, she draped her jacket over her right arm, held her helmet against her hip with her left and crossed the cracked sidewalk. He stepped back to allow her entrance, walking behind the bar to find her a menu and give her time to get settled. She paused for a moment, as if allowing her eyes to adjust to the diminished light indoors.

Then she strolled across the room to a table beside the plate glass window that looked out onto Main Street. Stowing her belongings on the chair beside the window, she sat on the adjacent one. Most women walking into a strange bar alone acted a little tentative, but every move this woman made spoke of confidence and attitude.

Lord, did she ever have an attitude.

Sylvia shot Cal an amused, knowing look. "Careful there, hon. You're about to drool in the lemon wedges."

Cal scowled at her. "Isn't it about time you went home and rested up for tomorrow? Thursday's usually real busy."

Chuckling, the waitress shook her head. "And miss the best show this town's seen in twenty years?" Her gaze drifted to the mirror behind the bar, and Cal knew she was watching the biker woman. A second later, Sylvia sputtered with laughter, then cupped one hand around the side of her mouth. "Don't look now, boss, but that gal's got a tattoo on her left bazoomba."

"What?" Cal jerked up his head, barely catching himself in time to stop a full-fledged stare.

Sylvia pounded one hand on the bar and hee-hawed at him. The other woman looked toward the commotion. When her eyes met Cal's, he felt a wave of heat rush up the back of his neck and into his face and ears. Sylvia cackled louder. Cal swore under his breath, grabbed a menu and stalked across the room to take the woman's order. He would not, absolutely would *not* look at anything below her chin.

"We serve food in here if you're hungry," he said, shoving the menu at her. "What'll you have to drink?"

"A light beer. Whatever you have on tap is fine." She flipped open the menu. Cal started to turn away, but she said, "Wait. I'll order a sandwich now, too."

He turned back around. The woman's head was bent over the menu. His gaze was irresistibly drawn to her hair, and then just sort of naturally followed the line of her bedraggled ponytail where it curved across her left shoulder and dangled in front of her…chest. In an automatic motion, she flipped the ponytail behind her shoulder.

The motion had been quick, but not quick enough to prevent her tank top from gaping and giving him a glimpse of a rounded breast and the top quarter inch of what had to be a tattoo headed for her cleavage. He'd seen a dainty, swirly thing, but he couldn't tell what it was or what it might be attached to. His fingertips itched to pluck the cloth just far enough away from her skin to let him see the whole design.

Suddenly the woman slapped the menu shut. Cal dragged his gaze back up to her face. Her eyes held a cynical, weary expression that plainly said she'd caught him studying her chest. He felt his neck and ears get hot all over again, though he couldn't have said why he should be embarrassed. A woman who'd get a tattoo there must expect folks to look at it.

"I'll have a cheeseburger and fries." She shoved the menu back at him. "Well done on the burger and hold the beer until the food's ready."

Before he'd finished jotting down her order, she pushed back her chair, grabbed her jacket and headed for the ladies' room. He watched her backside twitch back and forth under those snug jeans until the door swung shut behind her. Shaking his head in disgust at himself, he told Sylvia to hold the fort, hurried to the kitchen, hung the ticket on the cook's wheel, and dinged the bell. Nobody answered.

Emma Barnes sighed with sheer joy when she found the ladies' room unoccupied. Once finished, Emma washed her hands, then wet a paper towel and wiped away as much road grit as she could.

Her hair looked wild, but since she'd have to put her helmet back on, she didn't see any profit in combing out the tangles now. Those idiot cowboys would probably think she was trying to pretty herself up for their benefit. As if she would ever be *that* desperate for male companionship.

It was too bad Cal McBride was such a jerk, or she might have considered primping a bit for him. He was huge—six foot three at least, with a brawny build that made him seem even bigger. His jeans—sporting a sharp crease, no less—crisp white shirt, colorful brocade vest and black cowboy boots fit him as if they were tailor-made. Though she suspected he often wore a Stetson hat, he hadn't worn one today, and she was glad he hadn't. It would have covered up his thick, glossy black hair. The man could star in shampoo commercials.

As if all of that didn't make him attractive enough, he had a full, but neatly trimmed black mustache, coffee-colored eyes and swarthy skin combined with rugged features to make an interesting face rather than a pretty-boy one. Although, now that she thought about it, when he smiled, a boyish dimple appeared just below the left tip of his mustache. Not that he'd smiled much at her.

Ruthlessly honest with herself, if with no one else, she had to admit that when he hadn't been trying to see down the front of her shirt, he'd looked at her as if she were an alien being, rather than an attractive woman. Did she care what he thought of her? Not enough to worry. She'd come to Wyoming to do a job, not to find a man. Her feminine ego would just have to get over his lack of enthusiasm.

She wouldn't be here long, anyway. As soon as she finished doing her stunts for *Against the Wind,* she would go on to the next job. If her agent had managed to arrange another one for her. Of course, this was a higher caliber production than she'd ever worked on before. With luck she'd make good contacts on the set. She might even find a better agent.

Bracing herself to go back into the bar, Emma shouldered her way out of the rest room. The cowboys at the pool table stopped their game and stared at her when she emerged. She pretended not to notice them. She didn't see Cal McBride, but the woman wearing a pink uniform, white running shoes and carrying fifty extra pounds was still perched on a bar stool, smoking and studying Emma with intense interest. Jeez, didn't these people ever see strangers? All this attention was giving her the creeps.

Emma paused beside the bar and spoke to the other woman. "Excuse me? Do you know where the Flying M Ranch is?"

"Why, sure. Cal's part of the family that owns it." The woman's eyes sparkled and when she smiled, her round face and bow mouth reminded Emma of a naughty cherub. She stuck her hand out. "I'm Sylvia Benson. What's your name, honey?"

Emma gave Sylvia's hand a quick shake. "Emma Barnes."

"Glad to know ya, Emma. Sit down, take a load off, and I'll get you a drink."

"I've already ordered one, thanks."

"Where are you from?"

"Los Angeles."

Sylvia's eyes widened. "You one of those movie people we've been hearin' so much about?"

Emma nodded. "I work with the stunt crew."

"The stunt crew?" Sylvia's heavily penciled eyebrows shot up into perfect arches. "You mean you do all the dangerous stuff for the actresses? Why, honey, that's amazing."

Emma shrugged. "It's a living."

Sylvia let out an ear-splitting laugh. "Well, it's gotta be more exciting than slingin' hash."

"I've done my share of that, too," Emma said with a smile. "I'm supposed to report to the Flying M tonight. Will you tell me how to get there?"

Sylvia pulled a pen from her uniform pocket, grabbed a napkin off the top of the bartender's stack and drew a crude map, then quickly went over the directions. Tucking the map into her jeans' pocket, Emma thanked her, excused herself and returned to her table. She gazed out at the empty street, wondering why anyone would choose to live in such a place.

The jukebox suddenly roared to life, startling her half out of her wits. She swivelled around in her chair and nearly groaned out loud when she saw the two cowboys heading toward her. They each carried a beer bottle and a pool cue, and wore what were supposed to be charming grins.

The taller one tipped his hat to her. She mentally rolled her eyes but tried to keep an impassive expression on her face. The shorter man pulled a red bandana from his back pocket and wiped it across his forehead.

"Howdy, ma'am," he said. "Nice bike you've got out there."

"Thank you," she said cautiously. She knew how she would have handled them in L.A., but she sensed things might be different in Wyoming. She didn't want to offer any unwitting challenges to their masculinity. For some reason that she'd never been able to fathom, she tended to have that effect on men with dismaying regularity. Nor did she want to give them the least bit of encouragement.

"How about a game of pool?" the taller one asked.

"No, thank you," she said.

They both looked surprised. Then the bandana guy smiled. "We don't have to play for money. Just a friendly little game."

"No, thank you," she repeated.

"We'll even spot you a couple of points," the tall guy said.

Emma shook her head and shot an impatient glance toward the doorway leading into the adjoining restaurant. She'd never had much tolerance for inane chatter, and she certainly had nothing in common with these…gentlemen. For heaven's sake, where was McBride? Out back killing the cow or what?

"What brings you to Sunshine Gap?" Mr. Bandana asked.

"Why is that any of your business?" she replied.

His eyes narrowed, but the smile on his lips remained. "Well, I don't guess it really is. No offense intended. Just bein' friendly."

Emma looked from him to his friend, and then back at him again. "I have all the friends I want."

The tall one bristled. "No need to get snotty, lady."

Emma took a deep breath and silently counted to five. "I'm simply telling you that I'm not interested. I'll thank you for respecting my privacy."

Mr. Bandana leaned close enough to give her a blast of beer-laden breath. "Now there's a good one. A gal who looks like you don't come into a bar all alone lookin' for privacy, babe."

Emma climbed to her feet and pushed her chair against the table, giving herself more room to maneuver should it become necessary. "I came in here to have a beer and a burger, and that is all," she said, enunciating slowly and clearly. "Furthermore, I am *not* your babe."

"Well, you could be," the taller one said. He stepped forward with a smile that was too close to a leer for comfort.

Emma held up her palms. "I'll give you both to the count of three to back off."

"Oh, yeah?" Mr. Bandana's eyes danced with unholy glee. "And then what're you gonna do? Call the cops?"

The taller one laughed with Mr. Bandana. "There's only one in Sunshine Gap, and he's not in town right now. Guess you'd be outta luck if you tried to call him."

Without taking her eyes off either one of these goons, Emma called in a loud voice. "Sylvia, would you please ask Mr. McBride to come here?"

Mr. Tall laughed again. "Syl went to the can, *babe*. And Cal's probably in the kitchen, jawin' with his cook. Looks like we're all alone."

"That's supposed make my little heart go pitty-pat?" Emma asked. She'd done her best to be civil, but they weren't listening. Men so rarely did. "I don't think so, *boys*."

"Boys, is it?" Mr. Bandana smirked at his friend. "Looks like we got ourselves a wild one here." Mr. Bandana set his beer bottle and pool cue on the next table. Mr. Tall followed suit, and they both stepped closer to her.

"If you touch me, you'll regret it," Emma said.

"Now, come on, honey," Mr. Bandana said. "We won't hurt you. We'll just have ourselves a little fun."

Cal made a quick trip through the kitchen, storeroom and walk-in freezer, then headed back to the bar. The dang cook was gone, and he'd have to ask Sylvia to make up the order.

He was halfway across the café when Sylvia ran in from the bar, hollering like a maniac.

"Cal! Cal! My Lord, Cal, you've gotta get out here!"

The panic on her normally placid face aroused his sense of urgency more than her words did. With a crash pinpointing the trouble, he sprinted for the bar, praying he wouldn't have to see any blood when he got there. The sight of blood always grossed him right out. He heard another crash just before he cleared the doorway.

He skidded to a stop and stared at the scene before him. Good Lord, he hadn't been gone five minutes, and Ronnie Black lay unmoving beneath an overturned table in the center of the room. Two wooden chairs beside him were now kindling. Joe Wright had his back pressed tight against the near end of the pool table. Clutching his right arm, he cowered before the woman, who clutched the front of his shirt in one hand and brandished a broken beer bottle in front of his terrified eyes with the other.

Cal strode toward her. "Drop it."

Head whipping around, Joe gave Cal a desperate look. "Thank God you're here. We was just talkin' to her and she went plumb loco. Get her away from me, *please.*"

"*Please?* You actually *do* know some manners?" The woman leaned closer to Joe, making his eyes bug out farther. "Why don't you try using them more often?"

Holding his hands loosely at his sides, Cal stopped beside her. "Put down the bottle, lady. *Now.*"

She glanced over her shoulder and met his gaze, then shrugged and turned back to Joe. "In a minute. This disgusting worm hasn't learned his lesson yet."

"Don't let her hurt me no more," Joe begged. "She already broke my arm."

"I did not, you big baby." She looked back at Cal and said dryly, "He needs more bladder control, but he'll be fine in the morning."

Cal glanced at the front of Joe's jeans and had to choke

down a laugh when he saw she was right. He hated bar fights, but this one must have been a classic.

Inclining her head toward Ronnie, the woman said, "You might want to check on his friend."

"No, Cal," Joe wailed. "Don't leave me, man."

Cal didn't like the way Ronnie was lying so still, but if he went over there, she might decide to carve Joe a third nostril.

"I don't enjoy hurting people," she said as if reading his thoughts. "I just don't let them hurt me."

"Don't move, Joe." Cal hurried to Ronnie, knelt on one knee beside him and pressed his index finger against Ronnie's neck. The pulse was steady and strong, and the puffs of stale beer emitting from Ronnie's mouth made it plain that he was breathing. Cal shook his shoulder. "Hey, Ronnie. Time to wake up."

Groaning, Ronnie blinked and raised a hand to the side of his head. Cal helped him sit up, told him to stay put and be quiet, and went back to help Joe. If he could. The lady wasn't like any woman he'd ever met. God only knew what she might do.

"He's all right," Cal said. "You've had your fun now, lady. Put that bottle *down.*" He reached for her wrist, but she jerked it out of his reach and almost took off the tip of Joe's nose.

"Have you learned your lesson now?" she asked coldly.

Joe nodded. "Oh, yes, ma'am. I won't ever bother you again. I promise."

"You won't bother any other woman again, either. Will you?"

Joe whipped his head back and forth. "Oh, no, ma'am. I sure won't. If a lady says no, I'll go away."

"I said *woman,* not *lady,*" she insisted. "That means *any* female. It doesn't matter how old she is, how she's dressed, how much makeup and perfume she's wearing or how drunk she is. If she says *no,* you disappear. Have you *got* that?"

Joe nodded again, reminding Cal of those toy animals people put in their rear car windows, the ones with a long, metal spring for a neck and the head bobbing around all the time. "Yes, ma'am. I do. I sure as hell do."

The woman stared at him for another agonizing moment, then set the bottle on the floor and stepped back. Joe slumped against the pool table. Ronnie groaned and lumbered to his feet.

Cal dragged Joe away from the woman and deposited him beside Ronnie. Standing between the opposing camps, he propped his hands on his hips. Nobody moved or spoke while he surveyed the room, mentally adding up the damage to his property.

"Anybody need a doctor?" he asked.

Ronnie and Joe declined. The woman shook her head.

"Fine," Cal said. "Anybody want to press charges?"

Again, all three declined.

"Anybody want to tell me what happened here?"

Ronnie and Joe exchanged a quick glance, then shook their heads.

"Fine," Cal said again. "You can both leave twenty-five dollars on the bar for your share of the trouble, and then I never want to see either one of you in here again."

"Aw, Cal," Ronnie protested. "It wasn't our fau—"

"Save your lame excuses," Cal said. "You two know better than to act like that, and you knew the rules when you walked in my door. Get the hell out of here, and don't come back."

Grumbling under their breath, the cowboys left. Cal turned to the woman, who had watched the proceedings without a word. She gazed back at him, baby blues cool and showing no remorse.

He wanted to talk to her in the worst way, to find out how she had wiped the floor of his bar with not one, but two cowboys who were easily twice her size. He wanted to see her smile as if she meant it, sit her on a bar stool and hear her life story. He wanted to know what her tattoo

was and why she'd gotten it. At the very least, he wanted
to know her name.

But none of that was going to happen. He could see it
in her eyes. It irritated him no end, but there was nothing
he could do about it. He asked anyway. "You want to tell
me what happened?"

"You can figure it out," she said. "If you really want
to."

"Joe and Ronnie aren't exactly great guys, but they're
usually harmless. I've never seen you before, but I'd sure
like to hear your side of the story."

She appeared to consider the offer for a moment, but
finally shook her head. "No, thanks."

"All right. The same rules apply to you, then," he said.
"I don't tolerate fighting in my place, so leave your twenty-
five dollars on the bar and don't come back."

"Just like that?"

"Yup. No exceptions."

Her laughter held a mocking note as she walked to her
table, picked up her jacket and pulled a small wallet from
an inside pocket. She counted out several bills and put on
the jacket. Picking up her helmet, she carried the money to
the bar and dropped it beside Joe's and Ronnie's.

Sylvia touched Cal's arm, startling him halfway to a
heart attack. "Sure you're doin' the right thing? That Joe
and Ronnie aren't worth the lead it'd take to shoot 'em, but
she seems like a nice little gal."

Cal patted her hand. "Don't worry about it, Syl. She
probably wouldn't have come back here, anyway."

"But—"

The woman walked to the front door, paused and turned
back. "Nice meeting you, Sylvia. Thanks for the map."

"You're welcome, Emma. You drive real careful now.
It's gettin' dark and that old road's not the best."

The woman gave her a quick nod, then walked outside.
Sylvia hurried to the window and peeked out. Cal followed.

"Emma? Map?" he said. "What was that all about?"

"We chatted while you were gone, and she was real polite. Said her name was Emma Barnes. I tried to tell ya she's one of those movie people. She's heading for the Flying M."

"Aw, jeez," Cal said with a groan, hoping this wasn't a bad omen for future relations between the residents of Sunshine Gap and the production company. He'd called in every marker he'd owned to get the community behind this venture. If there was any significant trouble, he'd never hear the end of it.

The motorcycle's engine started, then revved to a noise level that made further conversation impossible. Cal watched Emma back out into the street. As if she knew she had an audience, she turned her head toward the bar for a long moment. Revving the engine again until it practically screamed, she spun the rear tire, sending up a noxious-looking cloud of smoke. Then she roared down the street without a backward glance. She might as well have flipped him off.

Laughing, Sylvia turned to Cal when the noise faded away. "Now *that's* the kind of a woman you oughtta be marryin'. One with real spark and sass."

Cal shot her a dirty look and went over to clean up the debris from the fight.

She ignored his lack of response. "You know I think the world of Sandy, but she's not right for you, Cal."

"That's *your* opinion," Cal said. "And I *didn't* ask for it."

She shrugged. "Yeah, but what's going to happen when Marsh comes back to work on his movie? You think he's just going to congratulate you two on your engagement?"

"Why not?" Cal muttered, though he'd admit she might have a point. Well, too bad. His cousin had had his chance with Sandy and he'd blown it. "Marsh broke up with her years ago."

"Yeah, but I doubt he expected it to be permanent." Sylvia crossed the room to his side, grabbed his left hand, stuck a coin on his palm and curled his fingers around it. "Here. Emma left you a tip. Look at that and tell me you don't want to see her again."

Refusing to give the old bat any satisfaction, Cal stuck the coin into his right vest pocket without looking at it and picked up a chair leg. Muttering a litany of cuss words, Sylvia stomped over to the bar, grabbed her purse and walked out the front door, slamming it behind her.

When she was gone, Cal fished out the coin. A reluctant grin tugged at his mouth. Emma Barnes had sure told *him.*

On top of that trick with her bike, the little brat had left him a penny, the ultimate insult to anyone in the restaurant business. He'd like to see her again, all right, but he'd cut out his tongue before he'd ever admit it to anyone else.

He dropped the penny into his vest pocket and went back to work, hoping like hell this stupid incident wasn't going to wreck his hopes for the future. He had a nagging suspicion that if she wanted to, Ms. Barnes could make a lot of trouble. Sunshine Gap needed the movie people's business and their goodwill. It was his job as the mayor to make sure the town got both.

Closing his eyes, he pictured that rear tire of hers spinning and spitting out smoke. He'd known she was trouble the instant he'd seen her. The question now was, just how much trouble was she going to be?

Chapter Two

Seething, Emma roared out of Sunshine Gap on the road indicated by Sylvia's map. The sun slid behind the mountains, softening the brilliant blue sky to the gentler shades of twilight. The air had cooled from hot to warm, and it carried rich, earthy smells she couldn't immediately identify. Instead of enjoying it, however, she kept thinking up things she could have said—no, *should* have said—to that jerk Cal McBride.

Where did he get off banning her from his stupid bar? It wasn't even classy. It was barely a notch above a dive. All that wood paneling and Western junk on the walls, not to mention all those stuffed animal heads...it was enough to make any civilized person shudder.

Which was all beside the point anyway, because *she* hadn't done anything wrong. If she ever saw him again, she would tell him so.

Fine, gritty dust from the gravel road billowed around her, hampering her vision and sneaking under her helmet visor, tickling the inside of her nose and making her eyes water.

She pulled over to the side of the road, letting Mama's engine idle. The jagged mountains to the west and the prairie to the east looked as if human occupation hadn't changed it at all. Not in any way that mattered. It was wild and lonely, and so big and open and free, it made her whole chest ache with a need to become a part of it.

But that wasn't like her. She'd never had a home and didn't want one now. She loved traveling with every job, never staying anywhere long. She didn't even have her own apartment anymore. For fifty dollars a month, her friend Diana collected her mail, took phone messages and let her use the spare bedroom in her apartment whenever she was back in L.A.

Many of the locations she'd worked in had been green and lush, and far more beautiful than this scraggly, dusty corner of Wyoming. But none of those places had ever held her. Why on earth would this one?

Revving the throttle, she told herself that it wouldn't. Yes, there was something here that tugged at her heart, a haunting sort of attraction she didn't understand. But sooner or later, the newness would wear off and—

Suddenly a black Chevy Blazer shot past her. She jumped, then automatically steadied her bike. She'd been so absorbed in studying the countryside, she hadn't even heard the vehicle approaching. That wasn't like her, either. She'd earned her street smarts the hard way. Rule number one had always been to be aware of everything going on around her.

Ten yards up the road, the Chevy Blazer stopped, then slowly backed toward her. She waved at the dust and felt her heart stutter when she spotted the insignia of a badge painted on the passenger door. Oh, great. Just what she needed. A local cop who undoubtedly would find it necessary to lecture her about how quiet his town was and how much he liked it that way. Bikers and other troublesome types really weren't all that welcome in sleepy little towns.

She took off her helmet and balanced it on the gas tank. The cop rolled down the passenger window, leaned across the gearshift and tipped back a gray Stetson hat. He had dark eyes, a black beard and a surprisingly friendly smile for a cop. He looked so familiar—good grief, he looked like Cal McBride, but with a full beard rather than a mustache.

"Afternoon, ma'am," the cop said. "Need any help?"

"No, thank you," she replied.

"Just lookin' at the scenery?"

"Something like that."

He smiled and nodded. "It's a pretty view from here all right. Where you headed? It's easy to get lost out here if you don't know the area."

"I have directions."

The cop's smile drooped at the corners and his eyes took on a speculative cast while he studied her. Then he pulled the brim of his hat back down to shade his eyes and gave her a nod. "All right, ma'am. You have a nice day now."

Without waiting for a response, he rolled up the passenger window and roared off, his rear tires spitting gravel and coating her with a thick layer of dust. Coughing and cursing under her breath, she rocked the bike forward, releasing the stand, then popped the clutch and pulled out behind the cop. When she saw him turn in at the big arching sign welcoming guests to the Flying M Ranch, she groaned.

Great. After Sylvia's remark about Cal's family owning the Flying M and with the cop looking so much like Cal, she should have guessed they were related.

If this was any example of the luck she would have on the shoot, she ought to turn around and head right back to L.A. If she wasn't so darn broke, she would have done just that. Unfortunately the twenty-five dollars she'd left on Cal McBride's bar had been the end of her last paycheck. Finding a way to eat until the commissary tent opened would be a challenge. Well, it wouldn't be the first time she'd gone hungry. Grimacing at the thought, she pulled into the long driveway.

The Flying M Ranch turned out to be everything she had imagined and more. There were barbwire fences, cows, horses and green pastures. The white ranch house stretched to three stories in places, with dormer windows and green shutters and a porch with a wooden swing hanging from the ceiling.

There were flower beds whose soil had been turned over, a pair of dirt bikes leaning against the side of the house and a basketball hoop attached to the front of an outbuilding that looked as if it might be a garage. She particularly liked the bale of hay with a plastic cow head sticking out of it sitting at the edge of the yard. The overall effect was warm, homey and welcoming. And the cop was nowhere in sight, thank goodness.

The barn was one of those big, red, stately numbers, complete with hay doors, a rooster-shaped weather vane and a motley pack of dogs who came running out to bark at the stranger invading their turf. Keeping a wary eye on them, she parked beside the house and knocked on the front door.

A second Cal McBride look-alike, clean-shaven this time, introduced himself as Jake McBride, making her wonder just how many more McBrides there were. He chatted briefly and handed her a map to another house on the property, pointing out a twisted fir tree to get her started in the right direction. She thanked him, then mounted her bike and drove away.

Things were looking up. Maybe the rest of the McBrides would be more like Jake than Cal.

She arrived at her destination five minutes later. This house was newer than the first one, but it had a distinctive character of its own. Two stories high, it was stained a dark green, and the intricate rock work helped it to blend into its surroundings.

Barry Jacobson, the stunt coordinator and her all-time favorite boss, came out the front door and hurried down the steps to greet her before she could park her bike. "Emma, you made it," he said. "How was your trip?"

She grinned. Barry was a legend among stuntmen though one couldn't tell it by looking at his appearance. At first, second, and even third glance, he was just an average, middle-aged guy. Still he took on the most dangerous stunts and was constantly challenging the crew to give him their best work.

He was thoroughly professional and an absolute fanatic when it came to the safety of his crew members. He was also one of the handful of people Emma trusted without question. He gave her a one-armed hug. She hugged his waist in return.

"The trip was fine, but I'm glad I'm finally here," she said, rubbing her tush with her free hand. "It was a long way."

"No joke. Most of our crew has checked in now. We'll start the planning sessions in a day or two."

Emma tilted her head toward the house. "Here?"

Barry shook his head. "All the facilities at the ranch are taken. We'll be meeting in town. Did you notice a pub called Cal's Place when you came through Sunshine Gap?"

Emma nodded, the first twinges of dismay swirling in her gut. "What about it?"

"It has a small banquet room behind the bar. We've been given exclusive access to it for the duration of the shoot." As if sensing her discomfort, he studied her through narrowed eyes. "Is there a problem?"

Emma felt her face heating. She cleared her throat, then shrugged. "Well, yeah. I've been…banned from Cal's Place."

"Banned?" Barry stepped away from her, his eyes narrowed even more. "Why?"

Feeling like a delinquent, she explained briefly. Barry

frowned while he listened, then sighed and ran one hand over the top of his head.

"Dammit, Emma. If you're going to double for the star, you've got to be at those meetings. You've seen how small the town is. We don't have options, here."

"I know. But all I did was defend myself, Barry. It wasn't my fault."

"It never is," Barry retorted. "But this kind of thing happens to you all the time, and I'm tired of bailing you out."

"What am I supposed to do? Let some creeps paw me?"

"Of course not. But there must be techniques other women use to make guys leave them alone without resorting to violence."

Folding her arms across her chest, Emma opened her mouth, then changed her mind, clamped her lips together and looked at him. She wasn't like other women, and she didn't have a clue about how they handled obnoxious men. Diana was the only close female friend she'd ever had, and men simply didn't hit on her the way they did Emma.

"Oh, no you don't," Barry said, glaring at her. "I'm your friend and you damn well know it. Don't you dare shut down on me like that."

"I don't know what else to do," she grumbled.

"I'll tell you what you're going to do. You're going to go back into Sunshine Gap tomorrow morning, and you're going to apologize to Cal McBride. If it's necessary, you're going to *beg* him to let you come back into his establishment."

"I can't do that," Emma yelped.

"Then you're going to have to find another job."

"But, Barry—"

"No. You created this problem. You fix it. You've got to learn how to get along with other people, because I don't have the energy or the patience for this anymore."

Defeat left a bitter taste in her mouth, but she gave him

a grudging nod. "All right. But could you float me a loan until payday so I can eat? I'm short on cash."

Barry scrunched up his mouth and studied her for what felt like hours. "Yeah, I'll give you a loan. Just as soon as you get yourself back into Cal's Place. In the meantime, you can eat with the rest of the crew."

He led her inside and down a long hallway to the left. He opened a door at the very end, revealing a small bedroom, furnished with a cot, a sleeping bag and an array of building materials stacked neatly along one wall. "It's not much to look at, but it's clean and private."

"It's fine." She carried in her belongings, and after taking a quick shower, she stretched out on her cot for a nap. Of course, she couldn't sleep, not with Cal McBride's mocking smile appearing in her mind every time she tried to close her eyelids.

The awful man. She was already dreading the prospect of seeing him again. He undoubtedly would make her apology as humiliating as possible and enjoy doing so.

At closing time Cal gave the bar one last wipe-down and checked around to make sure everything was ready for tomorrow. His gaze touched on the table where Emma Barnes had sat, and he grimaced at the memories that came to mind. He glanced over his shoulder at the wall phone behind him, wondering if he should call Jake.

The more he considered the idea, however, the less it appealed. As big brothers went, Jake was a great guy, but he'd probably dish out a lecture Cal didn't want to hear. Besides, it didn't take a genius to figure out the answers to the questions that had been niggling at him ever since Sylvia had gone home.

His cousin Marsh had written the script for the movie they were getting ready to film, and Cal had read it. There was only one female character who would need a stunt double: the movie's star, Blair DuMaine. Emma Barnes had the same coloring and build as Blair. She was about the same size, too, and she had great muscles in her arms...

And didn't that just figure? He couldn't tick off some lowly assistant nobody would listen to. Oh, no, he had to tick off the woman who'd been hired to stand in for the biggest star in the production.

He couldn't just ignore the problem and hope it would go away, either. The crew was supposed to do their planning in his banquet room. If Emma Barnes had to be at those meetings, he was going to have to make an exception for her, after all.

He rubbed the back of his neck while he considered several possible approaches he might use to smooth things over. Only problem was, Emma Barnes didn't strike him as a woman who was easily appeased once she'd been offended. No sir. Not that little gal.

Heaving a disgruntled sigh, he decided his only hope was to grit his teeth and apologize to her. Then he'd invite her to come back to Cal's Place any time she wanted and hope for the best. He'd go out to the Flying M in the morning, right after the town council meeting.

She'd probably make him eat a crow the size of a bull buffalo.

Hoping to avoid alerting Cal McBride to her presence before she was ready to deal with him, Emma parked three blocks down the street. Once she arrived, she would talk fast and he might think twice before ejecting her. It wasn't much of a plan, but it was the best she'd been able to devise during a very long, sleepless night.

She caught sight of her destination and mentally cringed. Every single slot in front of Cal's Place was occupied. Just what she needed—a restaurant full of people to witness her humiliation.

She gave the door a hard shove and slipped inside. The sudden dimness after the brilliant sunshine outdoors momentarily blinded her. She blinked rapidly, desperate to regain her vision before Cal saw her. She heard quick, heavy footsteps, however, and when her focus returned, he stood directly in front of her. All six feet plus of him.

She'd forgotten just how big he was, and his skin carried a faint aroma of some musky aftershave. But now was not the time to be noticing such things. He continued to stand there, silently studying her with an expression that made her want to squirm. She resisted the urge.

She searched for an appropriate opening remark and drew a total blank. Then the twin aromas of coffee and frying bacon filled her nostrils, triggering an audible growl from her stomach. McBride's boyish dimple appeared below the left side of his mustache, but his smile held none of the mockery she might have expected. Instead, he seemed almost…relieved?

"Sounds like you're hungry," he said. "Well, you came to the right place. Come on in, Ms. Barnes."

It wasn't easy to prevent her mouth from falling open, but somehow, she managed. "Excuse me? Yesterday, you said—"

He flicked one hand as if brushing away a pesky fly. "Aw, that was yesterday. Don't worry about it."

The back of Emma's neck prickled. That was odd. He looked almost as uncomfortable as she felt.

Before she could figure out what was going on, he took her elbow and escorted her to a booth. He called a waitress over and told her to give Ms. Barnes coffee and breakfast on the house. Then he turned away.

"Wait just a minute, McBride," Emma protested. "I didn't come here to mooch a free breakfast. I need to talk to you."

"I know. I need to talk to you, too." He turned back and cocked a thumb over his shoulder, indicating a big round table at the back of the room. The people seated around it all nodded at her. Not knowing what else to do, Emma nodded back. McBride grinned.

"That's the town council over there. When our meeting's

over, I promise I'll be back. In the meantime, relax and enjoy your breakfast. Have anything you want.''

Though she sensed something still wasn't quite right, Emma took him at his word and ordered hotcakes, eggs and bacon. Just because she hadn't expected a free meal didn't mean she wouldn't eat one. For all she knew, McBride was putting on a nice-guy act for the town council, and he'd throw her out again after they left.

Her breakfast was hot and delicious, the coffee fresh and strong. The waitress, whose name tag said Kate, returned to take Emma's empty plate when she was finished. Emma gratefully accepted a second cup of coffee and settled back against the vinyl booth to think about Cal McBride's new attitude toward her.

No matter how she looked at the situation, the sudden change made no sense. During her long and sleepless night, she'd finally admitted to herself that Barry had been right. She did get into these situations far too often. She supposed she *could* have been nicer to the cop, and Cal McBride probably *had* been justified to ban her from his business. Any bar owner in L.A. would have done the same thing and called the police as well.

After hanging around and talking for what seemed like an awfully long time, the town council people gradually stood and filed out the front door, nodding to her again as they passed. She returned their greetings. Suddenly impatient for her conversation with McBride, she glanced back over her shoulder and saw him headed in her direction.

Oh, dear. There was something awfully sexy about watching a big, good-looking man move with such a smooth, athletic stride. And having that friendly smile and it's accompanying dimple aimed straight at her was enough to give her heart palpitations.

''Sorry that took so long,'' he said, sliding into the seat opposite hers. ''Sometimes those meetings drag on and on. Was your breakfast all right?''

''Excellent.''

"Glad to hear it."

"Mr. McBride—"

He grimaced. "We've got an awful lot of Mcbrides running around Sunshine Gap. Why don't you save yourself a lot of confusion and call me Cal?"

She probably wouldn't have believed him if she hadn't already met two other McBrides. "All right," she said. "My name is Emma Barnes. But you already knew that, didn't you?"

"Sylvia told me." He flashed his darn dimple again. Had she been a suspicious type, she would have guessed that he was intentionally using it to disarm her. It was working. "Mind if I call you Emma?"

"No, I don't mind," she said. "If you'll tell me what's going on here."

His gaze slid away from hers. His laugh had a nervous edge to it. "Going on? We got off to a bad start, and I'm trying to make amends. That's all there is to it."

"Uh-huh."

His eyebrows shot halfway up his forehead. "You don't believe me?"

"No."

"Why not?"

"You were awfully emphatic when you told me not to come back yesterday. I had the distinct impression that you expected to be obeyed."

His cheeks flushed, and irritation sparked in his dark eyes. "Well, I was madder than hell at the three of you. It was a bad situation all the way around. With you waving that bottle like a maniac, someone could have gotten hurt. A lot of people in these parts carry guns, you know?"

Emma nearly smiled at his defensive tone. "Then why are you backing down?"

Bracing one forearm on the table, he leaned forward and gave her a scowl so ferocious, she would have backed up if she hadn't been sitting in a booth. His voice came out low and gritty. "Why don't you just accept it as a gift and leave it at that?"

She knew she should take his advice, but it was too much fun watching him struggle with his temper to stop bugging him yet. "Will you be inviting my opponents to return as well?"

"No."

She waited for him to explain, but he remained silent. She admired his implacability. A person had to be completely sure of his position to act that way. At the same time, it increased her impression that his attitude change was out of character.

"Are you letting me come back because I'm in the movie?"

He hesitated so long she expected him to lie and "make nice." To her surprise, he nodded. "That's right."

"Then if I wasn't part of the movie crew, you would have written me off as a troublemaker and forgotten me."

He looked surprised for an instant. Then his face relaxed and a deep, rumbly chuckle rolled out of him. "Well, you sure caused some trouble, but I wouldn't have forgotten you. You're something else, Ms. Barnes."

His words gave her a tingle of pleasure, making her realize she didn't want him to forget her. That was ridiculous, of course, but the pleasant tingle remained. She cleared her throat and forced herself to go back to the original issue. "It's all about money, isn't it? You'll tolerate a troublemaker like me in order to cash in on the movie's business."

"That's part of it," he admitted. "You got a problem with that?"

She did, but she doubted he would understand if she tried to explain it. Instead, she asked, "What's the rest of it?"

"Well, it's not just about my bank account." He glanced around in a way that was obvious he was making sure no one else could overhear their conversation.

"The whole town needs business," he said, quietly. "Every year a few more ranchers go under. A few more families leave to look for work. The kids who graduate from our high school don't even think about sticking around unless their folks own a decent-sized spread. If things don't start changing soon, there may not be a Sunshine Gap in ten years."

"You say that as if it's your responsibility to save it."

"It is. I'm the mayor."

He looked too young to be a mayor, but she refrained from telling him so. "You think hosting one movie crew for a couple of months will make a lasting difference?"

"Not financially, but I hope the experience will be good enough to open up some local folks to new ideas."

"I'm afraid I don't understand."

"It's just small-town life," he said. "Most of the people who live here have to work real hard to make a living. They don't have money for traveling or vacations. They like knowing everybody they see and they're comfortable with their town just the way it is. They really don't want anything to change."

"People are like that everywhere," she said.

"It's a matter of degree. In a town this size and this isolated, those feelings are stronger than you'll find in other places. At least half of the people living in Sunshine Gap didn't want the production company to come here, no matter how much money it brought in."

"Really. Why not?"

"Too many troublemakers from California." He'd said the words in a serious tone, but there was a wicked gleam in his eyes. Why, the man was teasing her—as if he actually had a sense of humor. She acknowledged his effort with a grin of her own, and he went on. "But if we don't start welcoming change instead of fighting it, this town is going to die."

"So, this is just a first step for you?"

"That's right," he said with a nod. "We've got to start somewhere, and this is it. If everybody gets along okay this time around, maybe we can attract some other kinds of businesses. I'll do whatever I can to make this thing work. Even make exceptions to my own rules.'' He paused long enough to scowl at her, then added, ''But don't push your luck.''

She met and held his gaze. ''Point taken, Mr. Mayor. For whatever it's worth, I came here this morning to apologize for my behavior yesterday. If you'll grant me an exception, I won't break your rules again.''

''Will you tell me what really happened?'' he asked.

''Those guys were hitting on me,'' she said with a shrug. ''I tried to discourage them, but nobody else was there and they didn't want to take no for an answer.''

His mouth hardened into a tight, straight line and anger flashed in his eyes. This was not a man she would ever want to cross. ''Did they hurt you?''

''No, but I believed they would have if I hadn't defended myself.''

''Did they actually touch you?''

She shrugged again. ''They tried. I gave them a fair warning, but they seemed to think a female alone was fair game.''

''From what you said to Joe, I'd figured as much. You sure convinced them otherwise, though.'' He shook his head, whether in admiration or amazement, she couldn't say. Then he admitted, ''And you sure scared the hell out of me with that broken bottle.''

''I honestly wouldn't have used it unless I had no other choice. But I can and do take care of myself.''

''Well, I'm sorry you had to do it in my bar. We really don't get much trouble in here. I thought Sylvia would stay put or I never would have left you alone with those idiots for a second. I'll be a lot more careful about that in the future.''

The sincerity in his eyes and in his deep voice touched her like a caress. At the moment he didn't seem like a jerk at all. In fact, he seemed like a decent, thoughtful man. As if to prove it, he offered his hand.

"I'd say that makes us even, Emma," he said. "Want to start over and try to be friends?"

Smiling, she gave his hand a firm shake. "I'd like that, Cal. I think I'd like it very much."

Chapter Three

It seemed to Cal as if someone must have fired a starting pistol in Hollywood to start the procession of trucks, trailers and every kind of car and van imaginable loaded with production equipment. Today it reached Sunshine Gap. The traffic on Main Street picked up around noon and with every passing hour it got worse.

Local business owners thought they'd gone to heaven without having to die first. The ranchers, who were used to taking their half of any road out of the middle, suddenly found themselves participating in a genuine traffic jam and wished every single one of those out-of-state drivers would go straight to Hades. And everybody in the whole town had to call the mayor and tell him what they thought.

Cal's cousin Grace called at five o'clock to tell him the entire family and six guests were coming to town for supper. Cal nearly objected that he was too busy for that, but shut his mouth at the last possible second. These movie folks would be gone in a few months, but his family and the local residents would be here forever. Maybe they'd all stay to dance, which would keep the bar filled with customers until closing time.

He worked like crazy until his fiancée poked her head out of the kitchen and waved to catch his attention. When he pushed through the swinging doors, Sandy grabbed his forearm and practically dragged him back to the storeroom, then shut the door and leaned back against it.

She'd obviously gone home after work and changed into a skin-hugging pair of jeans and a pretty, aqua-colored shirt he'd never seen before. Her shoulder-length, auburn hair had a row of furrows across the top, as if she'd been stabbing her fingers through it. Even with fresh makeup on, her skin was paler than usual. Her green eyes looked enormous and a little...haunted.

"What's wrong, honey?" he asked.

She started to speak, had to clear her throat and tried again. Her voice still sounded raspy. "Is he here yet?"

"Who? Marsh?"

"Yes," she said in a whisper. "Who else?"

Right. Who else? Cal blew out a disgruntled sigh. He'd been hoping this wouldn't happen.

"Well? Is he?"

The impatience in her voice irritated him. "Yeah, he's here, but so what? He's ancient history. Isn't he?"

Her eyes widened as if his question had shocked her. "Of course, he is. I'm sorry, Cal. That must have sounded awful. I just don't want to run into him...unprepared. You know?"

Cal opened his arms to her. She moved into them without any hesitation and hugged him. Her action touched Cal in a real tender place up under his heart. He should have realized this evening would be hard for her.

Sandy had been his cousin Marsh's sweetheart all through high school and college. But when he'd left to see if he could make it as a screenwriter in Hollywood, she'd stayed behind in Sunshine Gap. If anyone but the two of them knew exactly what had happened to cause the breakup, they'd never talked about it. To Cal's knowledge, however, Sandy and Marsh hadn't spoken privately with each other in the past ten years.

Cal's own relationship with his cousin put another wrinkle on the situation. Since they were the same age, he and Marsh had competed with each other for girls, sports and their family's attention.

"I understand," he murmured, gently stroking her hair. "Marsh can rip pieces out of your hide with words, but I doubt he'll cause any trouble for us now. If he does, I'll just deck him. All right?"

"That's a great offer," she said with a chuckle, "but please don't do that. I just wish we hadn't decided to wait until August to get married. It seems like forever."

"It'll be okay," Cal assured her. "We'll have a lot better time at our wedding when all the strangers are gone and things have quieted down around here."

Her smile looked tight, but the panic had receded from her eyes. "You're right. Of course, you're right." She stepped away from him. "I don't know why I even let this get to me. He's been gone so long, he probably doesn't even remember I exist."

"Baloney. No man in his right mind would ever forget you."

She flashed him a smile that reeked of gratitude, and suddenly he felt extremely glad about that August wedding date. He never would have proposed to her if he hadn't honestly believed she was over Marsh. Completely over Marsh. He'd obviously been fooling himself. Knowing it rankled.

He could handle a marriage without any passionate love involved, but he had his fair share of pride. He sure as hell didn't want to spend the rest of his life with a woman who secretly wished he was someone else.

Sylvia rapped on the door. "Better get out front, boss.

Dillon and his bunch are done eatin', and I think they're fixin' to leave.''

"Be right there," Cal called, then turned back to Sandy. "We need to talk more about this. How about after closing?''

She nodded and gave him a wobbly excuse for a smile.

"Are you okay?''

"I'm fine, Cal.''

"You're sure?''

Nodding again, she smiled with more conviction. "Yes. Go on now. I'll see you later.''

Cal kissed her cheek and went back to work, feeling a grim sort of anticipation for the evening ahead. One way or another, he figured it was going to be a night to remember.

Emma sat in Cal's Place later that night, sipping ginger ale. With her chair balanced on its rear legs and her back pressed to the wall, she had a great view of all the action— and there was plenty of it to watch. She kept telling herself she should go back to the Flying M and move her stuff into the little trailer that would be her home for the duration, but she couldn't make herself leave.

She wasn't much of a drinker, but since most contacts in the business were made over drinks after work, she'd accompanied the rest of the crew into the bar. While they were still swapping lies about other pictures they'd worked on and scarfing down free popcorn and pretzels, a four-piece band straggled in, set up their instruments and ripped into a medley of hard-driving country tunes.

People poured into the room from the café next door. At first the locals sat on one side of the room, the production crowd sat on the other and very few people danced. Then Cal brought in a second wave of people, many of whom had to be his close relatives. The rest of the group included Blair DuMaine, her cousin Hope DuMaine, who also happened to be a friend of Emma's, the director and various other muckamucks on the shoot.

Cal introduced people, firmly nudged a few of them toward the dance floor, and the party began. The Californians loved the way the locals danced. The locals loved teaching the Californians. The city-country divisions quickly faded as strangers bought each other drinks and sat down to visit while drinking them.

Whether he was helping the bartender fill orders, delivering drinks or dancing himself, Cal McBride was in his element. To Emma, it was like watching a master conductor drawing whatever he wanted out of an orchestra. It was the most entertaining, fun, sexy thing she'd seen in years. She actually wished he would ask her to dance, and she'd always hated dancing.

"Well, if ain't the Motorcycle Mama."

"Well if it ain't the Hollywood Hellion." Emma shot Hope DuMaine a wry smile and tilted the rim of her glass toward the lone chair at her table. "Have a seat."

Hope plopped herself onto the chair and set down a cocktail glass Emma knew darn well held only tonic water. Hope was a bestselling novelist of racy, Hollywood, tell-all novels, and had developed quite a reputation for being outrageous.

"Can you believe this place?" Hope said, giving Emma one of her dramatic eye-rolls. "I mean, have you ever seen this many straight, great-looking men who can dance in one room?"

"Not lately," Emma said dryly. "By the way, thanks for getting me this job."

Hope sniffed. "What makes you think I had anything to do with it?"

"You think I'm too dumb to figure it out?" Emma replied. Hope gave her quick but fierce scowl. "Don't worry, I haven't told anyone. I wouldn't ruin your rep."

Hope made a scratching motion in front of Emma's face

with her three-inch, metallic blue fingernails. "See that you don't."

Snorting at the threat, Emma indicated Hope's short, spiky, royal-blue hair. "Your new do is a real head-turner, but where did you get those clothes? Some bordello in Nevada?"

"Oh, don't be tacky, Emma, darling. Surely, you know Western chic when you see it."

"Evidently not, but it's nice to have you around to take the heat off of me." Hope raised an eyebrow, silently demanding an explanation. "Until you showed up, everyone in this town stared at me. Now they're staring at you."

A whoop from the dance floor grabbed Emma's attention. One of the McBride men was twirling Blair so fast, she was nearly a blur.

Hope sighed. Dramatically, of course. "Oh, look. Blair's dancing with her cowboy again. Isn't that absolutely the sweetest thing in the whole world?"

"What's so sweet about it?"

Hope glanced around as if checking for eavesdroppers, then leaned close to Emma's ear and murmured, "She's in love with him. Dillon loves her, too."

Surprised, Emma glanced at her, then turned her head for a closer look at the dance floor. "That's Dillon McBride?"

"Yes, ma'am," Hope said. "You haven't figured them out?"

"I only know there are a lot of them and they're all tall, dark and handsome. I've even seen a couple of women here tonight who have that McBride 'look.'"

"Not bad for an amateur," Hope said with a laugh. "Allow me to enlighten you. There are two McBride families who jointly own the Flying M. One has three children, Dillon, Marsh and Grace." She pointed them out for Emma's benefit. "The other family has four children, Jake, Zack, Alexandra and Cal."

"If some of them are only cousins, how do they all look so much alike?" Emma asked.

"Their fathers are brothers, and their mothers are identical twins, which makes all of their children double first cousins. Genetically, they're more like seven siblings, and that's how they were raised."

"I've never heard of that before." The music slowed to a dreamy ballad. Spotting Cal dancing with a petite, auburn-haired woman who'd spent most of the evening attached to his side, Emma casually leaned close to Hope and asked, "Who's the woman with Cal McBride? Do you know?"

Hope looked in the direction Emma had pointed. Then her eyes widened, her lips parted and she clasped her hands together, holding them in front of her breasts. "Oh, my gosh, will you *look* at that!"

"What?" Emma looked back at the dance floor in time to see Marsh McBride cut in on Cal. He did it rather forcefully in Emma's opinion, and of course, Cal refused to cooperate. Both men puffed up their chests and leaned forward, exchanging vicious glares and nearly crushing the petite redhead between them.

Though the band kept playing, an odd silence fell over the room while the other customers waited to see what would happen next. The woman planted a hand squarely on each broad chest and shoved them back. She looked from one man to the other, said something no one else could hear. Cal finally relinquished her hand and Red danced away with Marsh.

"Oh, good boy, Marsh," Hope murmured. "You did it."

"Did what?" Emma asked.

"He's gone after his one true love. I'm so proud of him."

"What? She's been with Cal all evening."

"She's been hiding behind Cal, but she doesn't really love him. How devastating for him. He must be terribly hurt."

Cal was still standing on the dance floor, gazing after Marsh and Red. Emma thought he looked angry and perplexed. She wasn't so sure about hurt. "That's too bad. He's an okay guy."

Hope turned to Emma, her eyes flashing, her body practically vibrating with excitement. "You know Cal? That's wonderful, Emma. Quick! Go out there and ask him to dance. The poor dear looks so lost."

"Wait a second," Emma protested. "Maybe you know what's going on, but I've missed some—"

"Later." Hope shoved at Emma's arm, practically knocking her off the chair. "If you don't get out there, he's going to be completely humiliated. Just do it. Hurry. Go!"

Emma went. Hope had a gift for digging other people's most private heartaches out of them, and she'd been a close friend of Marsh McBride. If Hope said Cal was going to be humiliated, Emma believed her.

Besides, Emma wanted to help Cal. They were supposed to be friends, and he was starting to look as if he needed one. She felt horribly conspicuous approaching him but ignored her own discomfort and tapped his shoulder.

"Hey there, Mr. Mayor. Want to boogie?"

He looked at her as if he'd never seen her before. Hope must be right. The poor guy was seriously out of it. She tried to speak softly enough to prevent others from hearing, but forcefully enough to get his attention.

"Dance with me, McBride."

He blinked, then shook his head. "Oh. Sure, Emma."

Taking her into his arms, he automatically maneuvered her around the dance floor. She didn't have to worry about her limited dancing ability; wherever his mind was, Cal had a strong lead. Emma decided that when the guy knew what he was doing, this dancing thing wasn't so bad, after all.

Cal didn't speak, and she knew he was watching Marsh and Red. In spite of his distraction, Emma felt increasingly aware of his nearness, the warmth and size of his body, his easy sense of rhythm. She especially liked his soft humming, which sounded in perfect pitch with the band and made pleasant little tingles tap-dance up and down her spine. The moderate attraction she already felt toward him took a sharp turn toward lust. In fact, she found herself fantasizing about doing all kinds of things with him she rarely thought about.

She wanted to slide her arms around his neck and press herself against him. She wanted to run her fingers through his thick, glossy hair and trace his bushy mustache, take playful nips at it. She wanted to tug his head down to her level and plant a big kiss on his tight lips, try to soften them up a little and then taste him, and...

Concerned that she might be going completely nuts, Emma shook her head. Cal shot her a quizzical glance. She smiled, desperately scrambling for a topic of conversation.

"So, um...nice party." Good grief, was that icky, perky little voice really hers? She *was* going nuts. "Business is really booming tonight, isn't it?"

"Yeah." Cal looked down at her, one side of his mouth lifting in a lopsided grin. "Having a movie star drop in for dinner brought out a lot of folks."

Okay, she'd started a conversation. Now she just needed to keep it going. Piece of cake, right? Not when he pulled her closer and his hard thighs brushed against hers with every step. It felt...nice. So nice, her brain was going to short-circuit if he didn't back off.

"What's it like here in the winter?" Oh, great, she'd brought up the *weather?* Damn, but she was cool tonight. See if she ever tried to do a good deed for anyone, ever again.

"Cold."

Marsh and Red shuffled by, so stiff and awkward, they reminded Emma of penguins. Marsh was scowling and talking at the same time. The woman held her head bowed, as if she were listening, but couldn't bear to look into his eyes.

Emma felt Cal's shoulder muscles bunch up. His expression turned thunderous, and he made a slight movement, as if he intended to stomp over there, punch Marsh in the face and reclaim the redhead. Convinced that had to be a lousy idea, Emma waved a hand in front of his face, and said, "Yoo-hoo."

When he looked down at her, she jerked the front of her tank top down far enough to give him a glimpse of her tattoo, then yanked it back up and grinned at him. "I knew that would get your attention."

"Oh, thanks. I really needed that," Cal grumbled. "What is that thing, anyway?"

"I'll never tell. And don't get cranky. You're supposed to be dancing with me, remember?"

"Yeah, yeah." His gaze drifted around the room again.

Exasperated, Emma picked up their previous conversation from where they'd left off. "So, it's cold in the winter, huh? You're so descriptive, McBride."

"You want descriptive, buy a travel guide," Cal said in a near-snarl. "What do you care what it's like in the winter?"

"I don't. I'm just trying to help you."

"Help me? Why would I need your help?"

She resisted the urge to roll her eyes the way Hope did. Barely. "Beats me. I've stopped doing personality transplants."

His chuckle sounded reluctant, but it was still a chuckle. Whether he knew it or not, she *was* helping him not to make a fool of himself in public. Uh-oh. Marsh and Red were headed their way. Honest to Pete, she'd never had to work this hard to hold a man's attention before. Tightening her grip on Cal's hand, she pushed him off balance and used his momentum to turn him in a different direction.

"Hey," he protested. "I'm supposed to be leading here."

"Do a better job of it, and maybe I'll let you."

He rewarded her with another chuckle. She smiled up at him, their gazes met, and for one sweet moment, she felt a jolt of connection between them. Before she could even begin to savor it, however, the band concluded the song.

Cal raised his head and scanned the room. Emma did likewise, quickly spotting the couple a mere four feet to Cal's left. Red said something to Marsh and practically ran from the room, her eyes glistening as if a flood of tears was imminent. Marsh reached one hand out as if to stop her, then dropped it against his side and moved off in the opposite direction, his face nearly as distraught as Red's had been.

Cal stared at the door she had used to make her exit. He started to pull away, but Emma had had enough of wondering what this weird situation was all about. She grabbed his forearm and held on tight. He stopped, glaring pointedly at her hand. She wasn't letting go until she got a little information.

"Is she your girlfriend or what?"

"She's my fiancée."

Chapter Four

The last customer finally left around two-fifteen, the other employees at two-thirty-five, still chattering about the great tips the Californians had left. Cal went into his office and sat at his desk to prepare the bank deposit. There was so much more cash than he was used to handling, he added it up three times to make sure he hadn't made a mistake.

When they'd found out the production company was coming for sure last winter, he'd asked Bill Weber at the bank to put in a night drop, but the old-timer hadn't done it. Ah, the joys of small-town living. Now Weber would have to open the bank for him tomorrow and Sunday, too, because keeping a deposit this size in his own safe was a bad idea. Lord, there was so much to do, so many things he hadn't thought of...

Settling into his high-backed leather chair, he shut his eyes and sighed deeply. Since he hadn't been able to catch Sandy when she bolted from the dance floor, he'd better drive by her house on his way home and make sure she was okay.

A sharp tapping at the back door nearly made him jump right out of his own hide. Bolting upright, he shoved the bank bag out of sight and grabbed the pistol he kept in a secret compartment of his desk. He tucked it into his jeans at the small of his back, then stepped into the hallway. "Who's there?"

"It's me. Sandy."

Feeling foolish for having overreacted, he quickly unlocked the door and ushered her into the kitchen. Neither of them spoke while he made a cup of tea for her and reheated sludgy leftover coffee for himself. She looked pale but composed. A puffy redness around her eyes told him she'd been crying. A lot.

He'd expected as much, but Sandy was usually so strong and self-contained, it was still sort of shocking to see her look so...fragile. What a mess. Once he found out what Marsh had said to her, he'd drive on out to the ranch and rearrange his cousin's face for him. But first he had to get Sandy to talk.

Deciding the kitchen was too uncomfortable, he picked up their cups and led the way into the café, flipping on a few lights with his elbow. They slid into a back booth facing each other. Sandy took a sip, set her cup down with the careful precision she used when bandaging an injury or giving an injection, then inhaled a shaky breath and lifted her gaze to meet his.

"I'm sorry," she said softly. "I'm so sorry, Cal."

"What happened, honey?" he asked.

Linking her fingers around the cup, she lowered her gaze and studied the pale liquid inside. "It doesn't matter."

"Like hell it doesn't." He paused, suspecting she would retreat into silence if he let his temper show too much. When he was sure he could speak in a reasonable tone, he continued. "It's my responsibility to protect you. Whatever happened, that's the last time he's ever going to make you cry.''

She met his gaze again. ''He didn't say anything mean, Cal. He just asked if I was positive I was doing the right thing.''

''By marrying me?''

''That's what he meant,'' she said with a nod. ''But Marsh didn't upset me. Facing the truth did.''

''Which is?''

''Our engagement is a mistake, and it always has been. We have to call it off.''

Her words stunned him. He'd considered that very possibility earlier, but somehow, hearing *her* say those words out loud felt worse than thinking them himself. Just because he wasn't crazy in love with her, didn't mean he wanted to lose her, either. ''Why?''

She shrugged, then fiddled with the cup, flipping the handle back and forth between her index fingers. ''Marriage is tough for most people. You must see that all the time when you're at the bar. I see it at the clinic. It's tragic how many couples don't make it through the hard times.''

''You don't think we could make it?''

''The couples who do, always have such a deep love and respect for each other, they're willing to put up with anything, do whatever it takes to keep going. We don't have that, Cal.''

He conceded that point with a grudging nod. ''Okay. But why does it matter so much all of a sudden? Earlier tonight, you were wishing we could have the wedding sooner.''

''I was wishing it was already over and done with. It's not the same thing.'' Leaning closer, she rested her right hand on the table. Her slender fingers curled into a fist. ''I was afraid to face Marsh again unless I was legally committed to you.''

''To me? Or would anyone do?''

''I don't know. I just…didn't want to have any options, any choices to make.''

"But you do now?"

She uttered a strained laugh. "Not really. I don't want to get involved with him again. I doubt he wants that, either." Tears welled in her eyes and her voice wavered. "But I can't marry you, Cal."

"Hey, don't cry." Reaching across the table, he wrapped his hand around her fist and gave it a gentle squeeze. "Let's take our time and think this through."

"There's nothing to think through." Sniffling, she jerked her hand from beneath his and sat up straight. Raising her chin, she scowled at him, a crease forming between her eyebrows. "We were insane to think it might work. Both of us."

He scowled right back at her. "Insane? That's a little harsh. Our engagement might've been unusual, but—"

"Stop rationalizing, will you? We don't love each other *that* way. We don't even kiss *that* way."

He was starting to feel mildly annoyed, now. She didn't have to make it sound so awful. "We could, if we wanted to."

She stared at him for a moment as if she couldn't believe he really was this stupid. "But we *don't* want to. We're best *friends,* not lovers, and that's exactly my point. There's no...sizzle here."

"Sizzle doesn't last. Friendship does."

"It won't if we abuse it this way. We both got tired of waiting for someone more interesting to come along, so we gave up. Don't you see? We've just...settled for each other."

Settled for each other? No way. Well, all right, so maybe he'd felt like he would be "settling" by marrying Sandy, but only a little bit. He'd never realized she felt the same way about *him.* Oblivious to his smoking ego, she went on.

"Doesn't that strike you as being awfully pathetic?"

Now she'd gone too far. "Pathetic? Hell, no, it's not pathetic. We were just facing reality."

"Calm down, Cal."

He ignored her attempt to interrupt him. "Living out here in the middle of nowhere makes it damned unlikely that we're ever gonna meet many marriage prospects. I thought we respected each other and enjoyed being with each other. And we both want kids before we're too old to enjoy raising them. I still think we could build a good marriage on that alone."

"We could have tried it, but *I'll bet* we'd be miserable together in six months."

"Well, thanks a lot. You think I'd be a lousy husband, don't you?"

She vigorously shook her head. "I don't think that at all. For anyone you really loved, you'd be a wonderful husband. We've been friends for so long, I'm more like a sister to you than a lover."

"Oh, well, thank you so much for sharing *that* piece of insight," Cal grumbled. "I think you're just saying all of this to avoid talking about the real issue here."

"Which is?"

"Marsh. After everything he did to you, you're still in love with him."

"Don't, Cal," she murmured.

"Don't what? You got to tell your version of the truth. Don't I get to tell mine?"

"Not if you want to hurt me with it." Her voice cracked, but she added in a ragged whisper, "I didn't say any of this to hurt you."

The pain in her eyes and in her voice cooled his anger as rapidly as it had flared. Sandy had been his best friend for as long as he could remember. She was gentle and caring, and just about the sweetest woman he'd ever known. Of course, she hadn't been trying to hurt him. That just wasn't in her.

He exhaled harshly, as if that would heal his wounded ego, then forced a smile onto his mouth. "I know. And I don't want to hurt you, either. I'm sorry I came at you with Marsh, like that."

"Well, what you said is true," she admitted. "When I started dancing with him tonight, it all came back. All those years we spent together, our hopes and plans and dreams. I felt alive again. And even though being in his arms hurt, it felt wonderful, too."

"That's why we have to break the engagement?"

She pressed her lips tightly together and after a moment's thought, she nodded. "I'm not willing to live the rest of my life without some sizzle to liven things up. You shouldn't, either. Our relationship is wonderful in its own way, but it's a poor substitute for the real thing. It wouldn't be fair to either of us. We both deserve better."

He had to admit that what she'd said made sense. Might as well save whatever he could from the situation. "Are we still gonna be friends?"

Her quick smile eased his anxiety. "Of course. Why wouldn't we?"

"Beats me," he said, returning her smile. "But I was afraid maybe we'd wrecked our friendship, too. You just never know how another person will react to something like this."

"Oh, relax. I don't know what I'd do without you. Who else would I talk to all the time?"

Cal chuckled at her, then adopted a more serious mood. "What's your plan, then? Are you going to try to get Marsh back?"

A shudder rippled over her. "No. I don't think there's any future for me and Marsh, either. I'm just a small-town nurse. I'm past thirty, ten pounds overweight, have no sense of fashion and was probably doomed to spinsterhood at birth. I'm not crazy enough to think I can compete with the kind of women he dates now."

"He sure wanted to dance with you, tonight," Cal said. "He tapped my shoulder so hard when he cut in, he probably left a bruise."

She snorted. "That didn't mean a thing. You two have

always competed with each other. He was just marking his territory out of habit.''

The mental image that remark brought to mind made Cal laugh. ''That sounds like something Alex would say, but I always thought you were more proper than that, Ms. Bishop.''

''Yeah?'' She rolled her eyes at him. ''And what did being proper ever get me? The prize for being the most boring woman in Sunshine Gap?''

Concerned by her negativity, something which seemed out of character for her, Cal reached across the table and tucked a wayward strand of hair behind her ear. ''Now, cut that out. You're being way too hard on yourself, and I won't stand for it. You're not boring, overweight, dowdy or old.''

Her cheeks turned pink. ''Oh, Cal—''

''No, I mean it,'' he said. ''I happen to have excellent taste in women and I asked you to marry me because you're a vibrant, intelligent, attractive woman. There's no reason to get down on yourself because Marsh can't or won't see that. In my not-so-humble opinion, he's an idiot.''

She laughed softly for a moment, then suddenly her eyes puddled up, and she dashed the tears away with the backs of her hands. ''Maybe he is at that. But dammit, I really thought I was over him. I feel like such a fool.''

Sliding out of his seat, Cal moved around to the other side of the table. He put his arm around Sandy's shoulders and cuddled her against him.

''If you're a fool, you're in real good company,'' he said, gently stroking her hair. ''You wouldn't believe how many folks I talk to who are still carrying a torch for a love they lost years ago. That's why I've always been so dang scared of it, I guess. Falling in love is a huge risk.''

Sniffling, she nodded, rubbing her cheek against the side of his chest. ''But it's worth it, Cal. Even when it doesn't work out, it's worth it.''

''If you say so,'' he said, smiling when she retaliated by

digging her elbow into his ribs. If she still could do that, she was going to be fine. He leaned down and pecked her cheek, then slid out of the booth and helped her to her feet.

"Go home, Bishop," he said. "It's been a long day, and I need my beauty sleep."

She eyed him up and down. "Yeah, you're uglying up something terrible, all right."

He took a mock swing at her rump. She dodged it, and they walked to the back door together. She turned to face him there, her expression once again somber. Tugging off her engagement ring, she took his right hand in hers and dropped the ring into his palm, curling his fingers over it.

"I really am sorry, Cal."

"No need for that, but you'd better promise you'll call if you need me."

"Cross my heart." She made the appropriate hand motions over her chest, gave him a quick, fierce hug and slipped out into the night.

Gripping the ring tightly in his fist, Cal walked into his office and sank into the chair behind his desk. He placed the ring on the blotter for a moment before picking it up again and sticking it onto the tip of his index finger. Turning it this way and that, he studied the diamond's inner fire.

Hmm. The woman he'd asked to marry him had just backed out on him. Shouldn't he be feeling sad or lonely or disappointed? Or angry? Probably. But he didn't feel any of those things.

Instead, he felt…relieved.

Did that mean there was something wrong with him? Or was it just that Sandy had been right, and he'd unconsciously known all along, that this engagement wasn't going to work? Probably a combination of both. And that was more than enough self-analysis for one night.

Shaking his head at himself, he tucked the ring into his vest pocket. It clinked against something metallic. He poked his finger into the pocket and felt around. Dragging out a coin, he held it up to the light.

It was the penny Emma Barnes had left him when he'd banished her from Cal's Place. He must have been wearing this vest that day, stuck it into his pocket and forgotten about it. Until now.

Sandy's words about a relationship needing sizzle came back to him, bringing images of Emma with them. That temper of hers carried a hefty dose of sizzle all by itself. Then there was her snotty side and her helpful side. Both were entertaining, and he had to smile when he remembered how she'd rushed to his rescue on the dance floor.

What a gal. And what a good friend she'd tried to be tonight. She could be a lot of fun, too. He hadn't experienced it much firsthand, but he'd seen her cracking jokes with Sylvia, heard her whooping with a boisterous laughter that had made him want to laugh along with her, when he hadn't even heard the joke. And she was a *fine*-looking woman. Yeah, Emma had sizzle to spare.

He'd worked real hard to ignore his attraction to her because of his engagement. But that was over, and he was a free agent again. If he asked Emma out, would she even be interested? He thought she might, but there was only one way to find out. He didn't plan to fall in love with her, or anything, but he sure would love to get a better look at that tattoo.

When she'd flashed it at him on the dance floor, he'd been too distracted to pay attention. Next time, he wouldn't miss a thing.

For the next five days Emma refused to spend even one second more in Cal's Place than was absolutely necessary. She missed hanging out after work with the rest of the crew, but whenever she so much as glimpsed Cal McBride, she remembered that awful moment on the dance floor when he'd revealed his engagement, and she had to get away.

She'd felt completely mortified for entertaining lusty thoughts about another woman's future husband. Granted, nobody else knew what she'd been thinking and feeling, but *she* knew. And she had no intention of finding any other opportunities to make a fool of herself.

Cal must have laughed himself sick over the things she'd said to him that night. What on earth had possessed her to think she could actually help him? And the things she'd done to distract him from watching his fiancée....

She could hardly believe Cal hadn't sought her out for the sole purpose of razzing her about flashing her tattoo at him. She would die of embarrassment if he did. Which was exactly why she intended to go on avoiding him for as long as possible.

Focusing her attention on the movie, she hid out at the Flying M. It wasn't exactly a hardship. It gave her a perfect opportunity to become more acquainted with Blair Du-Maine. She also got to work with Dillon McBride, the former rodeo star who'd been teaching Blair to ride and do ranch chores. He didn't say much, but she absorbed every word he uttered and learned a lot about horses and roping from watching him work.

She also made a new friend in Grace McBride Kramer, and her sons, Riley and Steven. The little devils were into everything, and they'd practically adopted Lori Jones's son, Brandon. Lori was one of the wranglers, and Emma enjoyed working with her, too. She wasn't as friendly as Grace, but Emma hadn't met many people anywhere who were as friendly as the McBrides.

She thought about that for hours, wondering what made them so special. She eventually reached the conclusion that their friendliness was a product of knowing exactly who they were and where they had come from. After the original homesteaders, four generations of McBrides had grown up on this ranch.

They knew and were known by everyone in their community. They belonged here, and they had the luxury of knowing they always would.

She envied that kind of confidence to the depths of her soul, but refused to let it interfere with her new friendships.

It wasn't the McBrides's fault they'd been so lucky. They hadn't chosen their parents any more than she had, and they were incredibly likable. Even Zack, the cop, had turned out to be a stand-up guy. Emma had noticed him hanging around Lori lately, acting more like a love-struck teenager than a big, tough cop.

Personally, Emma still liked Cal the best. If only she hadn't acted so…aggressive that night, but, she couldn't change the past. She could only go to her meetings, do her job and try to stay out of his way.

She'd started parking her motorcycle behind the café to prevent any mishaps with people too curious to keep their hands to themselves. Late one afternoon when she'd begun to believe Cal had forgotten all about her, she put her head down and hurried toward the café's back door. He came out of his office unexpectedly, and she ran into him so hard, she bounced off his chest. She would have fallen if he hadn't grabbed her arms.

"Whoa, there," he said, steadying her. "Why, Emma, long time, no see. How've you been?"

"Um…fine." Lord, she couldn't look into his eyes. Her heart was pounding so hard she could barely speak at all. "Really fine."

His fingers lightly swept back and forth, raising gooseflesh on her arms, even through her leather jacket. "Where were you going in such a hurry?"

"Oh, just, um, back to the ranch. It's been a long day, and I need to spend some time with my horse. It was nice seeing you, Cal."

When she started to pull away, he tightened his grip just enough to hold her in place. "Now, why don't I believe that?" he asked with smile warm enough to melt her toenail polish. "Could it be because you've been avoiding me? Yes, I think it could."

"I'm not avoiding you," she lied. "I have other things to do besides hang around your bar every day."

"Oh, yeah? Like what?"

"Like…learning to fall off a galloping horse without getting killed. Little things like that."

"Uh-huh. So why aren't the other guys practicing that stunt, too?"

"Maybe they already know how."

"Right." His grin turned wicked, stealing most of her breath. "And how many hours a day are you practicing it?"

"As many as I can stand," she retorted. "It's not so easy to learn."

"I'm sure it's not. But really now, Emma, why are you avoiding me?"

"Why would you care if I was?" she countered.

"Well, I thought we were going to be friends." His big, dark eyes took on a wounded-puppy expression that tugged at her heartstrings, even though she knew he was using it on purpose. "It's hard to be friends with a gal who scampers away like a terrified squirrel every time you come around."

"I've never 'scampered away' in my life," she said. "I have professional responsibilities to fulfill, and practicing happens to be one of them."

"Don't you ever get any time off?"

Emma watched his dimple appear and felt a sinking sensation in the pit of her stomach. Whatever he was up to, she really hoped she wasn't going to fall for it. She cleared her throat and looked away from his darn sexy eyes. "Not much," she said. "It depends on the shooting schedule. What's your point?"

"I'd like to spend some time with you. I've been trying to catch you for days so I could ask you out."

Emma yanked herself out of his grasp and glared at him. "Excuse me? Aren't you forgetting something important?"

He bit his lower lip and wrinkled up his eyebrows as if he were solving calculus problems in his head. "I can't think of anything. You want to know where we're going?"

She wanted to smack him but knew she didn't dare.

"You lousy, cheating slime. I wouldn't go to a dogfight with you if you were one of the contestants and favored to win."

His whole body stiffened and his face flushed a dark red. "What the hell are you talking about?"

Making no effort to hide her disgust, she pushed past him and banged through the screen door to the alley. He charged after her, catching up as she mounted her bike.

"Wait a minute. Where do you get off calling me that?"

"Cheating slime? Gee, Cal, if the name fits, why shouldn't I? Of course, maybe your *fiancée* doesn't mind your dating other women, but I don't mess around with engaged or married men. You got that, McBride?"

He tipped back his head and laughed so long, Emma started the engine and picked up her helmet. Reaching his long arms over and around the handlebars he grabbed the ignition key with one hand, and her helmet with the other. She lunged forward, grabbing at them, but he easily held them out of reach. Then he straddled her front wheel and leaned down, gazing straight into her eyes with an intensity that made her insides quiver. She lowered herself back onto the seat.

"I think I get your drift, all right. I'd even say your attitude is admirable. But, honey, you've been so busy avoiding me, you've missed out on all the juicy gossip."

"What gossip?"

"I don't *have* a fiancée anymore. Sandy gave back her ring the night you saved me on the dance floor."

Her face burned, and she looked down at the handgrips, struggling for composure.

He gave her another wicked grin, bringing out his dimple. "I wanted to tell you how much I appreciated your efforts. If I'd punched out Marsh the way I intended to, I *would* have made a complete fool of myself, and I'd never be able to enforce my rule about fighting again, either."

Emma frowned thoughtfully, trying to figure out what

was wrong with this picture. "She dumped you for Marsh?"

He shrugged. "Not exactly. It's a long story. If you're really interested, have dinner with me tonight and I'll tell you all about it."

"Oh, I get it," she said, relaxing a little. "This isn't a real date. You just want somebody to listen to you."

His eyes narrowed, giving her the impression that he was calculating odds. What on earth was he up to, anyway? Then he said, "If that's the way you want to look at it, fine by me."

"What do you mean?"

"Nothing." He backed off a step. Though his smile seemed genuine enough, she didn't completely trust it. She raised an eyebrow at him, and he hastily tacked on, "Honest, Emma. I could really use a friend to talk to right now."

"Why me? You've got tons of friends who know you better than I do."

"Most of them wouldn't be able to stop themselves from blabbing everything I said all over town. I don't think you'd do that."

"Of course not," she said, indignant at the thought of anyone betraying a friend's confidence in idle gossip.

"Well, then, have dinner with me tonight."

She gazed deeply into his eyes and saw only a sincere desire for her company. How could she refuse? "All right. Just remember I don't do the dress-up thing. Make it a place where I can wear jeans."

His smile warmed her all the way through. "You've got yourself a deal. I'll pick you up at seven and have you home by eleven. Will that do?"

Nodding, she returned his smile. "Fine."

He held out her key and helmet. When she reached up to take them, he leaned down, planting a gentle, but delightfully sweet kiss on her lips. Though the contact was quick, it startled every nerve ending in her mouth to complete awareness and created a melting sensation low in her belly.

When he pulled away, it took considerable effort on her part to stop herself from protesting. More flustered than she wanted to admit, she crammed on her helmet, started Mama and drove off. She felt his gaze boring into her back all the way to the end of the alley, and heaved a sigh of relief as she turned onto the road to the Flying M.

What had she gotten herself into now? Cal's kiss had been nothing more than a friendly gesture. Of course it had. She had to remember that. And she would.

But if he could do that much to her with a friendly little smooch, what would it be like if he ever really kissed her? And meant it?

Chapter Five

Cal drove out to the ranch and followed the path until he came to the trailer with a familiar motorcycle parked beside it. He climbed out of his pickup and walked over to study Emma's motorcycle. Jeez, she must polish the thing every day. He didn't know that much about Emma, but he knew she hated for anyone else to touch her bike.

He heard a clanking noise from inside the trailer, then a soft curse that made him grin. And suddenly big, wing-flapping butterflies invaded his stomach. A cold, sticky sweat covered his palms. Oh, great, he didn't need this. It was just a date.

God knew he'd been on plenty of them in the past. Of course, it had been a long time since he'd dated a woman he barely knew, but that shouldn't make him feel this nervous. He could talk to anyone, and nobody had ever accused him of being bashful.

Emma stepped outside then, smiling when she caught sight of him. Cal tried not to gawk at her, but damn, she looked as fresh and appealing as a frisky, newborn filly. She might not ''do the dress-up thing,'' and she wasn't beautiful in the strictest sense of the word, but what she did to a pair of snug jeans and a blue, scoop-necked T-shirt that matched the color of her eyes nearly gave him a heart attack.

With her hair down around her shoulders and shining in the waning sunlight, her eyes warm and welcoming, a delicate silver locket around her neck and tiny sliver hoops in her earlobes, she looked real pretty in a girl-next-door kind of way.

But then, a guy couldn't help noticing her firm curves and long, shapely legs, and the girl next door ripened into an extremely desirable woman. The final kick came when he saw her leather sandals. Who would have guessed that under those clunky hiking boots she always wore when she rode her bike, she had such slender feet with dainty toes and bright red toenails?

He'd never had a thing for feet, but the vanity of those painted toenails struck him as being incredibly erotic. It also made him wonder what other delights—besides her tattoo—might be hiding under her clothing. She appeared to have a surprisingly soft and feminine side to her personality.

''Hi,'' she said.

''Hi.'' He tipped his hat to her. ''Ready to go?''

She reached back inside the trailer, grabbed a small purse and locked the door behind her. ''I am now.''

He swept one hand in front of himself, indicating his barn-red-and-black, vintage Ford pickup. ''Right this way, ma'am.''

Her eyes widened when she saw his truck. She walked all the way around it, oohing and ahhing over every little special touch he'd put into the restoration. ''She's gorgeous, Cal. Nice colors, too. Oh, I can hardly wait to see how she rides.''

Cal opened the passenger door for her, sneaking a peek

at her cute little rump as she scrambled onto the high seat. Then he hurried around the front and climbed in beside her. She fired questions about the truck at him all the way to Cody.

Marveling at her wide-ranging knowledge, he could barely believe his ears. Most of the men in Sunshine Gap maintained their own vehicles, did basic plumbing and other household repairs and fixed appliances out of necessity. Nobody living forty or fifty miles from the highway wanted to spend a fortune on service calls or waste time hauling a washing machine into town. They could handle any regular mechanical jobs that came along, and were justifiably proud of their skills.

But Emma spoke confidently of pulling engines and ring jobs, transmissions and drivetrains, gear ratios and torque the way other women talked about recipes. In Cal's eyes, she was a rare and special woman. Hell, she probably knew more about engines than he did. Strangely enough, he didn't find that annoying or intimidating. He found it…exciting.

Cody's streets always were busy during the summer months, but Cal found a parking space two blocks from their destination. He took Emma's hand while they walked along. She shot him a wide-eyed look, as if to say friends don't hold hands. He told her he just didn't want to lose her in the crowd. She raised a doubtful eyebrow at him, but left her hand in his.

"Oh, my," she said when the old Irma Hotel with its lighted roof line and balcony came into view. "What's that?"

"That's where we're having dinner," Cal said. "Buffalo Bill Cody himself built it for his daughter around the turn of the century. They put out the best prime rib in two hundred miles. In Wyoming, that's saying something."

"It's beautiful." She looked up at him, her forehead wrinkled in a frown. "Are you sure we can wear jeans in there?"

He laughed. "We can wear jeans just about where we want. I doubt there's even a restaurant down in Cheyenne that doesn't allow customers to wear jeans. They'd go out of business."

It was fun watching Emma's quiet appreciation of the grand old hotel's elegant interior. Even more fun watching her face when the first bite of prime rib landed on her tongue. Her eyelids drifted shut as if the combination of garlic, salt, pepper and juicy meat gave her tastebuds a pleasure so intense it was nearly sexual.

Cal figured that was an idea that deserved further thought, but not just yet. He had little doubt they would get there soon enough, and he would enjoy every single second of holding her in his arms when they did. For now, he just wanted to show her a good time and help her to feel comfortable with him.

By the time the waiter cleared away their empty plates and served steaming cups of coffee, Cal felt content and relaxed. Until Emma asked about his broken engagement. He sat up straighter and gave her a coaxing smile.

"Let's talk about you, instead."

"Let's not," she retorted with a grin. "You said you needed a friend to talk to, so talk, McBride. What happened?"

"This is just between you and me, right?" Emma gave him a solemn nod and he continued. "Sandy's still in love with my cousin Marsh, so she called off our engagement."

"That's terrible, Cal. I'm so sorry." Emma reached across the table and laid her hand on his forearm, giving it a sympathetic squeeze.

Maybe telling her about his broken engagement wasn't such a bad idea after all. A few sympathy points actually might come in handy. He shrugged one shoulder. "I'll live. It was a calculated risk at best. She was Marsh's girlfriend first, but they hadn't seen each other in years. We both thought she'd gotten over him, but we were wrong."

"Has he gotten over her?"

"You'd think so after ten years, but maybe not. He sure was ticked off when he found out about our engagement. Funny thing is, Sandy says she doesn't want to get back together with him. She just couldn't marry me while she still loves him."

"Why did they break up in the first place?"

"Nobody knows but them, and they're not talking."

"That doesn't sound good," Emma observed.

"Well, you just never know," Cal replied. "Maybe now that I'm out of the way, they'll be able to work it all out."

Emma pinned him against his chair with a glinty-eyed stare. "You don't seem very heartbroken."

"I'm not," he admitted. "My relationship with Sandy was never a heavy-duty love match."

Clearly shocked, she stared at him. "But you were going to get *married*," she sputtered. "Why would either one of you agree to that?"

Cal squirmed at the appalled expression on her face. He wasn't sure he could explain it to her in a way she would understand. "We were both ready to settle down and have kids. We'd been best friends for a long time and there wasn't anybody around setting either one of us on fire, so it...seemed like the thing to do."

"But you're so young. Early thirties I'd say?"

"Thirty-four," he said. "Both of us."

"Then what's the big rush? You have plenty of time to have children."

"Yeah, if we were living in a city like L.A., we'd probably look at it that way," he conceded. "But out here, most people get married and start having babies in their late teens or early twenties. This is a family-oriented culture, and kids are really important. As far as Sunshine Gap is concerned, Sandy and I are a pair of oddballs because we've never been married."

Emma's scowl deepened into a full-fledged frown. "That's no reason to marry someone you don't love."

"We love each other. Hell, we're best friends. I can think of worse things than being married to Sandy."

Emma's cheeks turned pink and she held her hands palms-up, as if begging him to see the error of his thinking. "But it's not really what you *want*, is it?"

"Next time you're in Sunshine Gap, look around," he said. "You don't have thousands of people in your age range to choose from. When you live here, you marry the most compatible person available and make the best of it."

"Baloney! Go on a trip. Take a cruise. Get yourself on a national talk show. There's a great big world out there with millions of people you could love. Make a little effort and find one."

Cal had to smile at her impassioned speech. He wasn't sure why she was getting so riled about his love life, but he found it endearing that she cared enough to try to set him straight. Here was a woman with strong convictions. While he admired that, she was so darn earnest, he couldn't resist poking at her a little.

"Excuse me, honey," he drawled, "but I don't see any ring on your finger. If falling in love is so great, why aren't you doing it yourself?"

"Two reasons," she said. "I don't have time, and I rarely stay in one place long enough to get involved with anyone."

"Then what makes you qualified to give me advice?"

"Well, I've had a few relationships, *honey*." She leaned forward, bracing one elbow on the table and thumping her opposite index finger in time with her words. "I do know how it's done, and I would never *marry* some guy just because he was the best one available. I wouldn't even pick out a bike that way, much less a husband. Are you and Sandy both nuts?"

Cal chuckled. "Could be. How did you choose your bike?"

She shot him a reproving look, no doubt for chuckling

at such a serious topic. Honestly, she should have been a school teacher or a librarian, maybe even a cop.

"The way I choose anything," she said. "I figure out exactly what I want, and then I save my money until I can afford to buy it."

"No compromises?"

"No compromises. I did too much of that when I was growing up, but I don't have to do it anymore. And I won't."

"So, you're waiting for Mr. Absolutely Right to come along?"

"It's bound to be better than settling for Mr. You'll-Do."

Cal laughed again, drawing a glare that should have singed his mustache. Of course, that only made him laugh harder, and the harder he laughed the madder she looked. But it felt wonderful to laugh, and he couldn't rein it in just yet. Emma sat back again, folded her arms across her breasts and simply stared at him until he regained his composure. Then she started pelting him with questions again.

"Have you ever lived anywhere besides Sunshine Gap?"

"I spent fours years in Laramie going to college."

"What's your degree in?"

"Business administration."

She nodded her approval and he almost started laughing again. He couldn't remember the last time he hadn't been able to predict both sides of a conversation. He had no clue where she was headed with this one, and it was exhilarating.

"What did you do after college?"

"Worked in Denver for a couple of years."

"Why didn't you stay there?"

"I didn't like corporate America."

"What does that mean?"

"I was too naive about office politics and some other things. Let's just say I decided to take some time off and figure out where I'd gone wrong."

"You never went back?"

Cal shook his head. "I bought my business and decided to see if I could make it work."

"Which, it obviously did," she said.

He nodded. "Then the next thing I knew, I'd been talked into running for the town council, and now I'm the mayor. I doubt I'll ever be able to leave now."

"But is this what you really *want?* Or have you just…settled for what's available again? Your life's ticking away, Cal. Where do you want to be five years from now? Ten years from now? Do you know?"

He thought about her question for a moment, then slowly shook his head. "Can't say that I do, Emma. It's a good question, though. I'll give it some thought."

"Do that, McBride."

She gave him an enigmatic smile, but before he could ask her about it, the waiter delivered the check. Cal stuck an adequate wad of cash into the leather folder. Emma pushed back her chair and stood, indicating she was ready to leave.

Cal thought about protesting. They still had plenty of time, and he was reluctant to end the evening early. On the other hand, some exercise would feel good after such a heavy meal. He could take her on a walking tour of downtown Cody.

Emma immediately agreed with his suggestion, and when he took her hand this time, she didn't even blink. Smiling with satisfaction, Cal escorted her outdoors. And came face-to-face with none other than his cousin Marsh and Marsh's blue-haired friend, Hope DuMaine.

Emma nearly groaned out loud when she recognized the other couple. It had been a nice evening until now. While Cal and Marsh puffed themselves up on testosterone and adrenalin and played dueling eyeballs, she gave Hope a long, cold stare.

Hope stepped closer to her and whispered, "Oh, stop.

I'm sorry about the other night, but I didn't know that would happen."

"Oh? Lose your crystal ball while you were out cruising on your broom?" Emma taunted.

With a pointed glance at Cal and Emma's joined hands, Hope sniffed. "I don't know what you're whining about."

"It's not like that, Hope."

"Of course it's not." Hope's smile turned wicked. "I know the drill. You're just friends."

When Hope trotted out that much sarcasm, Emma knew it was time to retreat. Her primary means of defending herself was physical; Hope's was verbal, and her tongue could be as cruel and sharp as any wildcat's fangs. Even if she'd had an appropriate response in mind, Emma doubted Hope could have heard it over the men's voices.

"What're you trying to say, Marsh?" Cal demanded.

"You know damn well what I'm saying," Marsh answered. "If you didn't love Sandy any more than this—" he paused to give Emma a scathing glance "—you had no right to ask her to marry you. She deserves better."

Cal snorted. "Coming from you, that's rich. Tell me all about how you treated Sandy so well. You stupid jerk—"

Marsh's right fist smashed into Cal's nose. Blood gushed down the front of Cal's T-shirt and dripped onto the sidewalk. Cal turned deathly pale, his eyes rolled back until only the whites showed and his knees sagged.

"Aw, hell." Marsh shook his hand as if trying to ease the pain. "Catch him!"

Emma freed her fingers and whipped her arm around Cal's waist. She struggled to keep him upright, but he was out cold and his dead weight pulled her off balance. It happened so fast, she could only try to cushion his fall. With no time to use her professional training, she hit the concrete hard, and a second later, Cal landed on top of her.

The impact vibrated the length of her spine, driving the oxygen from her lungs and reminding her in graphic detail why it was important to tuck and roll. She lay on the

ground, cradling his head against her breasts and fighting
for breath. Marsh and Hope loomed over her, their eyes
filled with worry. Marsh grabbed Cal's arm as if to pull
him off of Emma, but she tightened her grip on him.

"Don't move him," she wheezed. "Head injury. Call
paramedics."

Marsh flashed his version of the McBride grin at her.
"It's not a head injury. He just can't stand the sight of
blood. Passes out every time."

"You're sure?" Emma asked.

"Yup. I'm more worried about you than that big hoss."
Marsh carefully rolled Cal onto his back and off of Emma.

She inhaled a series of long, deep breaths. When her
lungs functioned normally again, she propped herself up on
one hand. Hope went into the restaurant to get a damp cloth
and an ice bag for Cal's nose. While she was gone, Emma
watched Marsh intently.

He sat on the sidewalk, supporting the back of Cal's head
with one hand and warding off the foot traffic around them
with the other. Of all the McBride men she had met, Marsh
had the most classically handsome face. He had dark circles
under his eyes at the moment, however, and there were
lines of strain radiating from his nose and mouth.

"Did you really have to hit him?" Emma asked, tilting
her head toward Cal. His eyelids twitched as if he were
starting to come around.

"Seemed like it at the time," Marsh said with a sad
smile. "But I wish I hadn't. We used to be best buds."

Cal groaned, then tried to sit up. Marsh put his free hand,
fingers spread wide, in the center of Cal's chest and held
him down. "Hold on there, cuz. Give yourself a minute."
He glanced over at Emma. "You hurt anywhere?"

"I'm fine," Emma assured him. She'd probably have
bruises the length of her spine, but she doubted anything
was hurt enough to require medical attention. She brushed
an unruly shock of hair out of Cal's eyes, then pointed at
the front of his shirt and her own. Both were liberally

soaked with bright red blood. "Will he pass out again if he sees this?"

Marsh shrugged. "Hard to say. I've seen it happen, but he doesn't always."

"Stop talkin' about me like I'm not here," Cal grumbled. He grabbed Marsh's hand and flung it off his chest, then struggled into a sitting position. He glanced up at the crowd of curious onlookers and glared at all of them. "Show's over, folks. Go on about your business."

"Sure you don't need an ambulance here?" a man asked, his Brooklyn accent thick enough to slice.

"He's all right," Emma said.

With obvious reluctance, the man moved on down the sidewalk, his companions slowly following him. Hope arrived with a white dish towel and the restaurant's manager carrying a bowl of water and a plastic bag filled with ice cubes. Emma dipped the towel in the water and cleaned Cal's face. Though he was clearly uncomfortable, he tolerated her ministrations well enough—until she banged his nose with her knuckle while scrubbing his mustache. Jerking back, he scowled at her.

"Ow, dammit! That hurt."

"Duh, McBride," Emma retorted, rinsing out the towel and going after a speck of blood on the side of his chin. "You'll be lucky if it's not broken."

He cautiously put his thumb and forefinger on either side of his nose and slowly worked them down to the tip, then slid them back up to the bridge. "I'm in luck then. I think it's okay."

Marsh squatted down and studied Cal's nose for himself. Nodding in satisfaction, he met Cal's angry gaze. "I'm glad it's not busted. And I'm sorry I hit you."

Cal stared at the hand Marsh offered him, then ignored it and climbed to his feet under his own power. He swayed there for a moment, making Emma want to hit him for being so blasted stubborn. Dropping the towel, she scrambled to her own feet and wrapped her arm around his waist to steady him.

Marsh lowered his hand to his side and gave Cal a pained look. "Come on, man. Let's make up and move on. We can't solve anything with a feud between us."

"What is there to solve?" Cal took the ice bag from the restaurant manager and held it up beside his face. "Sandy and I are still good friends, and we're always going to be good friends. Seems to me you're the one who's most liable to hurt her now, but you'd better not do it. If you're not really committed to working things out with her this time, leave her the hell alone."

"And if I don't?" Marsh demanded.

"Then be prepared to protect that pretty-boy face of yours. You got in a lucky punch tonight, but you know damn well you won't get another one. I'm not going to sit back and watch you play with her head again."

Hope frowned at Cal, then at Marsh. "All right, boys, you've had your fun. Enough already." She reached out and nudged the ice bag toward Cal's nose. Tucking her other hand into the crook of Marsh's elbow, she pulled him toward the restaurant. "Let's go, sweet cheeks. I'm hungry."

Breathing out a silent sigh of relief when the heavy door closed behind Marsh and Hope, Emma gathered up the towel and the bowl, handing them back to the manager. "Thank you. We'll be going now."

When the other man left, Emma took Cal's free hand in case he needed steadying and headed back to his vintage pickup. Once there he handed her the keys without protest, slumped against the passenger door and held the ice bag to his nose. And then, he started to laugh. And laugh. And laugh some more.

Emma tolerated it until they reached the outskirts of town. Pulling into a tavern's parking lot, she shifted into Neutral and let the engine idle. "Stop acting like a demented hyena, or I'll find the hospital and have you admitted to the psych ward. What on earth is the matter with you?''

Shaking his head and wiping at the outer corners of his eyes, Cal straightened up and turned to face her. "Sorry," he said, though he didn't look the least bit sorry to her. "There's nothing wrong with me. It's just Marsh looked so surprised when I wouldn't shake his hand back there. I've got him right where I want him, and one of these days, he'll thank me for it.''

"For what?''

"For making him see that he still loves Sandy, and he might lose her for good if he doesn't pull his head out of…well, never mind.''

"You mean…you and Sandy were just setting Marsh up with your engagement?''

"I'm not quite that devious," Cal said with grin. "And Sandy's not devious at all. The engagement was real enough. If Marsh hadn't come home, I'd say chances were better than even the wedding would have gone off without a hitch.''

Hopelessly confused, Emma huffed at him. "But you sound as if you really want Sandy and Marsh to get back together.''

Cal shrugged. "I love both of them, Emma. I want 'em to be happy, and as long as they're apart, I don't think they ever will be. They just seem to belong together.''

"You're really okay with that?''

"Yeah." Holding her gaze, he reached across the darkened cab and stroked her cheek with the backs of his fingers. "I really am. Now I can go after exactly what I want.''

His touch was incredibly gentle, but her skin tingled wildly wherever his fingers moved. Her heart thumped hard against her breastbone. Her mouth dried out. Surely, he wasn't saying… *Oh, don't be ridiculous, Em. Of course, he's not saying he wants you.* But for an insane instant, she almost wished he *was* saying that. The realization prompted her to break eye contact and drive back onto the highway.

Cal chuckled and brought the ice bag back to his nose. Emma enjoyed driving his pickup immensely, but the silence began to grate on her nerves.

"How's your nose?" she asked.

He pulled away the ice bag and leaned across the seat to give her a closer look. "Right now it feels damn cold. How ugly is it?"

She shrugged. "A little puffy and red, but it's okay otherwise. Does it hurt?"

"Not much." He sat back and laid the ice bag on the seat beside him.

"Do you really always pass out whenever you see blood?"

He muttered a word that made her chuckle. Since the light had grown dim and he immediately averted his face, she couldn't be certain, but she thought he was blushing like a ripe strawberry. He shifted his weight and cleared his throat before answering. "Yup. And I'll be damned if I know why."

"People give you a hard time about it?"

"Oh yeah," Cal said with a disgruntled laugh. "If you want to know the truth, that's why I'm not working the ranch with Dillon and Jake."

"Is there that much blood involved in ranching?"

"Branding and calving are the worst. The whole family thinks I'm a ninny."

"Lots of people have that problem," Emma said. "Don't they know that?"

"They know it intellectually. And it's fine when it happens to somebody else. But it's never been okay when I'm the one who's out cold."

"I thought Marsh handled it well enough tonight."

Cal shrugged one shoulder. "Yeah, I guess he did."

"He told me you two used to be best buds."

"We were." A nostalgic smile softened his features.

"Our birthdays are only a week apart. Everyone called us the twins."

"When did that change?"

"About the time he took off for Hollywood to be a big screenwriter and left Sandy behind. I never understood how he could break her heart that way. He's bugged me ever since."

"Maybe he wasn't meant to stay here and be a cowboy, Cal."

"That's not the issue. I left the Gap too, but I didn't walk away and act like nobody here mattered anymore. When he did come home, all he could talk about was Hollywood this and movie stars that, and L.A. was super cool, and Wyoming was the armpit of the nation. He was damn irritating."

Emma smiled. "I can imagine. But isn't it interesting that his first screenplay to make it into production is about the founders of the Flying M? I heard that he absolutely insisted on shooting in Wyoming."

"You think that means something?" Cal asked.

"He did an awful lot of work trying to bring the Flying M to life if he has no respect for it."

"I hadn't thought of it that way before," Cal said in a thoughtful tone.

"Whether you believe it or not, he loves you," Emma said softly. "I saw it in his eyes when you were unconscious."

Cal grunted, then looked away. "Yeah, well, he's not such a bad guy. He just doesn't understand women."

It was Emma's turn to crack up.

"What?" he asked indignantly. "You think I *don't?*"

Emma forced herself to pay attention to the road. "I didn't say a word."

"With all that hee-hawing, you didn't have to," Cal grumbled.

"It's nothing personal. You really can't help it because you're a guy. You're wired differently than we are."

"That doesn't mean I can't understand anything."

"Of course, it doesn't." Laughter threatened to overwhelm her again, and she had to take a deep breath to steady herself. "It just makes the likelihood that you will, much more remote."

"Give me one example of a time where I've missed the boat."

Do you want a list? "The engagement was your idea. You talked Sandy into it, didn't you?"

"How'd you know that?"

Oh, just a wild and crazy guess. "You really had to sell her on it, didn't you?"

"Yeah," he said cautiously. "Why is that a big deal?"

"Because no woman in her right mind would have dreamed up a scheme like that. The idea reeked from the beginning."

"Hey, I explained all of that."

"And it made perfect sense from a rational viewpoint. But you forgot about all the history between you and Marsh, and Marsh and Sandy that hasn't been resolved. If they haven't made up after all these years, they're not even close to being rational, and it's perfectly clear that neither one of them is ready to move on."

"That's easy to see in hindsight."

Emma rolled her eyes. "Only if you're a guy. You don't give feelings the respect they deserve, and then you're surprised when they come back and trash your big plans."

He was quiet for what seemed like a long time. Comfortable with the silence now, Emma drove on. The old truck had no air-conditioning, but the breeze coming in the open windows was cool and sweet, and carried a hint of sagebrush. Every now and then she glimpsed a flash of something slinking into the brush at the sides of the road, a coyote, maybe or a raccoon or even a skunk.

She smiled and took her right hand off the steering wheel long enough to pat her tattoo through her shirt. Suddenly she felt his gaze boring into her breasts, and her face felt hot at the memory of flashing him on the dance floor. So, maybe guys weren't the only ones who did idiotic things.

"I think I see what you mean," he finally said. "Now that you've pointed it out, it's damned odd neither one of them would ever make the first move to be friends again. Marsh has been home for a week or two almost every summer, but they've gone to amazing lengths to avoid each other."

"My point exactly." She turned her head and smiled at him. "So what are you going to do now?"

"I was thinkin' about huntin' up a sexy, hot-tempered gal to console me." He waggled his eyebrows at her. "What do you think of that idea?"

Emma snorted. "Forget it, dude. The last thing you need right now is another romance."

"Uh-huh. What's the first thing I need?"

"You need a good friend to blast you out of this huge rut you've fallen into. Lucky for you, I'm available."

His deep, rough chuckle reached across the bench seat and warmed her clear through. "How do you plan to do that?"

She glanced across the darkened cab at him and gave him a small, and she hoped, mysterious smile. "Telling you would spoil half the fun. Guess you'll just have to wait and see."

Chapter Six

During the next two weeks Cal developed a healthy respect for the wide range of creativity and deviousness residing in Emma's mind. When she decided to blast a guy out of a rut, she assaulted every piece of his comfort zone without mercy. No routine was too mundane to be disrupted, no habit too ingrained to be left unchallenged, no part of his life too personal to escape her scrutiny.

Did she even have the decency to work alone? Noooooo. Of course not. From day one she enlisted the help of his staff, making up alternative menus for the cooks and waitresses on duty to follow.

If he ordered his favorite bacon-and-egg breakfast, he ended up with a bagel, cream cheese and fresh strawberries instead—a neat trick since bagels weren't on the menu at all. An order for a club sandwich turned into a seafood salad. A burger and fries? A grilled chicken breast, rice and a green salad. And just when he thought he'd figured out her system, she changed the whole thing and he had to start all over again.

It was no better in the bar. If he ordered a beer, he got a margarita. If he ordered a margarita, he got a gin and tonic. If he ordered a gin and tonic, he got a whiskey ditch. He considered waiting on himself, but he was too fascinated to see what she would do next.

Deciding he didn't get enough exercise, she dragged him away every chance she got and introduced him to the dubious pleasures of trail running. If there were any trails in the area built for that purpose, he wasn't aware of them. Such minor details never deterred Emma.

One day she led him into the woods at the edge of town and followed deer paths, stomped through brooks and dodged boulders with the glee of a kid on a waterslide. The next day he followed her across rough prairie terrain, using cow paths or dirt bike trails to avoid sagebrush and thistle patches. He warned her about the ticks and snakes in the brush, hoping to convince her to run on the relatively level back roads.

No such luck. She told him the ticks and snakes would just have to watch out for themselves, and off she went, wearing nothing but a tank top over a sports bra, running shorts, shoes and socks. He sweated gallons and suffered multiple sore muscles trying to keep up with her, but he focused his attention on her shapely behind and kept on going like a greyhound chasing the mechanical rabbit. The woman had endless stores of energy. He could think of better ways to use it.

When he complained about spending too much time away from his business, she insisted that what he really needed was an assistant manager to run the place when he was gone. Shortly thereafter she started campaigning on Sylvia's behalf. Cal resisted the idea with everything he had, but figured it was only a matter of time before she wore him down enough to convince him.

The movie folks took Sundays off. Emma didn't. One

Sunday she roared up on her Harley-Davidson while he was eating the waffle and melon salad he'd received in place of the Denver omelette he'd ordered. Clad in leather, she strode through the café and took the chair opposite his, an excited smile stretching across her face.

"Morning, Cal. Hurry up with that," she said. "We don't want to be late."

"Late for what?" he asked, though he wasn't too sure he really wanted to know. He wouldn't put it past her to take him hang gliding.

"We're going white water rafting. I've made the reservations, but we'll have to go Dutch."

"Aw, Emma, *please*," he said, "I don't want to do that."

"Have you ever done it before?"

"Well, no, but—"

"Then it's high time you did, McBride. People rarely try out the tourist attractions in their own backyards, and you've got some great ones here.

"I don't swim very well," Cal said.

"That's okay," she said, waving his concerns away. "I've got my lifesaving card. You fall in the water, I'll save you."

"Oh, jeez, Emma."

"Cal," she said, mimicking his whiny tone. "Come on, you've been such a good sport so far. Don't wimp out on me now."

Damn woman always knew how to hit him smack in the ego. Honest to God, she was worse than his brothers or his cousins. Still, he had to admit it worked.

"All right," he grumbled. "But I'll have to go change."

She eyed his leather vest and boots, then grudgingly nodded. "Okay. But put a rush on it, will you?"

She followed him to his house. His miniature poodles, Yip and Yap, burst through their doggy door and raced along the fence, barking their fool heads off. Yip was black, Yap was champagne colored, and both were spayed females. Exclaiming with delight, Emma ran to the fence. "Hello, you little sweeties," she cooed, driving the dogs into a wilder frenzy.

Cal's neck felt warm. Now she'd ask him why a big guy like him had two tiny dogs instead of a Doberman or a German shepherd. Well, he wasn't going to explain. He probably would have chosen a bigger dog for himself, but he'd inherited Yip and Yap when old Mrs. Hayes had sold him the house and moved into the nursing home in Cody. Though the poodles were spoiled and noisy, he'd become real attatched to them.

He opened the gate and strode through, then guarded the opening while Emma joined him. Given any opportunity at all, Yip and Yap escaped and ran around the neighborhood, decorating everyone else's lawn. It made them less than popular, as did their tendency to bark incessantly. Emma dropped to her knees on the grass and held her arms out to them.

Yip ran right up her legs and jumped again and again, trying to lick her face. Yap ran circles around her, barking all the way. Cal snorted in disgust and headed for the house.

"Want to come in?" he asked Emma.

"No, thanks," she said, scooping Yap up with one hand and cuddling her close. "I'll just stay out here with these little darlings. Put some trunks on under your jeans and coat yourself with sunscreen. Bring a towel and a dry set of clothes to keep in the car, too, and some ratty tennis shoes to wear in the raft."

"Yes, mother," Cal said, giving her a snappy salute.

"I'm just trying to make sure you have fun and don't have to pay any nasty consequences later," she said mildly.

He shut up and went inside. By the time he was ready to go, his mood had lightened, mostly due to the sound of Emma's laughter coming through his bedroom window. She was throwing a rubber baseball for the dogs now, and everything they did seemed to please her no end. When he went back outside, she scrambled to her feet and wiped her hands on the seat of her jeans.

"Will Mama be okay here?" she asked, pointing at her bike.

"Why don't you bring her around back by the garage? Then she won't be so noticeable from the street."

Her grateful smile warmed him, and he realized he always felt a delicious undercurrent of anticipation when he was around her. With Emma along, outings he'd always considered too much trouble turned into adventures.

The trip to Cody seemed shorter than usual. They arrived at the meeting place in plenty of time to buy their tickets, change into old shoes and pick out life jackets that fit. The guide selected Cal and Emma to take front positions in the raft and handed them each a paddle.

Cal glanced around at their fellow passengers and immediately understood why they'd been chosen. The majority of the others had children with them or sported white hair. One of the seniors told him they were all on a bus tour from Maine.

The ladies tittered nervously when the guide handed them plastic buckets and told them to bail when he gave them the signal. Once they were in the water, he started his spiel, pointing out wildlife and other points of interest along the river's banks. Gradually, their speed picked up, and the guide began shouting directions to the paddlers and the bailers. Cal found himself working hard to keep the raft headed straight down the river.

He glanced over when Emma let out a loud whoop and a laugh, and felt his groin tighten. Slicing the water with her paddle, she was the picture of vitality. Her hair glistened in the bright sunshine, her long, tanned arms moved with sureness, her rippling muscles showed strength and skill.

She clearly was having the time of her life, and it was the sexiest thing Cal had ever seen. Thank God he kept getting splashed with frigid water every two minutes. If some of those elderly ladies had any idea what he was thinking, they'd probably faint and end up drowning in the water collecting in the bottom of the raft.

Lord, Emma's tank top was soaked now, and the cold water had a predictable effect on her nipples. Cal's mouth went dry and for a second, he forgot to paddle, The raft drifted sideways under the power of Emma's unopposed stroke. The guide yelled at him, and Cal had to laugh at himself while he struggled to straighten the raft out again.

Then they hit a series of rapids that made the raft bounce around like a writhing snake. Cal and Emma paddled as hard and fast as they could. The kids and the senior citizens shrieked and laughed and held on for dear life until the guide hollered at them to start bailing again.

Two hours later they headed for shore, tired but exhilarated, soaked to the skin yet thirsty enough to lower the river level, and ready to eat like there was no tomorrow. Lunch had been included in their trip's price, and the rafting company had set up a pair of picnic tables and two barbecue grills working full tilt.

Since children under six weren't allowed in the rafts, the company also provided a baby-sitting service. There were lots of happy squeals from the little ones when they were reunited with their families.

Cal and Emma sat across from each other at one of the tables, grinning like fools and filling their stomachs with burgers, potato salad, baked beans and pickles. A family with four children sat next to them, and Emma seemed to get as big a kick out of the kids' excited chatter as he did. The smallest child, a little girl of two or three, stood up on the bench and looked at Cal with big, heart-melting blue eyes.

With her head tipped to one side, she studied him carefully, then climbed onto his lap, stuck a thumb into her mouth and rested her head against his chest. Looking mortified, her mother reached across the toddler's older brother, but Cal waved her hands away.

"I don't mind," he said, smiling down at his little friend. "Go ahead and enjoy your lunch."

The woman shot him a doubtful look, but her daughter snuggled closer to Cal and her eyes drifted shut. Cal stroked her tousled curls, liking the feel of her warm, solid little body against his. Suddenly, he felt Emma's gaze zeroed in on him. When he looked at her, he saw tears shimmering in her eyes.

"What is it?" he asked softly.

"That's the sweetest thing I've ever seen," Emma whispered, swiping at her eyes with her fingertips. "She's so…trusting."

"Maybe she just knows a good guy when she sees him."

Emma nodded, then murmured something he couldn't quite catch, but he thought it sounded something like, "And so do I."

Before he could ask her to repeat it, she carried their dirty plates to the trash barrel and brought him a chocolate ice-cream cone from the serving table. The moments they spent quietly licking the ice cream and enjoying the warm breeze were darn close to perfect. He pretended for an instant that Emma was his wife, the toddler was their child, and it felt…right.

It was weird to find himself thinking that way, but for once, he didn't question it or try to analyze it. He just relaxed and savored the feeling. That was something Emma had taught him lately. To live in the moment, experiencing every sensation to the fullest.

All too soon lunch was over. Cal handed his little buddy to her daddy and joined Emma in the back seat of one of the vans provided to take them back to Cody. The bus was warm, the passengers full, the atmosphere perfect for an afternoon nap. Emma leaned toward Cal until her arm rested heavily against him.

He freed his own arm and wrapped it around her, gently pressing her head down on his shoulder. She sighed and snuggled in, just about the same way the toddler had done, and a wave of tenderness washed through Cal's heart.

Emma was so like a child in some ways, going after every experience with a wide-eyed excitement and boundless enthusiasm. But he was always aware of her as a woman, too, a strong, vibrant, sexy, woman he was beginning to want like hell on fire. Her moods were so changeable, he never knew quite what to make of her or what to expect, but he wanted to know everything there was to know about her.

Heaving a soft, sweet sigh against the juncture of his neck and shoulder, she turned toward him. He brushed her hair back out of her eyes. Her lips curved upward, as if she enjoyed his touch, but her eyes remained shut. Unable to resist, he leaned down and kissed her sleepy smile. To his delight, her lips parted, and the tip of her tongue flicked out as if searching for his. He was more than happy to oblige.

When his lips touched hers again, she welcomed him with a soft moan, and he tumbled so deeply into the kiss, the driver and other passengers faded into a distant memory. It was like an omen, a cosmic neon sign flashing on and off in his brain. *She's the one* it said.

He told himself that he was being ridiculous. He and Emma were becoming good friends, and they were sexually attracted, but otherwise, they had little to nothing in common. Right now, however, he couldn't remember why that mattered. Man, oh, man, he could drown in her kiss, wanted to, in fact.

Fresh air and sunshine scented her hair. Her skin was warm and soft, her movements languid. She tasted of chocolate and a sharp hint of mustard. He wanted to swallow her whole.

She lay her palm flat against his chest and slowly moved it over him, exploring the indentations above his collarbones with her fingertips before moving them up and burrowing them into the back of his hair. He snatched off his hat to give her free passage, loving her touch and greedy for more of it.

When the van bounced into the unpaved parking lot, Emma's eyelids shot open. She jerked back from him, as if she'd thought she was only having a dream. Her eyes were dark, her cheeks rosy, her mouth sultry and plump from his kisses. His lower body hardened painfully. He couldn't hold back a soft groan. She glanced at his lap, then lifted her gaze to meet his. Her slender throat worked down an audible gulp.

"What's the matter?" he asked with a smile. "Didn't you ever make out on the school bus when you were a kid?"

She silently shook her head, her eyes enormous.

"Well, that's all that happened here," he assured her. "Don't look so shocked, honey. Even I can come up with a new experience once in a while."

She gave him a wry grin. "I guess you can, McBride."

"Everybody out," the driver called, sliding open the side door. He winked at them when they climbed out.

Laughing like a couple of naughty kids who'd been caught flipping spitwads in class, they ran to Cal's regular vehicle, a shiny red four-wheel-drive wagon that was eight years old, but looked brand-new. They peeled off wet sneakers and socks and took turns using the wagon for a changing room while they put on dry clothes. By the time they were ready to head back to Sunshine Gap, Cal wanted to stay in Cody.

"How about a drive farther up the canyon to look at the dam?" he suggested as he started the wagon. "Or we could walk through the Buffalo Bill Historical Center."

She shook her head. "Can't. I need to go back to the ranch and get in some more practice with old eagle eye."

Cal pulled out of the parking lot. "Who's that?"

"Dillon," she said with a laugh. "He can spot a mistake before you even make it. He must have been some bronc rider."

"Yeah, he was," Cal said. "He came real close to making the national finals a couple of times. Then he got his face all torn up in a stupid wreck, and he gave it up."

"He could have a career as a stunt coach any time he wanted one. I can't believe how much I've learned from him."

"I didn't know he was working with your crew," Cal said.

"He's not officially. I just bug him all the time, and he answers my questions. He's a nice guy."

"How'd you get into this business?" Cal asked.

"Blind luck. I was working in a garage in L.A. One day Barry brought his car in for a tune-up. We started talking and I told him I'd done tumbling and gymnastics in high school. He invited me to stop by and talk some more. I made a few calls to make sure he was legit. When I found out he was, I went."

"How long have you been doing it, Em?"

"Ten years now."

"Do you ever worry about getting hurt?"

"I'd have to be a fool not to," she said. "But I'm careful who I'll work with. If I don't think a gag's been thought out well enough, I won't do it until I'm satisfied it's as safe as we can make it. After that, you grit your teeth and go for it."

"How much longer do you plan to stay in the business?"

"'Til I get too old and arthritic to fall off buildings and crash cars," she said. "Or until I'm endangering my co-workers."

The more Cal thought about her crashing cars and falling off buildings, the less he liked the idea, but he was wise enough to know she wouldn't appreciate any expression of concern on his part. Emma was fiercely independent. Judging by her dedication to practicing and remaining at a peak level of fitness, she was completely committed to her career. Besides, he had no right to criticize her choices.

But suddenly he wanted the right to at least question

them. He lapsed into silence, troubled by the direction of his thoughts. Appearing to be perfectly comfortable without conversation, Emma settled back against her seat and gazed out the side window with what looked like fascination. Cal could understand that.

He'd driven to Cody and back hundreds, maybe thousands of times, but he still saw something new with every trip. To the east, the prairie stretched out forever. The horizon shimmered in the midday heat. A ghostly, grayish shape darted across the road, disappearing into the brush.

"What was that?" she asked. "A wolf?"

Cal grinned. "Well, they did bring wolves back into Yellowstone a while back, but they're bigger than that little fella was. That was just your basic garden-variety coyote."

Emma twisted around in her seat as if straining for another glimpse. "Really? I've never seen one that close before. Sometimes they come into residential areas in California and eat cats. Are they dangerous?"

"Not usually," Cal said. "There's plenty of wild game for them to eat out here, and not as many people crowding their habitat as there are in California. Of course if you come across one that's rabid or seriously hungry, I'd be damn careful."

They chatted easily for the rest of the trip. Neither of them mentioned those luscious kisses they'd shared in the van, but Cal hadn't forgotten them, and he doubted Emma had, either. It just sort of bubbled there below the surface, a rich stew of sensations and feelings neither was ready to discuss. Discuss them they would, however, and if Cal had anything to say about, it would be sooner, not later.

He could hardly wait.

Other than messing with Cal's menus again and switching the country-and-western tapes in his office with rock-and-roll tapes she'd collected from the crew, Emma basically left him alone for the next week. His bar and restaurant stayed so busy he had to hire more help.

Emma had less free time, as well. Blair DuMaine had discovered the lead actor and half the stunt crew had exaggerated their riding and roping skills. She'd hired Dillon McBride to coach them, and the whole stunt crew was doing double practice sessions now.

While she missed Cal's wry sense of humor, Emma welcomed the excuse to let things cool off between them. The problem wasn't that she hadn't enjoyed kissing him; it was that she'd enjoyed kissing him far too much. In the space of a few delicious minutes, he'd confirmed every one of her earlier suspicions about the effect a real kiss from him might have on her.

His warm, firm lips and exploring tongue had made her so hot, she'd nearly melted into a grease spot on the van seat. Her mind had kept telling her to stop before she did something stupid, but her body had rebelled. The possibility of losing control in such a situation scared her more than any stunt she'd ever done.

She'd never kissed a man who'd reached so deeply inside her before, and she'd loved the experience. If she wasn't careful, kissing Cal McBride could become an addiction. In fact, now she felt extremely curious about what it would be like to make love with him. She wasn't at all sure she liked wanting anyone that much.

Still, when the next Sunday rolled around and she had a day off, she couldn't resist taking the opportunity to see him again.

Since Barry occasionally rode with her and he always had to be talking, he'd sprung for a pair of helmets with microphones. He'd given her the red one for her last birthday. He carried his own helmet and a set of protective leather gear with him.

His jacket would be too small for Cal, but maybe the rest of the stuff would work. She asked around and found out Dillon had an old leather jacket Cal could use. She borrowed it and Barry's gear on Saturday night, and rode Mama up to the back door of Cal's Place the next morning.

Sitting at his usual table, he looked up when she entered the café from the kitchen, and gave her a broad, welcoming smile that set off warm, curling sensations in her lower abdomen. Ignoring them, she smiled back at him, and snatched a piece of bacon from his plate before she took the chair opposite his. "Morning, Mayor McBride."

"Morning, yourself," he said. "What kind of torture have you got lined up for me today?"

"Torture?" Emma placed one hand over her chest as if she couldn't believe he was accusing her of any such thing. "When did I ever torture you?"

"You want a list?"

"No." She got up and headed back the way she'd come.

"Emma, wait," Cal said, coming after her. "I was just teasing you."

She stopped and grinned at him over her shoulder. "Really? So was I. Gotcha, McBride."

Returning to the table and Cal ordered her a waffle, a side of bacon and coffee. When the waitress took off, he looked straight into Emma's eyes. "I've missed you, Ms. Barnes."

Those curling sensations returned. She wrinkled her nose at him. "I've missed you, too, Mr. Mayor."

"I mean it, Em," he said, suddenly serious. "I've missed seeing you every day."

Tingles of alarm danced through her veins. His words warmed her all over again, and they made her feel special. But she couldn't afford to get used to hearing those things from a man. Any man. There simply wasn't room in her life for one. "I've been busy. We're going to start shooting next week."

"I know. And that means I'll see you even less often. So what are we going to do today?"

She raised an eyebrow at him. "What? You're not even going to give me a token whine this time?"

"Nope. Whatever you choose is fine with me."

"Great. We'll go skydiving."

His face paled and his eyes widened. "Hell, Em, I don't like heights much—"

"Relax. I was just seeing how far you'd go. I've jumped twice, but it's not high on my list of fun things to do either."

His laugh sounded sincerely relieved, but she suspected he really would have gone skydiving with her if she'd demanded that of him. Even if it scared the devil out of him. What a guy.

"Okay," he said. "So what *do* you have planned?"

Emma's breakfast arrived. She arranged her place setting to her satisfaction, then asked, "Want to go for a ride on Mama?"

Cal's whole face brightened. "No kidding? I've always wanted to ride one of those things, but—"

"You don't get to drive," she warned him, just in case he had any ideas about doing so. "Not today."

"No problem," he said with a shrug. "I'm not licensed for it, anyway. But if I like it well enough, I might think about buying a bike myself."

"First you have to survive today. I left some gear in your office. Why don't you go see if any of it fits while I eat? Then we can get on the road."

He took off like an eager kid. When he returned, she had to bite down hard on her lower lip to keep from laughing. Barry's green helmet looked okay, but the jacket was short in the sleeves and rode up above the waistband of Cal's jeans. The chaps were several inches short, too, and the overall effect was that of a gangly boy whose parents couldn't keep up with his growth spurts. He carried the elbow-length leather gloves as if he wasn't quite sure what he was supposed to do with them.

"Don't laugh," he warned her. "I know I look stupid."

"It's not that bad." He gave her an uh-huh look. "No, really. Besides, it doesn't matter how it looks. The important thing is making sure you're protected if we have an accident."

"Have you ever had an accident on a bike?"

"Only in the movies." She pushed back her chair and walked closer to him. "But I'm not naive enough to think I'll never have one, so I take what precautions I can."

She checked him all out, pronounced he would do, then asked if the boots he was wearing were his favorites. He shook his head, and five minutes later they were off, heading for the highway. Cal was a great passenger. He kept his weight centered over the seat, leaned into curves like a pro and held onto her without trying to grope her.

He didn't talk all the time the way Barry did, for which she was grateful, but he didn't try to be Mr. Cool all the time, either. He whooped in delight when she turned south on Highway 120 and opened up the throttle. On an interstate highway, she usually cruised at seventy miles an hour. On a two-lane, Wyoming state highway, she settled for sixty.

She slowed for the little town of Meeteetse, then accelerated again. When she hit cruising speed, Cal started singing. Had she said *singing?* No, it was more like a drunk belting out a song in a raspy voice with occasional grunting da-da sounds that evidently were an important part of the tune. The only lyrics she could make out were, "Born to be wi-i-i-ild."

"Hey, McBride!" she shouted. "Were you playing the air guitar back there, too?"

"Damn, you've got a smart mouth, woman."

They rode for hours, detouring on a whim, talking, teasing and sometimes, just enjoying the road, the sunshine and the scenery. Emma fell a little more in love with the back roads of Wyoming, and a little more in love with Cal.

There wasn't a thing she could do about it, nor did she honestly want to.

She refused to live in an all-or-nothing world. She couldn't have Cal or Wyoming forever, but she could enjoy them for a few more weeks. As long as she didn't get in over her head with Cal, she could continue to see him.

It was early evening by the time they returned to Sunshine Gap. Emma drove Cal home and accepted his invitation to come in and have a cold drink before heading back to the ranch. Yip and Yap raced out to greet her. Cal went into the house while she played with them. A few moments later, he brought out a tray of sandwich makings and a pitcher of iced tea, and invited her to wash up in his bathroom.

She'd spent enough time with him now, that sitting down across from him at the picnic table on his deck seemed perfectly natural. Hard to believe it had only been a month since he'd thrown her out of his bar. She smiled at the memory, then looked up to find him studying her with a decidedly lusty expression in his eyes.

She swallowed. Shifted on the bench. Uh-oh. If she didn't do something, he was going to melt her whole arsenal of resistance right here, right now, with only a look from those dark, sexy eyes of his.

Smiling enough to show his dimple, he reached out an index finger and ran the tip along the neckline of her tank top. She slapped his hand away as if she felt irritated rather than a confusing mixture of excitement and fear. Not fear of Cal, of course, but fear of her own response to him.

"What do you think you're doing?" she asked.

His grin widened. His dimple deepened. His gaze dipped to the center of her chest. "Your tattoo was showing a little. I just wanted to see what it was."

He raised his hand again. She batted it away again, then grabbed his hand and firmly pushed it to the table. Laying her own hand on top of his, she rubbed her fingertips over the backs of his knuckles. "I think not. Only my dearest and closest friends ever get to see it."

He brought out the sad-puppy expression that coaxed the most reluctant smiles out of her. "But, Emma, after the way you kissed me in the van last week, I thought I must be pretty dear to you. Pretty darn close, too."

Her toes curled inside her boots and suddenly there

wasn't enough oxygen to fill her lungs. "Nice try. I meant another kind of close."

"I'm a little slow about these things sometimes, Em." He leaned so close, she could almost feel his mustache hairs tickling her upper lip. "Maybe you could show me the difference."

Temptation on the hoof, she thought, borrowing a phrase she'd once heard Dillon mutter after Blair DuMaine had walked by. Now she knew exactly what Dillon had meant. The devil didn't have horns and a red outfit; he looked just like Cal McBride did at this very moment. God help her, the longer he sat there smiling at her, the more tempting he was. So much for not getting in over her head.

"I don't think so," she said, slowly climbing to her feet. "I'm only going to be here another month. I don't have anything more to offer you than a friendship, but I don't think that's possible anymore."

Cal stood up and came around to her side of the table. "Wait a minute, Emma."

She picked up her jacket from the deck railing and put it on. "There's nothing to wait for. We both know what's going on, and I don't want to play anymore."

He came closer. "Come on, Emma. I'll back off if you want me to."

Squashing an urge simply to turn around and run like hell, she chuckled and calmly headed down the stairs to the lawn below. "And that would last how long? You're fun to kiss, Mr. Mayor, but you are one dangerous man. Way too dangerous for me."

He kept pace with her across the yard to the gate. "I thought you liked danger."

"Not this kind." She went up on her tiptoes, grabbed the front of his shirt and planted a hot, wet kiss on his mouth, savoring the taste of him, pulling his scent deep into her lungs as if she could memorize both sensations. Then she released him, put on her helmet and swung her leg over Mama's seat. ''See you around, McBride. Stay out of ruts, will you?''

Without giving him a chance to answer, she drove away. Halfway up the street, she glanced in her rearview mirror. Cal was still standing by the gate, watching her. She really hoped he would give up on her now. She glanced in the mirror again. He was still watching. Suddenly the chorus of ''Born To Be Wild'' started thumping in her mind, and somehow, she just knew he was going to be difficult.

Chapter Seven

Cal watched Emma until she drove out of sight, then muttered a few choice words and scaled back into his truck. On the drive home...

Chapter Seven

Cal watched Emma until she was out of sight, then uttered a low, emphatic curse and headed back into his house, the poodles at his heels. When he stretched out on the sofa and put both hands over his face, the dogs jumped up onto his chest, emitting worried whines and nipping at the backs of his hands. He spread his fingers and peeked out at them. Yip barked and dug at the exposed heel of his left hand, determinedly burrowing underneath it.

Cal lifted both hands, and the dogs wiggled closer, their bodies trembling, their tiny tongues working him over, offering canine comfort. He scooted them down on his chest, out of tongue reach, and calmed them with slow, gentle pets. They curled up into two warm little fur balls and went to sleep.

Now that he felt calmer himself, he could formulate a new plan for dealing with Ms. Emma Barnes. That was the nicest kiss-off he'd ever received, but a kiss-off all the same. And he wasn't buying it. He'd never met a more confusing or irritating woman in his life. He wasn't even sure why he didn't write her off as being more trouble than she was worth.

He only knew that he couldn't do it. In four short weeks, she'd become an important part of his existence. It was nice to focus on another person instead of his business for a change. He also liked having "a life" for a change. It was something he never would have done for himself, but now he could see he'd really needed to get out and try new things, meet new people.

Closing his eyes, he pictured himself sitting on the back of the Harley, his hands on Emma's waist, the sound of Emma's voice in his ears. It had been a great day. A wonderful day. So what had he done to wreck it?

It wasn't as if she was an innocent eighteen-year-old and he was a lecherous old wolf trying to pounce on her. They were both adults, both single, both attracted. After holding onto her all day long on the bike, he hadn't thought twice about touching the neckline of her top that way. And she…well, talk about overreacting.

For God's sake, he hadn't grabbed the front of her shirt, yanked it out and satisfied his curiosity, although the thought had crossed his mind. He'd just been sort of…teasing her, the same way he felt teased whenever he caught a glimpse of that tattoo.

What on earth *was* that thing, anyway? Smoke from a fire-breathing dragon's nostrils? The feathery tip of some exotic plant or maybe a bird? A lion's tail or a tiger's whiskers? He always saw so little of it, it could be almost anything.

Why was she so determined to hide it from him? And what else might she be hiding? She knew damn near everything there was to know about him—his family, his business, his friends, his humiliating weakness at the sight of blood. But what did he know about her? Nothing. Nada. Zip.

It wasn't fair, and he didn't intend to put up with it

anymore, either. She couldn't ride into his life, take it over and shake it up the way she had, and then just ride off into the damn sunset. It was time somebody shook *her* life up a little.

The next Sunday afternoon, he decided to put his plan into action. He called the main house to find out exactly where Emma was. Jake said she was practicing her roping skills on Jethro, the plastic cow head stuck into a bale of hay in the yard. Cal tossed the picnic basket and a blanket into the back of his wagon, and drove to the Flying M.

Emma was still practicing when he parked beside the house. Today she looked more like a real cowgirl than even Grace did, with a straw Stetson hat covering her blond hair, a bright blue, short-sleeved, Western-cut cotton shirt, well-worn Wrangler jeans and dusty, beat-to-hell cowboy boots. When she first saw him, he could have sworn he saw a sparkle of gladness in her eyes.

Then she pulled her hat brim down in front, shadowing her face and making her eyes more difficult to see. So, she was a little uncomfortable at the prospect of facing him again. Seeing that as a good sign, Cal took his sweet time about climbing out of the vehicle and ambling across the driveway to greet her.

Mentally poking his tongue into the side of his cheek, he gave her his very best cowboy drawl. "Howdy, ma'am. You sure are a sight for sore eyes. How've ya been?"

A reluctant grin tugging at the sides of her mouth, Emma coiled up her rope and held it in one hand, propping the other hand on the curve of her hip. "Just fine, pard," she drawled back at him. "I'm real busy here, so I'd appreciate it if you'd state your business."

"Why, ma'am it's Sunday, and I don't see anybody else sweatin' and wearin' themselves out in this hot sunshine. You don't mean to work all day on the Sabbath, do you?"

"Haven't you got anything better to do than preach at me, mister?"

"Oh, he—ck, yeah, ma'am. That's why I'm here. I'm gonna go fishin'. Want to come along?"

She hesitated, then smiled just a little. "Maybe. Fishin' for what?"

"Trout. Rainbows, most likely. They're good eatin'."

"What are the terms?"

"Terms? You gotta learn to bait your own hook." Cal tipped the brim of his own hat back and rubbed his forehead as if he were thinking really hard. "You catch 'em, you clean 'em. That's a pretty standard rule. Think you could handle that?"

She paused, then slowly nodded. "I reckon. What else?"

Cal crossed his arms over his chest and eyed her warily. "I don't want you jumpin' all over me and tryin' to take advantage of me, lady. There'll be no pawin' or kissin' or hanky-panky. We'll just be fishin' buddies today. Agreed?"

Her voice took on a dry tone. "Yeah, I can probably handle that, too. When do we leave?"

"Soon as you put that rope away and put on some sneakers, and I collect some gear from the shed."

Emma nodded again, then turned and walked to the barn without another word. Delighted with the success of his plan so far, Cal hustled to the shed where they kept the Flying M's collection of fishing equipment. None of it was his, and he basically thought fishing was about as exciting as watching flies sit on the wall, but Emma didn't need to know that.

When they met back at the wagon, they set off on a narrow gravel road Cal remembered from earlier fishing expeditions with his siblings and cousins. While the others had competed fiercely with each other, he'd relaxed on the bank with a cooler of pop, a bag of chips and a stack of comic books, which, with adolescence, became a stack of girlie magazines. They'd been fun, too, and they sure had ticked off Alex and Grace something fierce. Always an added bonus for the boys in the family.

"You ever done this before?" he asked.

"Nope. This is a new one for me."

He nodded, pleased with her answer. If she didn't know much about fishing, he didn't have to pretend to be an expert.

The gravel road narrowed to a weed-infested dirt track. They bounced along from one bump to the next, neither saying much until he finally drove into a shady clearing on the banks of a crystal-clear creek. Emma climbed out and glanced around, stretching her arms over her head.

Lowering her arms back to her sides, she approached the water, looking upstream and down.

"Oh, wow," she said with an excited grin. "This is neat."

"I guess it's okay," Cal said.

"Okay? It's more than okay," she said, sending him a mock scowl. She strode back to the vehicle and joined him at the tailgate. "What do we do now? How can I help?"

He handed her the coffee can of nightcrawlers he'd paid the kid next door to catch for him. Grabbing a pair of cane poles with hooks, sinkers and red-and-white bobbers already fitted onto the lines, he led her a hundred yards upstream to a spot where the creek widened into a fishing hole. The gear he'd chosen was actually more suited to fishing in a pond or a lake, but he didn't care.

He told her to sit on the grassy bank and went down on one knee beside her. She accepted a pole and watched while he threaded a fat nightcrawler onto his hook. Without a bit of squeamishness, she dug out another fat worm and impaled it on the hook, looping it back and forth the way he'd shown her.

"Okay, now what?" she asked.

"Now you look around for a nice shady place to sit, throw your line in the water and wait for a nibble."

Her eyebrows wrinkled up in puzzlement. "Are you sure you know what you're doing? You don't even have to get wet?"

"Not the way I do it," Cal said with a shrug. "You can

make fishing all complicated and technical if you want, but I believe in giving the trout a fighting chance to live and spawn. To me, fishing's more about communing with nature than stomping through glacier-fed streams and catching your limit.''

Her eyes danced with amusement and a soft chuckle escaped her lips. "You're lazy, McBride."

Wanting to kiss her, he flicked a fingertip at the end of her nose. "Just because I'm not as hyperactive as certain folks we won't name, doesn't mean I'm lazy. Some people *do* relax, but maybe you don't know that. You're in such a deep rut—''

"Me?" She burst out laughing and eyed him with blatant disbelief. "I'm not the one in a rut. I do something new and different every single week."

"And that's exactly the rut you're in," Cal said. "You're an action junkie, Em. I'll bet you five bucks, you can't just sit there and wait ten minutes for a bite."

"It's not a question of whether I *can*," she said. "It's a question of why would I want to?"

"Uh-huh." Cal smiled and kept right on looking at her.

Her cheeks turned pink and her eyes narrowed. Finally she muttered something he suspected wouldn't pass muster down at the First Baptist Church and scooted closer to the creek. She made three awkward attempts to get her line into the water, then let out an impatient huff and scowled at him.

"You want to show me how to do this part, McBride?"

Lord, but he loved her temper. Trying not to show it, however, he climbed to his feet, raised the tip of his pole above his head and flicked his wrist just hard enough to send his line sailing over the middle of the pool. The worm-laden hook plopped into the water amazingly close to the spot he was hoping for. Smiling, he held out a hand, inviting her to take a shot at it.

She wasted no time in scrambling to her feet and trying to copy his movements. Her hook skipped across the surface of the water and landed on top of a big rock sticking out of the water. If only she would have asked, he gladly would have helped her,

But of course, her pride wouldn't allow her to do that. When she jerked the pole back with more force than was necessary, the only way he could prevent disaster was to drop his own pole, fling himself in front of her and cover her body with his own. He knocked her off her feet and onto her fanny, then couldn't stop himself from sprawling on top of her. Both of them grunted on impact. She smacked the heel of one hand against his chest.

Feeling her muscles bunch in preparation for shoving him off, he glared down into her furious eyes and practically snarled at her. "Give me credit for more class than this. I'm not jumping your damn bones."

She sucked in a harsh breath. "Then what are you doing?"

"I just saved you from hitting yourself in the face with a fish hook. Would you like to know where it is right now?"

Her eyes grew round with horror and she jerked her hands up beside her head, as if showing him she meant no harm. "Oh, jeez, Cal, are you hit?"

"Don't freak out," he said, striving for a soothing tone. "It's not in any skin yet. I think it's snagged on my belt or maybe a belt loop."

"What do you want me to do?"

She'd probably kill him if he told her the truth. It wasn't exactly a sexy position, but it was close enough to make any red-blooded man think along those lines. But that wasn't the purpose of today's outing and he had to get out of this before his anatomy got him in big trouble. Bracing his palms against the grass on either side of her shoulders, he lifted as much of his weight off her as he could.

"Lower the pole. Watch the line and try to get some tension out of it."

"Okay." She studied the line for a moment. Turning the

pole this way and that, she figured out which way she needed to move it. An instant later, Cal felt the pressure at the back of his waist relax. Emma reached around him, freed the hook, worm and all, and set it carefully on the grass beside her.

He slid off her and sat up. "Thanks, Em."

"Thanks?" Her voice rose an octave. She sat up, tossed her hat onto the grass behind her and ran a shaky hand over her hair. "I'm the one who should be thanking you. And you should be yelling at me for acting like such a klutz."

"It was an honest mistake. Could've happened to anybody."

"Has it ever happened to you?"

He probably wouldn't have admitted it to anyone else, but she looked so upset, his first instinct was to comfort her. "Yeah." He rubbed the old scar below his right ear. "But it's one of those mistakes you only make once."

"You didn't have anyone to save you, did you?"

Cal shook his head and grinned. "But I didn't have such a pretty face to protect, either. You want to fish some more?"

"Do you?" She looked as eager as a kid waiting for a shot.

"Not really. But I brought a picnic. Want to try that?"

She leaned over, clasped the sides of his head between her palms and gave him a quick smooch on the lips. "You are one special man. I've never met anyone like you before."

"Now what'd I say about hanky-panky?" he asked, adopting a prim tone Miz Hannah might use. "Keep your hands to yourself, lady. I'm not cheap or easy, you know."

Chuckling, Emma scrambled to her feet and headed for the vehicle. By the time Cal retrieved both fishing poles, and dealt with the worms, she had spread his picnic blanket under a tree and was unpacking the basket, chortling at each new discovery.

"Fried chicken. Macaroni salad. Deviled eggs. Dill pickles. Grapes. A pie? What kind is it?"

Cal took the pie from her hands and studied it. "Looks like rhubarb. Ever tried it?"

Her face fell. "Yeah. I didn't like it much, though."

"Well, shoot. I guess you'll just have to gag down a fudge brownie then. It's a dirty job, but somebody's gotta do it."

She laughed, and they fell back into the warm, relaxed companionship they'd shared the two previous Sundays. Cal watched the sunshine filtering through the trees dapple her hair and her skin and wanted to kiss her so bad, his lips ached. He restrained himself, however, and they whiled away the rest of the afternoon, talking and stuffing themselves with the picnic.

He hated to do anything that might spoil this easy atmosphere between them, but he wanted to know more about her. And he wanted to do it now, while she couldn't run away if she got mad at him again.

Lounging back on one elbow, he popped a grape into his mouth, chewed thoughtfully and swallowed it. "Were you born in California?"

She stiffened, scrutinizing him as if she suspected he might have some underhanded agenda behind his question. Cal waited patiently, and she finally answered. "Texas."

"Well that explains why you're such a good rider, I guess. That is, if you grew up there?" Cal grinned and popped another grape into his mouth.

Her gaze turned decidedly frosty. "Does it matter?"

He laughed and shook his head. "Of course not. I'm just curious. Did you grow up on a ranch down there?"

"I didn't grow up there at all."

Cal waited for further explanation. When none came, he pressed again. "So, where *did* you grow up?"

"I prefer not to discuss that."

"Okay," Cal said. "Do you have any brothers and sisters?"

She climbed onto her knees and started cleaning up the meal's debris. "What is this? Pry-into-Emma's-business day?"

He shrugged one shoulder. "No. I just don't know anything about you or your family. What you were like as a little girl."

"It's not that interesting. Compared to your family, mine is really boring."

"Why don't you let me decide that for myself?" Cal asked. "Do you have any brothers and sisters?"

"No." She rolled down the top of the paper bag she'd used for garbage and carried it to the wagon. Cal waited until she returned to the blanket before trying again.

"What about your parents? Where do they live?"

"They don't," Emma said, staring at him with no expression on her face. "They're dead."

Oh, boy. He'd really stepped in it now. "I'm sorry, Em," he said quietly.

"No reason you should be. It happened a long time ago. And I don't talk about it. Not ever."

"All right, Emma. I was just trying to be your friend."

"Where I come from, friends mind their own business. I want to go back to the ranch now."

"We can't even talk about this?"

"No." Grabbing the picnic basket, she carried it to the vehicle, shoved it in the back and slammed the tailgate. She propped her hands on her hips and tapped the toe of one sneaker, bristling with impatience. "Well? Are you coming or not?"

"Not." Cal rose to his feet and walked across the grass to join her. "I want you to stay here and talk to me. Really talk for a change. Let me know more of you than the outside package. Not that I don't admire the outside package."

"No wonder you're a politician," she said, her tone less than complimentary. "You are such a cajoler, I think you could coax the pit out of a peach. But I'm not interested, so take me back to the ranch."

"I don't get it, Emma," he said quietly. "We're good together. We have fun together. You know I'm not just after you for sex. Why won't you take a chance to see if something more than a friendship could grow between us?"

The look she gave him could have dropped a charging buffalo. Cal was not impressed. "What? No snappy comebacks?"

Her fingers curled into a pair of mean-looking fists, and for a second or two, he thought she might try to deck him. Then she blew out a disgust-laden snort, whirled around and walked toward the road.

"Emma, come back here," he called.

She kept on walking. Cal watched her for a moment, then swore under his breath, put away the blanket and climbed into the wagon. He caught up with her in less than a mile. When he approached, she jumped down into the shallow ditch beside the road, as if she thought he might run over her. Damn, stubborn woman.

He pulled up beside her, slowing to a crawl so he could keep pace with her. "It's fifteen miles back to the ranch."

She didn't look at him.

"There might be snakes down there." She shot him such a startled look he darn near laughed out loud. "This time of day, they're usually headed home after sunning themselves all afternoon."

She faced forward again and kept walking.

He let her march along for another half mile before trying again. For all the attention she paid him, he could have been a fence post. "Do you ever act like an adult?"

"Frequently," she answered, still refusing to look at him.

"Well, I'd sure like to see it sometime." He waited for her to take the bait, but she was too smart to do that. He continued, anyhow. "You know, an adult usually sticks around when she's got a problem with somebody. All I've ever seen you do is run away."

"It saves me a lot of aggravation."

Cal snorted. "Could be, but it's bound to leave you pretty lonely. It's damn hard to be friends with a person who won't even give you a chance to understand her."

"There's nothing to understand. I like my privacy, and I'm not giving it up to satisfy your stupid curiosity."

"What's so secret, you can't answer a few simple questions about your background? Was your dad a CIA assassin? Or maybe a serial killer? And maybe your mom was a bank robber. Or maybe *you're* wanted by the law. What did you do, Em? Rob a Harley-Davidson dealership?"

"Shut up, McBride."

"Aw, Emma, you're breakin' my heart." Lowering his voice, he tried for a Spanish accent. "You know you really want me."

She shot him a mocking look and tripped over a tree branch hidden in the long grass. Cal hit the brakes. "You're gonna hurt yourself stomping like that for fifteen miles. Don't you want at least try to keep yourself in one piece until you shoot that new stunt?"

She paused, then looked over her shoulder at him. "Yes, I do. But I'm not going to let you pry into my affairs, which you seem convinced you have a right to do. So, I guess I'll just have to keep on walking."

Cal took his foot off the brake and caught up with her. "You'd really risk hurting yourself, just to avoid my questions?"

"Yup."

"Was I even close to why you're so secretive?"

"Nope."

"Are you this rude to everybody? Or is it just me?"

"Everybody. I'm an equal opportunity rude person."

He put on the brakes again and called to her. "All right. Get in, and I promise I won't ask you any more questions."

Cal hit the gas and stuck a classic country-western tape into the player. Neither spoke the whole way back. When he parked beside her trailer, she turned to him, her eyes filled with a sadness that tugged hard at his heart. But he wasn't going to let that distract him this time.

"Cal, I'm sorry," she said.

He smiled at her. "No problem. I'm sure this isn't true, but you know, another guy might look at this situation and interpret it another way."

"What are you talking about?"

"Well, you know, maybe you just did what you had to do so you could attend your meetings. By pretending you wanted to be my friend and stringing me along, you guaranteed I wouldn't change my mind about letting you into Cal's Place. But now that you're not using my banquet room, you're free to dump me."

Her mouth fell open. Her eyes widened. She sucked in a soft gasp. "You don't really believe that."

Cal chuckled. "Who, me? Hell no. I'm just pointing out that some people might take it that way."

"I'm not a user, Cal."

"Of course not. I know you're scared you'll get hurt if you let me come too close, and I don't blame you for protecting yourself. But I'm a very patient man. I can wait until you learn to trust me. And you *will* learn to trust me, Emma."

"Don't start—"

Cal cut her off. "No, don't *you* start. I've only got one more thing to say, anyway. I'm a lot like you in some ways. When I see something that's exactly what I really want, I don't give up until I get it."

Emma frowned at him for a moment, then popped her door latch, climbed out and stomped into her trailer. Cal cranked the steering wheel hard to the right and peeled away from the trailer village, his rear tires spitting gravel.

Emma slammed the trailer door behind her, then dropped onto the tiny sofa, ripped off her sneakers and pulled on her hiking boots. Her eyes burned with unshed tears, and her throat ached with the need to let them fall, but tears only made you feel weak. She couldn't afford that.

The best cure she'd ever found for a desperate urge to fall apart was a long, fast ride on Mama. Putting on her protective gear in record time, she grabbed her keys and left before the walls could start closing in. Wanting to avoid Sunshine Gap, she took the short cut to the highway and turned toward Meeteetse.

The sun slipped behind the mountains to the west, but she raced on and on, searching for the sense of peace she always found with Mama. But this time, it didn't come, even though she went all the way to a little town called Thermopolis. She would have liked to have seen the world's largest mineral hot springs and the buffalo herd the signs advertised, but she had to go back to the Flying M.

With an early call tomorrow morning, she needed a good night's sleep to perform well on the set. Besides, riding a motorcycle at night was trickier than riding it in the daytime. She took off again, determined to outrun the visions of Cal's wounded eyes that had haunted her for eighty-some miles.

But it didn't work this time, either, and his statements about her running away from problems and being lonely echoed in her mind, as well. She would admit to the truth of some of his accusations. She'd learned the hard way that if you never let anyone get too close, they couldn't hurt you.

She'd been tempted to violate her rules of self-protection for Cal, but the habit of pushing people away was so deeply ingrained, she hadn't been able to stop herself from pushing him away, too. And why should she? She'd made it perfectly clear from the beginning that she didn't intend to be more than a friend. Hadn't she? She was sure she had.

Well, maybe those kisses they'd shared in the van had confused that point a little. But still, the second she finished her last stunt, she would be leaving Wyoming. What was the point in setting herself up for a painful, but inevitable separation?

And Cal— Hah! He thought he knew her so well, did he? He didn't have clue one about what it would take for her to learn to trust anyone completely. He could be as patient as he wanted, but it wouldn't do him any good. Except maybe to soothe his bruised ego. Big deal.

It wasn't as if he really cared about her or…loved her. He was still on the rebound from his broken engagement, and she simply happened to be the first woman to come along and distract him from his pain. Or maybe he was one of those guys who loved the chase, and her resistance was only inciting him to chase harder. If anyone was a user here, it certainly wasn't her.

Cal's not a user, either.

Ah, yes, the voice of her conscience. She should have expected it to show up right about now. She opened the throttle, hoping the increased engine noise would drown it out. It didn't work, of course. Nothing could ever drown out that hummer.

Maybe it was a good thing, but at the moment, it didn't seem a bit helpful. She needed a good reason to dislike the man, dammit. So, maybe he wasn't a user. But he *was* bossy and irritating. He wasn't above manipulating people, either. Just look what he'd done to Marsh that night in Cody.

Then why did you go fishing with him today?

Good question. If only she had a good answer. Before she could invent one, three deer jumped into the middle of the road. Then the idiot creatures just stood there and stared at her, as if their feet had been set in cement.

By the time Emma realized what was happening, it was too late to stop. Instinctively taking the only way that offered any hope of avoiding a major injury, she headed for the ditch. At the edge of the pavement, she straightened out the bike, riding the line between asphalt and dirt as if it were a tightrope. Honking her horn, she came closer and closer to the deer, thinking she was going to make it just fine.

Until she hit a crumbling patch of asphalt.

Suddenly Mama's front tire dropped onto the weedy verge. The rear end followed, and momentum carried the bike closer and closer to the steep slope leading to the bottom of the ditch. Emma strained with every muscle in her arms and shoulders to turn her bike back toward the pavement.

She hit a bump, and again the bike wobbled to the right. Emma yanked harder on the hand grip and put her left foot on the ground, fighting for control. But the tires simply slid out from under her and Emma had no choice but to slide with her bike. The footrest caught in the top of her left boot, snapping something in her ankle. Still, she fought to free her leg.

Mama kept sliding downward, dragging her over rocks and sagebushes, through litter, smashed aluminum cans and broken beer bottles. The rear tire slammed into a rock big enough to hold the bike in place momentarily. Emma's body pitched headfirst over the handlebar, but she couldn't complete the flip because her hiking boot was still hung up on the damn footrest.

The bike tipped, jerking her around as if she were a beanbag doll. She landed on her back. The front end of the bike crashed on top of her left leg. She cried out in agony.

Mama's engine flooded, stalled and died. The air reeked with gas fumes. Smelling them, Emma begged any higher power out there who happened to be listening, please, please, please, to keep it from igniting. She most definitely did not want to be a crispy critter. Then the stars, both inside her head and up in that big Wyoming sky abruptly went out.

When Emma awoke again, she had no idea how long she'd been lying there, but it was still night. Pain riddled her body, concentrating most fiercely around her left ankle.

She was shivering uncontrollably, and though she tried to be stoic, she heard herself wailing like a baby.

"Oh, God, how am I gonna get out of here? Am I even gonna get out of here alive?"

Hearing the rising hysteria in her voice made her realize the first thing she had to do was calm down. She shut her eyes and rested, inhaling the slowest breaths she could manage. Encouraged by that much success, she started looking for anything else she could do to help herself.

Her arms were free. She tried to move, to drag herself out from under the motorcycle, but her left leg was useless, the bike weighed over six hundred pounds, and from this position, she couldn't get any kind of leverage on it with her right leg or foot, whatever. It was so hard to focus…

"Well," she muttered, needing to hear the sound of a human voice. Any human voice. "That didn't work. What next?"

She felt woozy. And cold. In spite of her leather jacket and chaps and gloves, she felt cold right down to her core. And her ankle hurt bad. Really bad. Some other parts of her hurt, too, but the leg was the worst. Her stomach contracted, felt as if it might roll over.

Don't even think about that one, Emma.

She closed her eyes, took more slow breaths and the nausea subsided a little. There was no traffic on the road above her. No noises at all, but the wind rustling the weeds and a coyote howling his damn lungs out. Lord, she hoped he wasn't—how had Cal put it? Oh yeah. Seriously hungry. Or rabid.

She also really hoped all that howling was not a dinner invitation to his buddies, with her body headlining the menu. What if his buddies were actually wolves sneaking out of Yellowstone National Park, looking for an easy kill?

Or bears? There must be bears around here with all these mountains. Maybe even grizzlies. It was summer, too, their prime feeding time. *Hi, there, Smokey. How about some fresh stuntwoman? Tastes like chicken.*

Her laughter had a slightly maniacal edge to it. But, gallows humor seemed to fit this situation.

She heard a soft rustling in the bushes to her left. Her first horrified thought was that it could be gophers or field mice—whatever rodents lived out here—were coming to investigate the invader, which would be her. Or maybe it was one of the snakes Cal had mentioned, looking for something warm to cuddle up to in this cool night air. Her skin crawled at the possibility.

It was just so dark out here. The quarter moon looked pretty enough, but it didn't shed much light. Mama's headlight must be broken. *Oh, God, please help me.*

She could stand anything if she could see it. But even the thought of some unknown creature crawling over her when she was helpless made her want to scream and scream and never stop screaming. But who would hear her? Not one living human being, she was sure of that.

It seemed as if she'd been alone her whole life, but it had never felt this awful, this terrifying before. Maybe it was shock from the accident, or the hot, grinding pain working its way up her left leg that made her feel so desolate, so depressed, so utterly…alone. No one would miss her if she didn't come home tonight. Or any other night, for that matter.

If she died out here, would anybody even give a damn?

She refused to answer that question for fear she would sink even lower into this ditch, close her eyes and just give up. She didn't feel tough right now. And she was learning fast that she really wasn't much of a loner, either. Dammit, she needed help. She wanted somebody to care if the bears and coyotes and snakes got her.

And she was cold. So cold she was afraid of going to sleep.

Right now, she'd give anything to have Cal with her, holding her hand and telling her she was going to be all right. Even if she *wasn't* going to be all right, she knew that he would tell her she was. He'd tell her anything she needed to hear if it would prevent her from giving up. She could almost love him for that.

She didn't love him, though. She wasn't the type to love anyone—all right, all *right*. Since she actually could die tonight, maybe it was time for total honesty. And the truth *was* that she didn't know how to love anyone, didn't even know if she was capable of feeling the emotion. But if she ever could love a man, he would have to be an awful lot like Cal McBride.

Yes, he was bossy and occasionally irritating. But he was a good man. She could use so many words to describe him, but everything she knew about him led her to believe that *good* fit him best. He'd tried to be her friend, and she'd hurt him. Maybe she *had* used him. Not intentionally, of course, but intentions didn't matter if the result was the same.

Tears filled her eyes and spilled down her cheeks, and for once, she was too weak to stop them. A car whooshed by on the road. Screaming, Emma tried to sit up and wave her arms, anything to attract attention. Vicious pain in her left leg slapped her back down and made her gorge rise into her throat. She collapsed, panting, crying and cursing as she realized that nobody from the road could even see her, much less hear her.

It took considerable effort, but finally she managed to pry off her helmet. The cool air on her head revived her and calmed her stomach. She rested until she could breathe normally again. With one last burst of strength, she grasped the side of the helmet and flung it up toward the road.

She heard it bounce on the pavement once, twice, then nothing. Damn. Was it sitting in the road like a neon-red sign, where some driver might spot it and wonder what it was doing there? Or had it bounced off into the opposite barrow ditch? In which case, nobody would ever see it from the road, either, and she was no better off than before.

There was no way to tell. Sniffling, she lay back and

swiped at her tears with the backs of her hands. No more of that now. Self-pity was a luxury she couldn't afford.

Gazing up at the quarter moon, she whispered, "Cal McBride. Calling Cal McBride. If you were here, I'd tell you all about my stupid background if you still wanted to hear about it. I could use a good friend right now. And I really, really miss you, you big, dumb jerk."

Chapter Eight

Too restless to settle anywhere by the time he got home, Cal changed into running clothes and jogged a fast five-mile loop around the outskirts of town, hoping to burn off excess energy. It didn't help much. He kept wishing Emma was with him, harassing him every step of the way. He showered, put on fresh clothes and decided to walk down to Cal's Place.

Tom Truman, the weekend bartender, greeted Cal with a broad smile. The bar was empty, which was hardly unusual for a Sunday night. Bars closed at ten o'clock on Sundays in Wyoming, and most folks were home getting ready to face Monday morning. Cal settled onto a bar stool and ordered a beer. Tom grinned and reached for the blender.

Cal's heart wrenched. Darn that Emma. He wanted to lay his forehead right down on the bar and bang it a few times. Maybe that would help clear up the confusion in his brain whenever he thought about her.

Without a doubt, she was the orneriest, stubbornest, most unreasonable, most unpredictable, most adorable, exciting and desirable woman on the planet. If he wasn't damn careful, she'd turn him into a doormat. Good thing he was damn careful.

He'd blasted the ol' ball into her court today. All he could do now was wait and see what she decided to do with it. He never had liked waiting.

Tom set a frozen, strawberry daiquiri in front of him, making a damn poor attempt at hiding a smirk, in Cal's opinion. Cal snorted in disgust, then picked up the glass and took a sip. Not bad. Tasted more like some kiddie drink than booze, but it wasn't bad.

"What's up, boss?" Tom asked, crossing his forearms on the bar.

"Not much," Cal answered. He took another sip, then pushed the drink away and told Tom what had happened with Emma. Tom gave him a soda and listened intently, shaking his head and making the sympathetic grunts needed to keep Cal talking.

"Wow, boss," Tom said when Cal had finished his sad tale. "She wouldn't tell ya *nothin'?*"

"Not one blessed thing," Cal said.

"That sure seems strange. I talked to her a few times while the stunt folks were here. Seemed real nice to me."

"She *is* real nice," Cal said. "She probably had a lousy home life when she was growing up. Some kids have it pretty tough, you know?"

"That's a fact. I hardly ever turn on the news anymore 'cause the stuff people do to each other and their kids is enough to turn my stomach. And to think of little Emma goin' through any of that..." Tom sighed and shook his head as if there was nothing left to say.

Cal fell silent, too, and the longer he thought about what Tom had said, the guiltier he felt for what he'd done to Emma. He hadn't been wrong to ask the questions, but his timing had definitely stunk. It hadn't always been easy growing up in the McBride household, but he'd never known abuse or neglect, and he'd always known love. Had Emma?

Not likely. After the way she'd bristled all up on him today, he'd bet Cal's Place that there was some deep, painful wound inside that woman, something she'd kept secret for a long, long time. And after a month's acquaintance, he'd expected her to just open right up and tell him all about it. Oh, smooth one.

Good Lord, what planet had he been on? But it didn't feel like he'd only known her a month; it felt more like she'd been a part of him forever. When he wasn't with her, hardly a minute went by that he didn't think about her, wish he could see her smile, share something with her.

He owed her an apology. No excuses, no rationalizations, no getting around it. He owed her a big apology.

Glancing at the clock, he grimaced. It was almost nine-thirty. In Sunshine Gap, that was considered late for dropping in. But Emma didn't have a phone in her trailer, and she wasn't from Sunshine Gap. Maybe she wouldn't mind as long as he didn't stay too long. He left Tom a tip and hurried home for his wagon.

Emma's trailer was dark when he parked in front of it. Emma's motorcycle was gone. Uneasiness prickling the back of his neck, Cal walked up to the trailer and cupped his hands around his eyes, trying to get a glimpse of the interior.

He heard voices coming his way and turned around. Wouldn't it be his luck to get caught snooping in her window like a Peeping Tom? Barry Jacobson and two stuntmen stepped out of the shadows. They all stopped when they saw Cal. Then Barry came forward, peeling a paper off the top of a stack he was carrying.

"Hey, Cal. Good to see you. We've had a schedule change for tomorrow. Will you give this to Emma?"

Cal took the paper, but stopped Barry when he and his buddies would have continued on down the row. "Hold on.

I'd be glad to give this to Emma if I knew where she was, but—''

Barry did a double take. "What do you mean, *if* you knew where she was. Wasn't she out with you tonight?"

"We went fishing earlier, but I dropped her off around six-thirty. I haven't seen her since. I came back out here to talk to her for a minute, but her bike's gone."

Barry turned to his companions. "Take a quick look around the ranch and see if you can find her."

The men took off in opposite directions. Frowning, Barry watched them for a moment before turning back to Cal. "This isn't like Emma. She knew we had an early call tomorrow and she always goes to bed early so she's sharp and ready to work. She's the last one I'd expect to be out carousing tonight."

Cal's stomach contracted into a hard knot. "The bars are closing up right now. I don't think she's carousing."

"What do you think she's doing, then?"

Remembering his own need to vent his frustration after he'd gotten home, Cal sighed. "Maybe she's just out riding and blowin' off some steam."

Barry's eyes narrowed into a suspicious-looking squint. "Why would she do that?"

"We, uh...well, we had words this afternoon," Cal admitted. "She was pretty...ticked off when I left."

"Ticked off, or upset?" Barry demanded, stepping closer to Cal. There was anger in his voice, his rigid stance, his hammerlike fists.

Call straightened to his full height. "Both, I suppose."

Barry stuck out his chest and chin, and began to sound exactly like an outraged father ready to fight to protect his little girl. "What the hell did you do to her, McBride?"

"I didn't lay a finger on her, if that's what you're hinting at. I was just trying to get to know her better. Guess I asked too many questions about her background."

Groaning, Barry shut his eyes and slowly shook his head.

"Dammit, no wonder she took off. I thought you cowboy types minded your own business."

"Not when we're...making friends with somebody," Cal said. "I really like Emma, you know? I sure never meant to hurt her. I came out here tonight to apologize to her for being so nosy."

Barry's frown softened. "She's not an easy one and she never will be, but she's a fine woman, Cal. You can take my word for it."

"I don't need to take your word for it. I can see it myself. That's why I was trying to get to know her. She just sort of went ballistic on me."

Taking a step back, Barry gave him a sad smile. "She would have done that with anyone who asked questions about her family. There's no way you could have known."

"But I could've shut my mouth when she told me she didn't want to talk about it."

Barry studied him long and hard. "You're in love with her."

Hearing the other man say those words without even a hint of a question made Cal's gut tighten. He opened his mouth to deny it, but the words wouldn't come. Could it be true? No, of course not. He was just sort of...thinking about falling in love with her. He hadn't already fallen.

But if that were the case, why was he still standing here, talking to Barry and worrying his fool head off about Emma? Why did even the possibility, however remote, of never seeing her again make him feel so...bleak? And why did Barry's knowing more about Emma than he did make him feel jealous enough to want to kill the man? Before he could answer any of those questions satisfactorily, one of the stuntmen returned with Jake, and Grace's son, Riley.

"Kid says he saw her take off like a bat outta hell," the stuntman reported. "A little before seven."

Cal's stomach contracted again, then dropped clear down to the soles of his feet. Oh, damn, right after he'd left her. And he'd refused to listen to her apology...accused her of using him, which he really didn't believe…probably sounded like he intended to stalk her for God's sake. If anything happened to her, he would never forgive himself. Never.

Barry questioned Riley further, but couldn't get any more information out of him. There was no way to know if Emma went to the highway or not, or if she had gone there, which way she would have turned. Finally Barry gave up, and they all stood around in a group, waiting to hear from the other man.

When he couldn't stand the waiting any longer, Cal took Jake aside. "I've got a bad feeling about this one. I think we should rally the family."

Jake nodded, then said, "I'll help, and Marsh and Dillon will, too. But Alex has to be on the set early in the morning, Grace needs to stay with the kids and there's no way we're gonna ask Zack to leave Lori alone right now."

"Still no sign of her ex?" Cal asked. He'd had his employees handing out pictures of Lori Jones's ex-husband for the past week and asking if anyone had seen him. Lori and her boy had been hiding from the abusive SOB for four years, and she had reason to believe he was closing in on them. Cal didn't blame Zack for sticking close to home until the creep was caught.

Jake shook his head. "But we've got CBs in all the ranch rigs. We'll drive them and keep in touch with each other. I'll go back to the house and get us organized. We'll meet you up there after you've heard from the other guy. I'd discourage the movie folks from doing much searching on their own. They don't know these roads like we do."

Cal felt doubly grateful for his family right now. Mc-Brides fought with each other over all kinds of stupid things, but when there was real trouble, they all pulled together, no questions asked. Clapping Jake on the back, Cal nodded his agreement with the plan. Jake could organize an army in his sleep. "Thanks."

"We'll find her," Jake said.

He left without saying another word, but the compassion in his big brother's eyes confirmed Cal's earlier suspicions about himself. Yeah, he was falling in love with Emma Barnes, all right. It must be the real, scary, lasting kind of love if Jake recognized it so easily. Well, he couldn't worry about it now.

The other stuntman returned with nothing helpful to report. Cal told Barry and the others about Jake's plan. Barry agreed, but insisted he wanted to ride along with Cal. By the time they arrived at the main house, the rigs were gassed up, the troops were gathered and Jake had maps of the area marked for each search team.

Though Zack wasn't coming with them, he promised to call the other cops in the area and find out if any of them had seen or heard anything about a motorcycle accident. He would also alert Sandy Bishop to the possible need for an ambulance and coordinate search patterns with his own CB.

Cal and Barry drew the route from Sunshine Gap south on Highway 120. It was the same one Cal and Emma had taken the week before, and the one Cal suspected she would have taken this time, too. They searched all night, driving slowly and calling her name out the windows all the way to Thermopolis and back, investigating side roads along the way .

With every mile, Cal's uneasiness grew. Hearing the other teams report a similar lack of results on the radio didn't help his mood much, either. Dammit, this was all his fault. If he hadn't been so aggressive, she never would have done this.

But when a guy was…well, all right, falling in *love,* it was a natural reaction to want to know everything about his woman. God knew, he'd heard this kind of stuff hundreds of times across the bar at Cal's Place. And Emma certainly hadn't wasted any time in pulling his life story out of him, either. Did that mean she cared about him? At least a little bit?

He thought it did. If she didn't care at all, he figured she probably would've just told him to take a hike rather than getting so upset. Most people didn't get all worked up over stuff they didn't care about. If Emma was upset enough to take off on her bike the night before an early call—because of a stupid argument with him—she *must* care about him.

He held on to that slender thread of hope hour after hour. When the first fingers of dawn pierced the eastern horizon, Cal and Barry were both hoarse, exhausted and hungry, but neither was ready to quit. They made a pit stop at Cal's café, grabbed a thermos of coffee and a bag of doughnuts and set off again. Cal silently prayed that with the help from a little sunlight, they finally would find Emma.

Cal and Barry were too busy concentrating on looking to spare any energy for talking to each other. About five miles south of Meeteetse, Barry let out a raspy yell and pointed toward the fence line on the west side of the road. Cal jammed on the brakes, then slowly backed up until he spotted what had excited the other man.

Emma's helmet, red as a giant cherry, lay upside down on a patch of grass between two fence posts. Cal felt his heart racing so hard, he thought it had surged up behind his sternum. He yanked the pickup onto the road's skinny shoulder and jumped out.

Refusing to think about how badly she might have been hurt to lose her helmet, he shouted, "Emma! Emma, where are you?"

No answer.

Barry said, "I'll get the helmet," and plunged down the steep embankment and thrashed his way through weeds, stubby bushes and rocks to get there.

Cal scanned the east side of the road, first to his right. Nothing. But she was here, somewhere. He could feel her presence, could practically smell the scent of her hair. Fighting his own frantic impatience, he moved his eyes slowly, slowly to the left. Bingo.

"Barry, over here," he called, pointing at the patch of flattened bushes he'd found.

He sprinted for those bushes. His heart sank when he looked over the side of the road and saw Emma and the bike all crumpled up in a heap at the bottom of the ditch. No wonder they hadn't been able to find her. The damn ditch was at least three feet deep here. Maybe four. Emma looked pale and still, what if she was—

He couldn't finish that thought. Instead, he scrambled down the incline and knelt beside her, sliding his shaking fingers along her neck in search of a pulse. It was there, all right. He didn't have much experience to judge its strength, but at least he could feel it.

"Emma? Emma, can you hear me?"

No response. Cal shouted, "Barry, bring the first aid kit and blanket. Hurry!"

Turning back to Emma, Cal brushed tangled hair out of her face. Her skin was cold and clammy, but he didn't see any blood. Thank God. Of course, no blood didn't mean she wasn't hurt somewhere. "Emma, sweetheart, talk to me. Wake up and talk to me. You're going to be all right."

Barry skidded down the slope, blanket under one arm, the first aid kit under the other. He knelt on Emma's other side, found her pulse, then pulled up her eyelids with the pad of his thumb and shone a small flashlight at her eyes. "Pupils are reacting." Putting the flashlight aside, he lightly ran his fingers over Emma's head. "No scrapes or obvious bumps on her head. Must've been wearing her helmet like a good girl. Thank God for small favors."

Not trusting his voice at the moment, Cal nodded his agreement. Barry shook out the blanket and covered Emma with it, tucking it in around her.

"She's in shock, but on the surface she looks like she'll make it to me."

"How do you know so much?" Cal asked.

"I'm a stunt coordinator. I've seen accidents a hell of a

lot worse than this one. I could probably pass an EMT test if I wanted to."

Cal tipped his head toward the bike. "Shouldn't we get that off her?"

Barry moved toward Emma's legs, squatted on his heels and studied the motorcycle from three different angles. Then he beckoned for Cal to join him. "She's not tangled in it anywhere, so let's give it a shot. But we really don't want to move her or drag it across her legs. We'll just lift it straight off her, but if we hit any resistance at all, we quit and set it right back down where it was. All right?"

Cal nodded and positioned himself where Barry directed him. Between the two of them, freeing Emma proved to be a surprisingly quick and easy maneuver. While Barry studied Emma's legs and covered them up, Cal rolled the bike out of the way. He came back and looked down at her, gulping at the huge, jagged lump in his throat. Lord, was she ever going to wake up?

"What else can we do for her?" he asked.

"I'll go call for the ambulance," Barry said. "You stay with her and keep trying to wake her up. If she does, try to keep her calm and reassure her, but don't give her anything to drink. Not water, not anything."

Barry climbed up to the road. Cal opened the first aid kit and set it beside Emma's head. He stroked her forehead and her hair. "Emma," he said, "Emma, sweetheart, it's me, Cal. Can you hear me?"

Her eyelids fluttered and she crinkled up her forehead as if even that much movement hurt her, but her eyes stayed shut. He tried again. "Emma, wake up, now. Let's see those pretty blue eyes."

She uttered a soft whimper, then tried to lift her head.

Cal slid his hand under the back of her neck, intending to prevent her from moving it herself until the ambulance arrived. "That's it, Emma. Wake up, honey, but don't try to move. Help's on the way. You're gonna be just fine."

For some unfathomable reason, she smiled, then opened

one eye at a time. Squinting as if she were having trouble focusing, she looked at him with the vacant sort of expression newborn babies sometimes had.

"Knew you'd say that, McBride," she murmured, her voice as croaky and hoarse as his own and Barry's were.

"You did?"

"Heard your voice...all night."

"We've been out here looking for you all night."

"That's nice." She grimaced, then exhaled a shallow breath. "Water?"

"Can't help you there, hon. Barry'll nail my hide to the barn door."

"He's here?"

"Oh, yeah. He's calling the ambulance right now. Been acting like a demented daddy all night."

She coughed, though it may have been an attempt to laugh. Cal couldn't tell for sure. She ran her tongue over the fronts of her upper teeth and made a face. "Tastes like dirt."

Cal poked around in the first aid kit and came up with a moist towelette. He opened it and gently wiped it over her face. Beneath the layer of dust, he noted that her skin looked sort of pasty white, and her lips had a bluish tinge to them. Her breathing sounded odd, too. Kind of shallow and fast.

Concerned, he glanced up toward the road. No sign of Barry yet. Well, he'd try to keep Emma talking. She slurred some of her words, but so far, she was making pretty good sense. That must be a good sign.

"Where do you hurt, Em?"

She rolled her eyes at him. "Everywhere."

He tried to smile at her, but it was damned hard. "Yeah, I'll bet you do. Where does it hurt the worst?"

"Leg. Left one."

"Okay," Cal said. "Anywhere else in particular, hon?"

She lifted her right forearm, then let it drop as if she just didn't have the strength to hold it up. Cal leaned closer for a better look. The sleeve of her jacket had shredded into strips. Beneath it, her glove's leather gauntlet reached almost to her elbow.

Unable to see any obvious sign of injury, he gently ran a fingertip across the area she'd indicated. She winced, and he pulled back immediately. A dark reddish stain covered his fingertip.

Blood. Cal shut his eyes and sucked in a deep breath. He would *not* pass out. Emma needed his help, and he was not going to wuss out on her. No damn way.

Gritting his teeth, he opened his eyes and looking through the ribbons of leather above her gauntlet, saw a trail of drying blood and followed it up her bicep to a two-inch chunk of brown glass deeply embedded in her flesh. To have soaked the leather gauntlet that much, the wound must have bled a lot, but she wasn't bleeding now.

Strangely enough, Cal's urge to faint passed, and he could almost look at the wound rationally. Amazing what he managed to do whenever he was around this woman.

"You okay?" she asked.

"Fine, sweetheart. You hang in there."

Barry came back down to join them. "Hey, you're awake," he said, going down on one knee on Emma's other side. "That's great. The ambulance is on the way."

"Sounds like…a party," Emma said. "How's Mama?"

Barry scowled at her. "Who cares? I told you that thing was too dangerous."

Emma huffed. "You jump off buildings…get set on fire. You call a little ol' motorcycle dangerous?"

Barry grinned slightly. "Still got that smart mouth. I was hoping you'd gotten that knocked out of you."

"You wish."

He reached out and stroked her cheek. "It's going to be all right, kid. Ten minutes tops, and you'll be on your way to the best orthopedic surgeon I can find."

She nodded, coughed, then moaned. Cal thought Barry turned a little pale under his California tan. Before he could be sure, the stunt coordinator said he had to watch for the ambulance and hurried back up the hill.

Cal carefully took Emma's hand, ignoring the dampness on her glove. She looked up, silently regarding him with an expression in her eyes he couldn't interpret.

"What is it, Em?"

"Nothing." She glanced down, sniffled and slowly lifted her chin to meet his gaze again. Tears glittered in her eyes, but she made no attempt to hide them from him. "Glad you're here. Talk...later?"

He heard the scream of a siren coming from a distance and resigned himself to waiting until she was well on the road to recovery. He leaned closer and brushed away the tears for her. "Any time you're up to it. Don't worry about a thing, sweetheart. I'll be right beside you all the way."

She gave him a crooked smile. "Thanks, friend. Good ones hard to find. Ya know?"

"Yeah, I know, Em. That's why I'm not goin' anywhere."

Jeez, she looked so pale and fragile, it was a good thing the ambulance had arrived. There was all sorts of commotion up on the road, but Cal never looked away from Emma for a second.

Her gaze clung to his with an intensity and a sense of trust that squeezed on his heart like an iron fist.

Life sure had a perverse sense of humor sometimes. A month ago, he'd thought he couldn't fall in love—really, head-over-heels, 'til-the-end-of-our-lives kind of love— with anyone. Especially not with some hot-tempered biker babe. He couldn't have been more wrong.

Now that he'd seen the real woman behind those black leather duds and that in-your-face attitude, he was falling in love so hard and so fast, he could barely keep up with his own emotions. He wanted to hold her and kiss her, pamper her and fuss over her, just plain take care of her. He figured she might put up with the pampering part until she started getting well.

After that, he had no doubt whatsoever, that she'd fight his help, and any attempt he made to lure her into any kind of a commitment. Well, too bad. She could fight like a hellcat for all he cared. She could be as independent as a skunk waving its tail in warning and she undoubtedly would. But she was in for one big surprise.

Compared to Cal McBride, she didn't even know the meaning of the word *stubborn*.

Chapter Nine

Emma blinked, and when she opened her eyes again, the world had changed. New faces loomed over her, blocking out the sun, and their voices mixed together in a jabbering, unintelligible mess. Who were they? What did they want? Her heart raced, her stomach roiled and she was scared. Really scared. Where was Cal? She hadn't been so scared when he'd been with her. She needed him.

She tried to reach out, but somebody was holding her hand. Another face floated into view, but she was too confused to focus on it. A clammy sweat broke out on her forehead and under her arms, and she shivered. Was somebody counting? Dammit, she wanted to know what was going on. Why couldn't she understand anything?

Someone was pushing fingers against her wrist. Someone else fastened a cervical collar around her neck. By the time she figured out these new people must be paramedics, she heard somebody counting again. Hands, how many she couldn't tell, held her steady as something slid beneath her.

When the hands released her, she was lying on a flat board instead of lumpy ground.

Then she heard a woman's voice say, "Get out of here, Cal. I need room to work."

"Cal?" Emma called.

A strong, warm hand gently squeezed hers. "I'm right here, sweetheart. I've got to let these folks help you now, but I'll be close by. I promise." His hand released hers and she so felt bereft, she wanted to cry.

Then a woman's face appeared. She had reddish hair and looked awfully familiar, but Emma couldn't place her.

"Hi, Emma. I'm a nurse and I'm going to take care of you. My name's Sandy Bishop."

Emma nearly swallowed her tongue. "Sandy...Bishop?" she said faintly. "You're Cal's...?"

"I was."

"Never touched him," Emma said. "Well, I kissed him, but that's all. I mean, he's hardly been used at all. By me, anyway. Good kisser, isn't he?"

Sandy chuckled and held Emma's wrist while looking at her own watch. Unable to stop herself, Emma babbled on.

"Wasn't trying to steal him. I mean, you did see him first. If you want him back..."

"It's okay." Sandy pried open Emma's eyelids and shone a penlight into her eyes. "If you want Cal McBride, honey, he's all yours."

"Really?"

Sandy stuck a needle into Emma's arm and attached a tube to it. "Really. Now stop worrying about that big lug and let's get you to the hospital. Can you tell me what day it is?"

Emma answered correctly. The questions and the poking and prodding went on forever.

Emma knew it was her fault. She kept drifting in and out of her brain or something. They still wouldn't give her any damned water, her stomach kept threatening to revolt and her leg throbbed with every heartbeat.

A sudden draft of air along the outside of her left sleeve drew her attention. To her horror, she saw Sandy slashing at her beloved jacket with a pair of scissors.

"Stop," Emma said. "Damn, stop cutting. Leather costs a *lot*. Knew you hated me."

"I don't hate you." Sandy smiled, but kept right on cutting. "I've got to see your injuries, Emma. This stuff's pretty well shot, anyway, though. Don't worry about it."

"Easy for you to say."

"Yeah, it sure is. I happen to think your life is more important than a jacket, but, hey, I'm just a nurse. What the heck do I know?"

Emma laughed, then gagged.

"She's vomiting." Sandy shouted.

Strong hands grabbed her, immobilizing her head and turning her onto her side, board and all. God, it was humiliating. She'd never been this helpless, and she hated it, hated it, hated it. Sandy cleaned her up with a calm, matter-of-fact manner but Emma still felt mortified.

"Sorry," she murmured when she'd been turned onto her back and could breathe normally again.

"Happens all the time," Sandy said. "We just don't want you to breathe that stuff into your lungs. Now *that's* messy. Okay, where was I? Oh yeah. Slicing up your favorite jacket."

Emma cleared her throat and beckoned for Sandy to lean closer. "Cut off…everything?" she whispered.

"Pretty much. Not bashful are you? With a body like yours, I'd run around stark naked every chance I got."

Emma started to shake her head, but the instant giddiness made her freeze in place. "Just don't let…Cal see tattoo."

"Where is it?" Sandy whispered.

"Chest."

Sandy winked at her. "No problem, hon."

Everything got sort of fuzzy again. She could feel Sandy's strong, but gentle hands touching her here and there, and more drafts as the rest of her clothing fell beneath the chomping scissors. There were voices, too, but they were talking so fast, she couldn't catch it all.

She inhaled a deep breath and opened her eyes. The blue sky, what she could see of it, was so beautiful it made her want to cry. Somebody cut the laces on her boot. She heard somebody say, "Oh, God..." The boot came off, jostling her left foot. The pain flashed behind her eyelids, ripped a scream from her throat and Emma was gone again.

Cal sat in the hospital's waiting room, scanning an ancient copy of *Time,* flipping Emma's penny over and over with his fingertips and quietly going out of his mind with worry. Since Cody's orthopedic surgeon was vacationing in Australia, they'd had to transport Emma over a hundred more miles to Billings, Montana in order to find another one. Sandy had ridden in the ambulance with Emma, but she'd already gone back to Sunshine Gap.

He'd stopped at the ranch long enough to grab a bag Grace had packed for Emma, stopped by his own house to pack a few things, arrange care for the dogs and ask Sylvia to manage his business until he returned. Finally, after driving like he didn't believe in speed limits for an hour and a half, he'd arrived at the hospital just in time to squeeze Emma's hand before they wheeled her into surgery.

She'd been in there almost two hours now, the longest two hours he could remember. Tossing the magazine onto an end table, he got up and paced across the room. As much as these places charged, you'd think they could afford current magazine subscriptions.

He'd already hit the hospital's gift shop and the cafeteria. He wished he could go somewhere else. Do something. Anything. But Emma's surgery should be over soon, and he didn't want to miss talking to the doctor or being there when Emma woke up.

The surgeon arrived five minutes later, filled Cal in on the surgery, then hurried off to his next patient. Saying a silent prayer of thanks, Cal tucked Emma's lucky penny into his vest pocket and hurried off to the nearest pay phone. Barry answered on the first ring. The instant Cal identified himself, Barry asked, "How's Emma?"

"Her surgery went fine," Cal said. "Took a while to get her ankle put back together, but the doc said that if she takes care of herself and stays off that cycle, she should make a full recovery."

"What about her career?"

"I asked about that," Cal said, "and he said it's too early to tell. She'll have to watch that ankle, though."

Barry remained silent for a moment, then sighed. "Yeah. I'd already guessed that. Damn."

Cal allowed his anger at Barry's less than enthusiastic response to creep into his voice. "Hey, she'll be able to walk, jog and do almost anything she wants. Considering how bad off she was when we found her, I'd say that's good news."

"Of course it is," Barry said. "But if that ankle's not a hundred percent, it's going to limit the jobs she'll be able to accept. In our business, that's a problem. She won't like it."

"She's smart. She'll find another way to make a living besides falling off galloping horses and crashing cars."

"If it comes to that, I'm sure she will. When will she be released?"

"A couple of days. She has to stay off that leg for about two weeks, though. Is there anyone I should call to come and help her?"

"Not that I know of. If we were in California, I could organize something, but we're in the middle of a shoot, and—"

"I'll work it out," Cal interrupted. "I have to go now, Barry. If there's any more news you need to hear, I'll call."

Indignant on Emma's behalf, Cal hung up and headed for the elevators. So, she was part of the movie crew's "family," but only as long as she was willing and able to risk breaking her neck for the sake of "the shoot." Now she was badly hurt and out of a job, and nobody had any time or resources to help her.

Cal jabbed the button for Emma's floor with more force than necessary. Oh, he knew he was probably overreacting. The production company did have millions of dollars invested in this movie, after all, and they stood to lose a small fortune if Barry couldn't find a replacement for Emma soon. Every day of delay was money lost. When it all came down to the bottom line, an injured stuntwoman was nothing more than an inconvenience.

Business was like that, and business always came first. Cal's former employers had tried to tell him that when they ordered him to ''downsize'' half the employees under his supervision, starting with everyone over fifty. If the order hadn't been a vile example of age discrimination, and if the company had been in dire financial straits, he might have been able to carry it out.

But the company had been in great shape. Most of the targeted workers had kids in college, and they'd faithfully served the company for twenty years or more. They were being downsized for no other reason than sheer greed, and Cal hadn't been able to stomach it. He'd been fired for refusing to do so, but he'd never regretted his decision.

He liked earning money as much as the next guy, but he'd sworn that he would never let pursuit of the almighty dollar become more important than the well-being of another person. He'd lived by that principle ever since. He would never be as rich as he could have been in the corporate world, but he could meet his own eyes in the shaving mirror every morning without flinching. If Emma's employers and co-workers couldn't see their way clear to help her now, by God, Cal McBride would.

He'd intended to do it anyway, but now he didn't have to worry about anyone's tender sensibilities but his own and Emma's. The thought made him smile. What an opportunity.

* * *

Roses. She must have died and heaven smelled like roses. Only, she didn't feel dead, exactly. And how did being dead feel? Emma didn't know. But she still didn't feel dead.

If she smelled roses, and she did, then where were they? And where was she? It seemed like a long time since she'd been sure of anything.

Focusing what little strength she had, she opened one eye, then the other. Beige walls. Beige blinds at the windows, open at the moment. Night sky outside. TV bolted high on the wall. Empty hospital bed on the other side of the room. Hospital bed? She looked down at herself. Hmm. She was lying in another one, and there was a tube coming out of her left hand.

Okay, she was in a hospital, and now that the rest of her body was starting to wake up, she suspected she was hurt, rather than ill. If only her memory wasn't so foggy. Her mouth tasted incredibly dry, and she wouldn't mind a visit to the bathroom, but she was strangely reluctant even to try to move.

Cautiously rolling her head to the other side of the pillow, she saw the roses. A huge bouquet, two dozen at least, half red and half white, arranged with a mixture of baby's breath and ferns in a crystal vase. Goodness. No one had ever given her flowers before. Who would have done this?

Turning her head an inch farther to the right, she saw him. Cal. The mere thought of his name made her feel warm inside. But seeing him here, sprawled in a chair that looked far too small for him, his eyes closed, the back of his head resting against the wall and his chin covered with more than one day's worth of stubble made her ache and smile at the same time. Soft, snuffling noises that weren't quite snores slipped from his parted lips.

Oh, dear, he looked exhausted, and he had one of his long arms wrapped around an adorable stuffed teddy bear. How long had he been here? And why was he here? For that matter, *where* was here?

As if he'd felt her scrutiny, Cal jerked upright, rubbed one hand down over his face and turned to look at her with such concern in his eyes, she wondered if she'd been expected to live. Then his gaze met hers and a slow, sleepy, absolutely wonderful smile spread across his face.

Pushing himself out of the chair, he crossed to her bedside, leaned down and caressed her cheek with the backs of his knuckles. "Hi, there," he murmured, his voice husky, whether with sleep or emotion, she couldn't tell. "How do you feel, Em?"

"Don't know yet. I'm afraid to move. What happened?"

His eyebrows came together in a worried frown. "Don't you remember?"

"Some, but it's all pretty fuzzy."

He reached for something beside her head. "Let's get the nurse in here."

"Wait. Please, just tell me, okay? I need to know."

He hesitated, then lowered his hand back to the bed rail. "All right. Last night you wiped out, and we didn't find you until early this morning. You're just waking up after surgery. Any of that ring a bell?"

Emma nodded, slowly. "It's coming back. Deer on the road and went for the ditch. Didn't work out. Where am I? Besides in the hospital."

"Billings, Montana," Cal said. "Biggest medical center for hundreds of miles in any direction. They've got a fine reputation and nice folks working here."

Twinges of pain gnawed at her left ankle. "How much surgery did I need?"

He scrunched up his face and shrugged. "Not that much. Nothing we can't handle."

"I'm starting to feel it," she said, letting her tone imply her lack of patience with his less than artful dodging. "I know there's something wrong, so tell me the truth. All of it."

"Don't get excited," he warned her. "The doctor says you should have a complete recovery."

"Recovery from what, dammit?"

"Well, you busted your ankle in a couple of places. Your right arm also had a nasty encounter with a broken beer bottle. Took ten stitches to close it up."

Emma grimaced, more at the realization of what those injuries might cost her in time and lost job opportunities, than from any real pain at the moment. She risked a glance at her lower leg. She couldn't see much but a lumpy looking ace bandage, stretching from her toes to her knee.

Whether he honestly thought she was in pain, or he just didn't want to answer any more questions, Cal rang for the nurse. Before Emma could protest, a sturdy, middle-aged woman who looked as if she might have done a stint in the marines entered the room. Her name tag said she was Mary P. Williams, and she bustled around with a big smile and brisk efficiency.

Within the first thirty seconds, she shooed Cal out of the room. Then she proceeded to check Emma's vital signs and dressings, taught her how to use a PCA pump to dispense her own pain medication, and introduced her to the horrors of using a bedpan. She also administered a bed bath, brushed out Emma's hair for her and handed her a toothbrush.

Unused to so much personal attention, Emma pulled every trick in her arsenal of intimidation techniques, but Mary P. had mastered the fine art of bullying patients into doing what they were supposed to do. And she did it with such cheery good humor, her patients didn't know whether to hug her or kill her. By the time she left, Emma felt as if she'd gone nine rounds with a very sweet sumo wrestler, but she was considerably cleaner and more comfortable, as well.

Cal poked his head back into the room, warily checking all four corners as if he expected Mary P. to be lurking somewhere, waiting for a chance to throw him out again. Chuckling weakly, Emma beckoned him into the room.

"Come in, you big coward. How could you leave me alone with that...dynamo?" Emma asked.

"You mean she's still alive?" Cal replied with a wicked grin. "I figured you'd take just about so much, and then you'd bash her over the head with a table or bust that vase and use it on her like you used your beer bottle on poor Joe."

"I thought about it," Emma admitted. "But she's too nice to threaten. You know?"

Scooping up the stuffed bear and a brown paper bag, Cal returned to the side of her bed. He rested an elbow on the bed rail, then set the bear on her right side, away from the IV tubes coming out of her left hand. "Thought you might like some company while you're laid up here."

Feeling strangely shy under his scrutiny, she stroked the bear's soft brown fur, studied the black embroidered eyes and nose, smiled at the bandana tied around its neck, the brocade vest and cowboy hat. "You know, he looks familiar. I think I'll call him...Calvin?"

Cal shook his head. "Not if you're naming him after me. My full name's Caleb. Caleb John McBride."

"Oh. That's nice," she murmured, then couldn't think of another thing to say to him. Something had shifted between them, but she wasn't sure what it was.

His dimple appeared below his mustache. He held up the bag. "Grace went into your trailer and packed a few things for you. Want me to open it? Or you can wait until they make you sit up tomorrow. Might be easier for you to handle then."

"Tomorrow's fine. You didn't have to do all of this."

"I know that, Em. So it must mean I wanted to do it," he said. "It's nothing anybody else wouldn't do."

She didn't believe that. And she couldn't look away from his smiling face. He appeared to be having the same problem, only in reverse. Having him so close warmed her inside and pushed the niggling fear and worry over her future to the back of her mind.

Noting the weariness in his face, she said, "You look like you need more sleep. Did you get a motel room?"

"Not yet, but Billings has plenty of places."

"Then go find one and get some rest."

"I'll do it on one condition."

"What's that?"

"Promise you won't start fretting. In the first place, it won't solve anything. In the second place, you're gonna get through this, one way or another. I'll be around to help you for as long as you need me. Deal?"

Unbearably touched, she slowly nodded. "Deal."

He leaned down, kissed her cheek and headed for the door. When he got there, she had to ask him one last question.

"Cal? How's...Mama?"

To her surprise, he didn't laugh at her. He held his Stetson hat in one hand and stuck his other hand into his front jeans pocket. "She's dinged up and scratched, and her headlight's busted. I don't know any more than that, but she looked fixable to me."

"Thanks."

He promised to come back in the morning and left. Suddenly, the room seemed awfully big, awfully quiet and awfully empty. Her stomach clenched in alarm. She always took care of herself. She couldn't allow herself to need Cal or anyone else.

She glanced at her lower left leg and sighed. The size of her bandage alone made it clear she was going to need *some*body's help, at least until she could get around on her own again. Sometimes life just didn't play fair, and all you could do was go with the flow. She might as well do it with as much grace and dignity as possible.

Cal arrived at the hospital ten minutes before visiting hours were supposed to start, but he went right up to Emma's room, anyway. Holding his hat, he knocked on the open door and called, "Hey, Em. You decent?"

"Reasonably," she called back.

"That'll do." He stepped into the room, took one look at her propped halfway to a sitting position and wearing the soft, cotton tank top and matching boxer shorts he'd bought for her and rocked right back on his boot heels. "Damn," he said, stretching the word into two syllables. "That's really purple."

She chuckled. "I think it's a great color."

"They had some pastel ones, but this one just seemed more like you."

"Good choice. I'm allergic to pastels."

"Well, I figured no matter what color it was, you'd like it better than those hospital gowns. I hear they're drafty."

He set his hat on the window ledge and approached her bed. Though Emma still looked tired and a little pale, there was more life and sparkle in her eyes. Her hair looked damp and carried the scent of her shampoo. Unable to resist, he leaned down and stole a quick kiss from her lips. "Truth is, that little outfit looks right fetching on you."

Her cheeks turned pink, and she glanced away, as if she felt flustered, which Cal enjoyed to no end. "Well, um...thank you."

"You're welcome." Thinking she was probably getting sick of looking up at everyone, he pulled the visitor's chair closer and lowered himself into it. "Have you seen the doctor today?"

"Yes. I can go home tomorrow if I continue to improve."

"That's great. Is there anyone I should call for you, so they don't worry if they don't hear from you?"

She sank her front teeth into her bottom lip, then slowly shook her head.

"All right," Cal said, his tone as casual as he could make it. "Then you're coming home with me."

She opened her mouth, but he wasn't about to let her get a word of protest in. Raising one hand like a traffic cop, he plunged into the speech he'd practically written in his sleep.

"I've got a guest room and a bathroom on the main floor, so you won't have to worry about stairs," he said. "Sylvia's not far way, and neither is my sister Alex. The neighbors are all nice, too, and they'll check on you when I have to go to work."

"Okay."

Convinced he would have to wear her down with a long list of reasons she should agree, Cal waved the word away and rolled on. "The dogs'll keep you company, and I've got a satellite dish, so you can watch anything you want on TV. You'll get a lot more rest if you're completely away from the crew and all of that hubbub out at the ranch."

"Okay."

"And I promise I won't take advantage of you, Em. I mean, I don't hit on injured women even if they are sexy. I won't lay a finger on you unless it's to help you move around or something like that, you know?"

"I know."

"You need some help, and I'm happy to do it, so there's no reason to get all stubborn and independent about this," he went on, jabbing his index finger on the arm of the chair for emphasis. "You're staying at my house, and that's that. Don't give me any arguments. They won't do you a bit of good."

Her eyes glinted with laughter and her smile practically begged for a kiss. "All right, Cal. Whatever you say."

He paused, certain now that he'd missed something important. Or maybe he was hearing things. Surely, she hadn't given in this easily. Had she? "What do you mean, 'okay?'"

She laughed out loud. "Okay. All right. I'll do it. You can stop the sales pitch any time."

"You mean that?"

"It's a reasonable solution to a big problem for me. Why wouldn't I agree?"

Cal studied her for a moment, then pushed himself to his feet and pressed the call button. A nurse hurried into the room. She looked at Emma's face, then Cal's, then back at Emma's.

"Is there something I can do for you?" she asked, her voice wary.

"I'm not sure," Cal said. "Did you folks do any brain tests on her? She's not acting like herself at all."

Emma sputtered indignantly. The nurse glanced at her before turning to Cal. "In what way?"

"Well, there's gotta be something wrong with her. She's way too agreeable to be Emma Barnes."

Chapter Ten

"He did *what?*" Hope DuMaine demanded, gasping out the last word for the sake of drama, no doubt.

"You heard me," Emma grumbled, though even she was finally starting to see the humor in the situation. "He asked the nurse if I'd had any brain tests, because I wasn't acting like myself."

Hope giggled. "Because you were too—" she giggled again "—agreeable to be Emma Barnes?"

"That's right," Emma said, watching her friend with great anticipation. Hope was not easily impressed or amused, but if something truly struck her as funny, she had the most wonderful, maniacal, cackling laugh. Emma did her best to provoke it whenever possible.

"What did the nurse do?"

"The poor woman didn't know what to do. I tried to tell her I was fine, but that big dope went on and on, insisting that I always argued about every little thing and he kept a perfectly straight face the whole time. She finally gave up trying to make sense out of either one of us and called the doctor. I barely got out of there without a CAT scan.''

Hope lost it. She cackled, howled, snorted and giggled, shaking her head like a royal-blue dust mop. Emma sat back and enjoyed the show. Anyone else would probably think Hope was totally demented, but Emma knew better. Hope's laughing fits were actually a safety valve that allowed her to burn off energy she couldn't release any other way.

Yip and Yap jumped off Emma's lap, dashing around and around Hope, barking as ferociously as eight-pound dogs could manage. Of course, their barks were so little and squeaky, Hope merely laughed harder, wiping at her streaming eyes with the backs of her hands. At last, she pushed herself to a sitting position and scooped the little beasts into her arms.

''Oh my,'' she said with a sigh. ''I needed that.''

''I could tell,'' Emma said. ''What's going on with you?''

''Nothing terribly interesting. The ranch was been quiet since that plane crash.''

''What plane crash?''

''You didn't hear?''

Emma shook her head. ''I've been out of the loop for a week.''

''Well, of course you have.'' Hope immediately launched into the story of Lori Jones's abusive ex-husband catching up with her and her son, and his attempt to abduct them in a small private plane. ''Zack, Jake and Marsh showed up just in time to save her, and her ex crashed the plane right into a pine tree. Poor Lori was so brave—I was simply awed when I heard about it. Thank heaven she had a few McBrides there to help.''

Emma nodded. ''McBrides are awfully nice to have around when you're in trouble.''

''So tell me more about you and Cal.''

"There *is* no me and Cal," Emma said. "We really are just good friends."

"Mm-hmm," Hope said, but her doubtful eyes gave another message entirely.

"Don't start with me, Hopester."

"As if I would dare. Really, Emma, all I said was—"

"I *heard* what you said, and I can tell your dirty little mind is cooking up all sorts of ideas."

"Dirty *little* mind?" Hope climbed to her feet, dumping the poodles onto the sofa on her way up. "I'll have you know there is absolutely nothing *little* about my mind. It may be warped. It's undoubtedly dirty. But it is *not* little."

"Yes, oh queen of the universe," Emma said dryly. "As I was saying, there *is* no me and Cal. He offered me a place to recuperate, and since I had no other choice, I accepted."

Hope shook her head, then cupped one hand around her ear. "Excuse me? Did I hear you say, 'no other choice?' Of course, you had another choice, and she's standing right here in front of you. You think I'm just pickled oysters?"

"I wouldn't dream of bothering you right now. Blair needs you, and I know you're plotting your next book, and—"

"And nothing, missy," Hope scolded, bracing her fists on her skinny hips. "You're my *friend*, Emma. I would be honored to take care of you when you need help, so don't tell me you had no other choice than to stay with Cal McBride. As they say out here in Wyoming, it just won't wash."

"All right, I'll admit I thought about calling you, but—"

"But what?"

"Would you please sit down and stop looming over me like a vulture?" Emma said.

"But *what?*" Hope repeated.

"But you're rich and famous, and I didn't want you to think I only hang out with you because I want something from you. A lot people try to do that to you, and your friendship is too important to me to risk having you wonder if I'm like that, too.''

"I would never think that of you. For pity's sake, you saved me from that big, hairy biker dude with the black teeth and the nipple ring. That's a debt I shall never be able to repay.''

Emma chuckled at the memory of the incident to which Hope was referring. Oh, yes, Hope DuMaine certainly had gotten herself into a tight spot that night. "I don't know, Hope. Bowser Bob was quite a man. You might've passed up a real prince when you started screaming for help.''

Hope sniffed, but a smile lurked around the corners of her mouth. "Enough of that, let's get back to you and Cal.'' While Emma steamed, she glanced around the room, undoubtedly making a mental inventory of the furnishings. "He must be an awfully good friend to share his home with you. And I really do suspect that he's quite smitten with you.''

"Would you care to tell me why?''

Hope swept one hand in front of her, indicating the cluttered coffee table. "Look at all of those lovely gifts.''

Emma snorted, but finally couldn't hold back a hoot of laughter. "Those aren't from Cal,'' she said. "Pull the table over here. This, you have got to see.''

When Hope had completed the task and settled herself back on the sofa, Emma picked up the first item. It was a pint jar, filled with a substance whose color was somewhere between ruby red and a deep, rich burgundy. A slightly mashed pink bow that had probably graced at least one other present, had been taped to the lid. "Want to guess what this is?'' Emma asked.

Hope took the jar and held it up to the sunlight. "It's jelly.''

"Homemade chokecherry jelly, to be exact,'' Emma said. "The little old lady next door brought it over the first time she dropped by to check on me for Mayor McBride.

She and her husband went to the mountains and picked the berries themselves.''

"Oh, that's sweet, Emma," Hope said.

"Yeah. Real sweet." Emma picked up the next item, a huge round tin with an ethereal picture of angels painted on the lid and a note saying the enclosed fruitcake weighed three pounds. She popped the lid, then passed the tin over to Hope. "Check out these little goodies."

Hope selected one of the small, square bars covered with a chocolate topping and took a tiny bite. An instant later her eyes bugged out, she shoved the whole thing into her mouth and lunged for the tin. Anticipating such a response, Emma had already set it on the floor beneath her own spot on the sofa, safely out of Hope's reach.

"Careful, they're incredibly addictive," she said. "And fattening."

"Ambrosia," Hope murmured, still chewing the rich, gooey cookie and making faces and moaning sounds that suggested she might be in the throes of ecstasy. "Lord, you could make a fortune selling those in L.A."

Emma nodded. "But first you'd have to beat the recipe out of T. K. Montgomery across the street. She's extremely proud of it. Won a blue ribbon at the county fair three years running."

"Maybe we could take her." Hope shot a speculative glance out the living room windows. "How big is she?"

"Four and a half feet tall," Emma said, "and, about four and a half feet wide. She's got five kids and a laugh loud enough to make you go deaf." Smiling, she picked up the next item and handed it to Hope.

This gift had two identical pieces. Hope held up the first double-layered crocheted oblong with variegated colors in the orange-yellow-red part of the spectrum, and a pom-pom attached to one end, made of the same yarn as the... whatever the oblong thing was. Frowning at Emma, she said, "All right, I give up. What are they for?"

"They're slippers to keep my toes warm," Emma said,

as if nobody had ever had to tell *her* what they were, which was a long, long way from the truth. But Hope didn't need to know that. "Put them on your feet and walk around. See what happens."

Giggling, Hope kicked off her sandals and put on the slippers. With her first step, Yip and Yap cut loose with a frenzy of barking, dove off the sofa and onto Hope's feet, tugging, growling and nipping as they tried to kill those evil pom-poms. Every time Hope moved, the poodles attacked more ferociously, becoming, in effect, additional slipper ornaments. Giggling, Hope plopped her tush back onto the sofa, pried the dogs off her feet and handed the slippers to Emma.

Laughing herself, Emma folded them and tucked them back into their box. "You're never going to believe this, but Cal has another unique item made from the same lot of yarn."

"What is it?"

"Take a look in the bathroom," Emma said, graciously pointing the way. "And when you're done in there, check out the fridge before you come back."

Hope shot her a doubtful glance, then dutifully trotted off to the bathroom. Emma studied the second hand on her watch. Hope's shriek of delight came in exactly ten seconds. "I've heard about crocheted toilet paper covers, but I've never actually *seen* one before," she called on her way to the kitchen.

Emma heard the refrigerator door open and could only imagine Hope's dumbfounded expression when she saw the convention of Tupperware dishes gathered inside. Those amazing, colorful plastic dishes with the wonderful burping lids held casseroles, pies, puddings, salads, homemade soups and even a quart of stewed prunes in case she became...what *was* that term? Bound up?

The refrigerator door snapped shut, and Hope returned to the living room, looking almost as befuddled as Emma felt. Without waiting for an invitation, Hope poked through the other gifts on the coffee table, admiring everything from the embroidered pillow cases to the silky bed jacket, faded with age and smelling faintly of mothballs, a canning jar stuffed with fresh flowers from someone's garden. When she met Emma's gaze, her eyes were thoughtful, her smile wistful.

"They've given you the best they had to give, Em."

Her throat too tight to speak at first, Emma nodded. "I know," she said softly. "And I never intended to make friends of any of them. Almost everyone in this little town has stopped by to see me at least once. Some are just curious about the woman living with their mayor, but most of them sincerely want me to feel welcome. I mean, they act as if they really care about me."

"Why wouldn't they, darling? You're quite likable, you know. Even lovable."

"Maybe to people who really know me, but why *these* people?" Emma asked. "They don't know me at all. I don't dress or act or talk the way they do. And here they are, waiting on me, bringing me food and presents, and even play cards with me."

"Cards?" Hope said.

"Yeah. The ladies tried to teach me to play bridge, but I couldn't hack it. So they rounded up a bunch of retired guys to come over and play poker with me. Can you believe that?"

"It's wonderful," Hope said "You sound as if there's a problem here, but I'm not seeing it."

Emma thought about the situation, trying to pinpoint exactly what was bothering her. Finally, the only thing she could come up with was a plaintive, "It's like something out of a dream, you know? People helping the stranger in need and all of that. There's no way I can ever repay what they've done for me. What am I supposed to do with all this…kindness?"

Hope shrugged, then tucked her hands into the pockets of her fringed denim skirt. "Accept it. Enjoy it. Pass it on whenever you get the chance, which you would do anyway."

"But it's so weird, Hope. I'm used to taking care of myself, and all of a sudden, I have a town full of funny, wonderfully kind people bringing me this stuff, giving me manicures and pedicures and telling me they're praying for me. I'd cry my eyes out, except that they all seem to feel it's their Christian duty to tell me how crazy Californians are."

"Well? Just how crazy are we?"

"Trust me," Emma said with a laugh, "you don't want to know."

"I already do," Hope said, rolling her eyes. "Some of us even dye our hair blue. But let's get back to the juicy stuff. How do you really feel about Cal McBride?"

"Confused," Emma admitted.

"In what way?" Hope asked.

Yip and Yap climbed into Emma's lap and curled up for a nap. She caressed their warm, furry little bodies, finding comfort in the contact. "I've been here for ten days now, and he's been wonderful the whole time. I mean, he treats me like a princess, and he's really sweet with all the elderly people who stop by to see how I'm doing. And he's funny and charming and..."

"Handsome," Hope said. "And don't forget sexy."

"Yeah, yeah." Picturing Cal as he'd looked when he'd come back from his run this morning, Emma practically felt her hormones twitch. Scrunching her eyes tightly shut for a moment, she uttered a soft moan of frustration. "Lord, I've created a monster."

"Oooh, that sounds interesting."

Emma opened her eyes and gave Hope a warning look. "Listen, Miss Tell-all, anything I say here is strictly off the record. I don't even want to see a hint of any of this in your next book. Are we absolutely clear on that?"

Hope flicked a hand as if waving Emma's concern away. "Yes, of course, darling. You're not much fun to write about, anyway. You're simply not depraved enough. Now, about this monster?''

Emma told her about taking Cal jogging with her. "And now he's out there every morning, and when he comes home, he's all sweaty and he takes off his T-shirt and wipes his chest with it."

"And there he is in all his manly glory," Hope intoned, "wearing nothing but skimpy little running shorts, shoes and a smile. Be still, my heart."

Emma laughed, but Hope's description was essentially accurate. "Exactly. And he sort of...putters around the house like that until he's stopped sweating. And I just sit here, pretending to ignore him, sipping my coffee and trying not to drool or whimper."

"Poor baby," Hope murmured. "I suppose he treats you like a little sister?"

"Not exactly. He doesn't hit on me, but sometimes when he looks at me, I know he feels attracted, and he never does anything about it. I guess I really don't know what he wants."

"Well, you see, we have these little birds, and we also have some little bees—"

"Do you want to hear this or not?"

Hope returned to the sofa and tucked one foot under herself. "I do. I'm sorry, Emma. You were saying you don't know what Cal wants from you?"

Emma nodded. "I'm just saying that the sex thing is there. It's been there all along. But it's not really the issue. He's got something else that's higher on his agenda, right now, but I don't know what it is. Does that make any sense?"

"Given that lovely splint thing you're wearing, it certainly does. Not that an inventive couple couldn't work around it, of course. But maybe he's simply trying to give you a little space while you're healing. It sounds too good to be true, of course, so perhaps, he's lulling you into a false sense of security. When he decides to seduce you, you'll feel too safe and comfortable to resist.''

"I don't think he's quite that devious," Emma said with a chuckle. "I don't understand him, that's all. So what else is new?''

"Maybe you should be asking what you want to get out of this situation, Emma.''

"The only thing I want is to get healed up and go back to work. I don't want anything from Cal.''

"I didn't say from Cal. I said from this situation. There's an important opportunity for you here if you're smart enough to take it.''

"What are you talking about?''

Hope leaned over, picked up Yap and lifted the poodle onto her own lap. Yap rolled onto her back, silently begging for a belly scratch. Smiling, Hope obliged her, carefully using the blue talon on her index finger to accomplish the task.

"For as long as I've known you, you've lived your life on the move," she said without looking up. "You've used your career as an excuse never to stay in one place very long, or to become attached to anyone.''

"It's not an excuse," Emma protested. "That's the way this business is.''

"Other stunt people find ways to connect. Most of the guys on this shoot are married.''

"Well, goody for them," Emma said.

"Don't be bitter, darling. You could be married if you wanted. But once you move on to a new location, you never look back or try to continue any relationship you might have started.''

"So what's this big opportunity?'' Emma asked.

Hope nodded at Emma's elevated leg. "For once in your life, you can't simply roar off on your bike if people should start getting closer than you're used to. It might be good to expand your comfort zone a bit while you have time to sit and think about what you want out of your life.''

"I don't have to think about it. I want to be a great stuntwoman."

"A lovely goal, but a short-term one. Stunt work is for youngsters. You're incredibly fit, but you're not a youngster anymore. People Barry's age are rare, and they only get to hang around because of the technical knowledge they've picked up." She pointed at Emma's ankle. "That injury is the beginning of the end of your stunt career."

Emma looked away. "It is not. I'm only thirty years old."

Hope softened her tone. "Big deal. Your ankle will heal this time, but it probably will never be quite the same. And every time you use it full-out, you're going to wonder if this is the time you'll blow it to pieces for good."

"Oh, please," Emma said. "Aren't we being just a bit melodramatic?"

"Not this time," Hope said. "You've seen the guys who didn't get out of the business when they should have, and they're hobbling around on canes. Ask any retired pro football player who can barely walk if he's glad he took the risks he did. You're not any more indestructible than they were."

"You think I should quit right now?"

"I think you should *think* about quitting. It's got to happen sometime. Why not be prepared for it?"

"How do you prepare for a disaster?"

"If you have solid long-term goals, it doesn't have to be such a disaster. Didn't you ever have one really special dream? Something you've always wanted to do besides stunt work?"

Emma grimaced, inwardly debating whether she should tell Hope that much. "Well," she said after a moment, "don't laugh, but I loved being a mechanic. Now that you mention it, the stunt work was only supposed to be a lark. I took the first job with Barry, hoping to save tons of money fast so I could open my own shop. Somewhere over the years, the shop idea got lost."

"That's fascinating, Emma," Hope said. "What about goals for your personal life?"

"I don't have a personal life. How would you set goals for that anyway? Make a list? Find a guy. Have a baby. Dump the guy. Buy a dog."

"Come on, darling, think about it. Where do you really want to be in five years? In ten years? Do you still want to be living like such a gypsy then? Or would you like to have a home somewhere and a family?"

Emma glared at Hope, nearly hating her for saying such awful things and asking such hard questions, the kind of questions that could keep a person up all night, worrying and feeling scared and trying to figure out the answers.

"So, is this a multiple choice test, or what?" Emma demanded.

Hope laughed, set Yap on the cushion beside Emma and stood.

"The only right answers are the ones that work for you."

"And where am I supposed to find them?"

"Well, they're not in all those old *I Love Lucy* reruns you've been watching. They're all right there inside you, Em."

"Don't get metaphysical on me, okay? I'm not in the mood."

"Well, if those questions are too difficult, I suppose you could simply ask yourself the real reason you agreed to stay here with Cal." Hope picked up her purse and the keys to the rental car she'd borrowed. "And when you figure that out, you'll be halfway to knowing why it scares the devil out of you when anyone—especially Cal—acts as if he really cares about you."

"That doesn't scare me."

Hope shot her a pitying look. "Emma, darling, if your leg wasn't broken, you'd be running as far and as fast as you possibly could to get away from all of this...kindness. Don't you want to know why?"

While Emma was still sputtering, Hope calmly walked

out. Emma yelled after her until Yip and Yap darted under the coffee table and cowered there, trembling like mad. In sheer frustration, she grabbed the stupid pom-pom slippers and threw them at the screen door. The dogs charged from their hiding place, pounced on the pom-poms and shook them viciously.

Suddenly Emma wanted those stupid slippers back as much as if they were precious heirlooms. She called the poodles, but they were having too much fun to pay attention, and there was no way she could catch the little stinkers and take the slippers away. Well, maybe she just hadn't given them the right incentive.

Reaching beneath the seat, she pulled out the angel tin and opened the lid. Both furry little heads popped up and turned in her direction. Emma selected a cookie and waved it back and forth. "Here, doggies. Bring me the slippers and you can have a treat."

They didn't bring the slippers, but Yip and Yap raced over to collect their reward. Emma gave them each a small taste, then snuggled them into her lap, rested her head against the sofa back and shut her eyes, as if that could block out all of Hope's lousy questions. Yip let out a jaw-cracking yawn and licked Emma's fingers before settling in.

Emma's heart contracted at that tiny show of affection, and she immediately wanted to put both dogs off her lap. She restrained herself, however. Okay, so Hope was right. She did have trouble forming connections with other people. This period of forced inactivity could be an opportunity to think about what she wanted for her life and her future. As long as she could leave the past out of it, she would be more than happy to do that.

Chapter Eleven

Cal left Sylvia in charge of the bar and café the following Wednesday night and walked home. Business was still booming, and under other circumstances, he would have insisted on staying until Cal's Place was locked up tight for the night. But Sylvia had proven herself to be a good manager in his stead, and he wanted to get home. He was worried about Emma.

For the first two weeks after her surgery, her spirits had been great and she'd handled the adjustments to everything from the pain and the neighbors, to the dogs and the inactivity like a champ. But in the past few days, she'd become withdrawn and moody. For the life of him, he couldn't figure out why.

The surgeon had finally decided the swelling in her leg and ankle had gone down enough to use a cast boot on her leg. It was a padded, plastic and velcro contraption that looked sort of like a knee-length ski boot with an open toe, and it allowed her to walk without the use of crutches. She still needed to be careful, of course, but the cast boot also allowed her to bathe and take care of her personal needs much more easily.

Her pain had eased. She was making friends right and left. She even had her own poker group. So why was she acting depressed?

If anyone should be feeling depressed, it was him. He knew of at least three romances brewing between members of his family and the movie folks, and those were only the ones he knew about. Everybody else appeared to be making progress, and here he was, living in the same house with Emma, seeing her in those clingy little boxer shorts and tank tops every day and knowing he'd promised not to touch her. He'd kept his word so far, but he honestly didn't know how much longer he could continue to keep his hands to himself.

She was a deliciously sensual woman. When she ate, she dug right in and savored every bite until she was full. She loved textures, too. She could hardly look at something without touching it. He rarely saw her when she wasn't stroking one of the poodles, and while she wore jeans and black leather on the outside, the silky little panties he'd seen drying in the bathroom hinted at a much softer inner woman.

And speaking of softer, someone had given her a set of aromatherapy body lotions. Now every time he came near her, she smelled of some exotic flower, and her skin looked so smooth and touchable...

It all drove him nuts. While he took pride in his ability to control his baser instincts, he'd never pretended to be a saint. Never particularly wanted to be one, either. But he could hardly try to move his relationship with Emma onto a less platonic level when she was feeling so sad. That was how she looked most of the time. Sad.

Except for when she watched the *I Love Lucy* reruns; she loved those old shows so much, she could recite whole sections of dialogue. He thought it was amazing how many of those programs she could find with his satellite dish, but she couldn't go on distracting herself with ancient sitcoms forever. It was time they had a talk.

He took the steps into the house two at a time, opened the door and called, "Lu-cy, I'm ho-ome." It was probably the worst Desi Arnaz impersonation in history, but it made Emma laugh, so he did it anyway. Instead of a laugh, however, he heard only silence.

A horde of nasty images ran through his head. Emma had fallen in the bathtub and cracked her skull open. Emma had gotten curious about the basement and fallen down the stairs. Emma had called one of her friends for a ride, packed up her belongings and left for good.

He wasn't sure which possibility he feared the most, but anything that would take her out of his life terrified him. Eventually, her ankle would heal, and she would want to go back to work, but he wasn't ready to face that yet. He doubted he ever would be if it took her away. Realizing he'd been right about the consequences of falling in love— the pain the insecurity, the fear of losing one special person—was scant consolation. Being this vulnerable to anyone stunk.

He searched the house from top to bottom, but couldn't find Emma. Her clothes were still in the guest room, however, and her toiletries still cluttered the bathroom. So where was she?

Stepping out onto the deck, he scanned the backyard. He didn't see Emma, but he heard music coming from his garage. He hurried down the steps to the grass, then ran across the lawn, slowing as he approached the open side door. Emma was singing along with an old tune by the Oak Ridge Boys, and when he peeked through the doorway, he nearly whimpered out loud.

She wore indecently short cutoffs and a sleeveless, body-hugging T-shirt, which jerked his libido awake in the time it took for his eyes to send the image of her long, bare legs to his brain. Worse yet, she was standing on the front bumper of his vintage truck, bending way over with her head and three-quarters of her arms buried in the guts of his most cherished possession. She was really getting into the song now, and her cute little rear sort of bebopped back and forth in time with the drums.

Wait a minute. That was his truck, dammit. What was she doing, digging around in it? And what if she slipped off the bumper and hurt herself again?

He didn't dare walk in there from this angle, for fear he might disgrace himself, whether by grabbing her or spanking her, he couldn't say just yet. She had the rear door of the garage open, too, however, and he quietly walked around the building. Clearing his throat to give her fair warning, he stepped inside and ambled toward the pickup's front end.

At first all he could see of her was the side of her head, poking out from behind the raised hood. Her eyes widened when she spotted him, and she ducked back behind the hood like a little kid who thinks she can't get into trouble if her dad can't see her. Hah! Now he heard some furtive scrapes and clanks, as if she was hurriedly replacing something she didn't want him to see.

Making no attempt to hide his irritation, he said, "What the hell do you think you're doing?"

She poked her head out again, and shot him an ingenuous smile. A black spot of grease decorated the tip of her nose, and she had a wider streak of it across her right cheek. "Hi. You're home early tonight."

Cal walked faster. "Emma, what are you doing to my truck?"

"Doing? Oh, uh...nothing, really. I just couldn't resist taking a look at it. It's really gorgeous."

He reached the front of the truck. She was still bent over, bracing one hand on the grille. For once he wished she was wearing one of her tank tops; he'd have seen her tattoo for sure. Her other hand was still down inside his truck. She turned her face toward him and pulled her chin back closer to her chest, somehow managing to copy the guilty looks Yip and Yap gave him when he caught them misbehaving.

Fearing he would laugh when he really should be stern, he glanced over the rest of her. Lord, her hands, arms and the fronts of her T-shirt and legs were even dirtier than her face. He looked at her face again, and saw an impish twinkle in her eyes that melted his irritation in a heartbeat.

He'd never seen her look happier than she did at this moment. It startled him to realize he would do almost anything to keep her that way, including letting her play with his beloved '51 Ford pickup. But on second thought, why not? The truck was a great piece of machinery, but still only a piece of machinery. Emma owned his heart.

"I'm sorry, Cal." She sank one of her front teeth into her lower lip for a moment, then continued. "I know I should have asked for permission, but I felt so bored and useless sitting in the house, and I finally came out here to see what kind of tools and stuff you had in your garage, and the truck was just sitting here, and I...well, I really wanted to see the engine, and then I remembered this funny little noise I heard when we came back from Cody that night, and I started poking around a little."

She patted the old army surplus blanket she'd spread over the grille. "See, I even put this down so I wouldn't get grease all over the paint. I didn't hurt anything, honest."

Fighting back a smile, Cal moved closer to her. "How do you know you didn't hurt anything? That's a screwdriver in your hand, isn't there?"

"What? This?" She pulled her hand out of the truck and held it up, starting as if she was shocked to find her fingers tightly clutching such a thing. "Oh. Well, yes, I guess there is, but I was careful. I mean, what can you really hurt on a truck this old? It's just so...basic, you know? It's what trucks were meant to be before they started putting all the foo-foos on them."

"Foo-foos?"

"Yeah. You know, like carpeting and extended cabs, fancy sound systems and air-conditioning, power steering and cruise control."

"Don't forget shock absorbers," Cal said, remembering some of the old trucks he'd ridden in and driven when he'd been growing up on the Flying M. Shocks weren't seen as a real necessity, and they didn't work for long on the ranch roads, anyway.

"Oh, yeah," Emma agreed, nodding enthusiastically.

Smiling, Cal pointed at the screwdriver. "What did you do with it, Emma?"

"Nothing, really," she said quickly. Too quickly. Her cheeks flushed a rosy pink. She eyed him thoughtfully, then pursed her lips and exhaled a soft sigh. "Well, all right, I tightened a couple of screws. Checked out the fan belt and the radiator. And I took a look at the carburetor. You got a problem with that, Mr. Mayor?"

He moved even closer to her, plucked the screwdriver out of her hand and tossed it behind him on the workbench. "Yeah, I've got a problem with it, and I'm afraid I'm going have to call Zack and ask him to put you under arrest."

"Arrest?" She sounded horrified, but her eyes sparkled with playfulness. "On what charge?"

"Two charges. First one's illegal tinkering with a man's ride. Out here, we used to hang people for less than that."

Moving carefully, she turned around to face him and put her hands on his shoulders. "That was horses, and you had to steal them to get hung. I didn't steal your truck, and I didn't hurt it either, so forget about it. You'll never prove a thing. What's the other charge?"

Standing on the bumper, she could look him straight in the eye, which she did. Her lips were close to his, so temptingly close he could barely breathe. He slid one arm behind her hips as if he would catch her should she lose her balance, but it was just an excuse to stand even closer to her. He figured they both knew it.

She pinched his shoulder. "What's the other charge, McBride?"

"Illegal tinkering with a man's mind."

"Never heard of that one before." She sputtered with laughter. "And you'd have to prove the man had a mind to start with. Uh-uh. No way am I pleading guilty to that one."

He wrapped his other arm around her hips and pulled her against him. "You should. You've got me so confused half the time, I don't know what day it is."

"Cool," she said with a grin. "How do I do that?"

"Sometimes you just have to draw a breath in the same room as me. Or wear these little shorty shorts you like so much. That always gets me."

"Really?" She took off his Stetson hat, set it behind her on the grille and crossed her wrists behind his neck. "They're nothing special."

Her warm, sweet breath caressed his face, and his heart slammed hard against the inner wall of his chest. "Excuse me?" he said. "I happen to think they're fantastic."

She tested his forehead with the backs of her fingers. "Fantastic? These old things?"

"What old things?"

"These old shorts. I hacked the legs off this pair of jeans three years ago."

"I'm not talking about your shorts. I'm talking about your legs. They're just…" Helpless to resist, he cupped his hands around the backs of her knees and slid them up and up her thighs to the stringy hems of her shorts, which came within a whisper of exposing a little cheekage. "Lord have mercy, woman, they're fantastic. These muscles are…well they're gorgeous."

She gasped quietly. Swayed toward him. A darker, sleepier light softened the amused twinkle in her eyes. Her smile made him feel light-headed. Her husky voice stroked his ears with a rough texture that made his arm hairs stand up.

"Why, thank you. Now, is there anything I can do to convince you to drop your charges?"

He closed his eyes. Rested his forehead against hers. Inhaled a deep breath. Big mistake. Now his head swam with her scents, flowery soap, warm skin, a touch of car grease, pure Emma. He shuddered.

"Don't flirt with me, Em," he said. "If you want me to act like a gentleman, don't be so damned adorable, will ya?"

"You think I'm...adorable?"

The wonder in her voice prompted him to look into her eyes again. "Don't tell me you haven't heard that a hundred times before, from a hundred different guys. You must know you're an adorable, attractive...hell, you're downright sexy."

"I've been told I'm sexy in a lot of different ways, but it's not flattering." Her chuckle had a sad edge to it. "That's just a guy's hormones talking. He couldn't care less about my feelings or my thoughts or any part of me that makes me special. He just wants a female body to play with."

Cal felt enraged that anyone had ever treated her with such a lack of respect. Now he was fiercely glad she'd wiped the floor with those idiots, Joe and Ronnie, that first day she arrived in Sunshine Gap.

What really humbled him, though, was knowing he'd made the same stupid assumptions about Emma those cowboys had, all because of her leather jacket, motorcycle and tattoo. What a joke. That's what you got for hanging onto prejudices about a whole group of people, when the only person you needed to concern yourself with was the one standing right in front of you. It was a lesson he wouldn't forget. "God, Emma, I didn't mean it that way—"

She clasped her hands around the sides of his face and kissed the tip of his nose. "Of course, you didn't. You said I was adorable."

"You are, darlin'," Cal said. "The more I know you,

the more adorable you get. You're funny, you're sweet to elderly people and you're nice to stupid poodles. I can't remember a time when I've enjoyed living in my house half as much as I have since you've been staying with me.''

"You smooth talker, you." She slid her hands into his hair above his ears and lightly massaged his scalp. He all but purred, and he was not a man who liked cats. "But it's okay if you think I'm sexy, too."

She gazed deeply into his eyes for a moment. Then slowly, tentatively, she settled her mouth over his and kissed him. It was a whisper soft, achingly sweet kiss at first, the kind that took every lusty, romantic fantasy a person had ever entertained and brought them into the realm of possibility.

She traced the seam between his lips with the tip of her tongue. He opened his mouth for her, clamped one arm around her waist and cupped the back of her head with his other hand, groaning with pleasure when she skimmed the edges of his teeth, then explored the inside of his mouth so slowly, he wanted to take control and get on with it. But he sensed that she was enjoying herself, and the last thing he wanted to do was to scare her off by moving too fast.

But what if she only wanted to kiss him? He was already so hard, the thought of having to stop was enough to make him groan. She pulled back and, with a quizzical expression, searched his face.

"What's wrong?" she murmured.

"Nothing, really," he said. He inhaled a calming breath, only it wasn't calming at all, not with her in his arms. "It's just that this might not be a good idea."

"Why not?"

"I don't want to rush you into anything. But I *do* think you're sexy, and it feels like I've wanted you forever. I'm not sure my control's all it should be right now. Understand?"

"Oh," she said with a smile. "That's so sweet of you."

Damn, but he hated it when women called him that.

Made him sound like a little boy, and he hadn't been a boy for close to twenty years. He sure as hell didn't feel like one now.

"I'm not sweet," he grumbled. "But I promised I'd keep my hands off if you agreed to stay with me. I keep my promises."

He dropped his arms to his sides, moved back a step and shook his head at his weakness where she was concerned. "Well, I try to, anyway. I shouldn't even be kissing you."

"Oh, yeah?" She hooked a hand around the back of his neck and massaged it. "Well, I kissed you first and I've been wanting to do it forever. I don't see that you have anything to feel guilty about."

"Careful, Emma," he said, stepping closer again. "Some guys would interpret that to mean you were excusing me from my promise."

She draped her forearms around his shoulders and pulled him close enough to whisper against his lips. "What if I am? And what if I want you to lose control?"

He swallowed, then raised his hands to her arms and gently rubbed them over her soft, bare skin. "Be sure, darlin'. If I get started kissing you and loving you, you might have to hit me with a brick to make me stop."

"I'll take my chances." Her low, husky laugh danced across uncharted nerve endings. She leaned closer still, forcing him to put his arms around her and balance her weight against him. "On your mark," she said with a sultry smile that sent his pulse racing into double time. "Get set." She dusted butterfly kisses over his eyelids, his eyebrows, his cheekbones. She tightened her arms around his neck and propelled herself off the bumper, wrapping her legs around his waist as best she could with the clunky cast boot on. "Go."

A gold-embossed, printed invitation couldn't have been any plainer. Supporting her bottom with one forearm, he cupped the back of her head with the opposite hand and kissed her. There was nothing tentative about this kiss.

It was deep and voracious, a kiss that burned straight through him like a double shot of good whiskey on a snowy night. Her head fell back against her shoulders beneath the force of it, her mouth opened wider to accept him, her arms and legs tightened around him, erasing the smallest air pockets between them.

His body surged against hers, straining at the confines of clothing. She moaned and rocked herself against him, tangling her tongue with his. He opened one eye, shifted right and left, looking for a likely spot to finish what they'd started. But all he could see was the gaping maw of the truck and the cluttered workbench. No way.

Someday, they would christen this old truck together, but not their first time. This one should be special, a time she would remember with smiles and sweet sighs, not giggles and groans at the thought of discomfort, awkwardness and bruises in unlikely places.

But Emma—being Emma—had other ideas.

He turned sideways to carry her around the side of the pickup and kept on moving in the interest of preserving the mood. As he walked past the driver's door, she grabbed the handle and held on as if it were her last link with freedom, forcing him to stop.

"No," she murmured, kissing and nibbling up the side of his neck to his earlobe. "Can't wait that long. Here. Now."

What an absolutely wonderful woman. And who was he to argue, when he didn't want to wait, either? He wasn't that stupid. Thank heaven he had a condom in his wallet. He wasn't *that* stupid, either. She found his mouth again, and kissed him until he felt weak in the knees.

Each mind-bending kiss, each moan, each fervent caress sucked rational thoughts from his brain and further aroused him. He fumbled the door open and studied the opening.

Because of the cast boot, Emma's left leg didn't curve around him as well as the right one did. It took a little fancy maneuvering to get her into the pickup without banging her leg around, but he managed it. He set her down on the bench seat, catching his breath and nuzzling the sweet curves where her neck flowed into her shoulders.

She lay back and opened her arms to him, looking like his very own perfect woman—a grease monkey goddess who wanted him too much to care about getting dirty or messing up her hair. If she was willing and eager to make love here, the possibilities for the future were limitless. A surge of lust hit him hard, sending the blood from his head to his groin so fast he felt dizzy with it.

Ducking inside the truck he leaned over her and dove into another kiss. She was so delicious and the seat was just about the right height. He slid both hands under the hem of her T-shirt and ran his fingers over her back and her sides. Her skin was hot to the touch and so supple, so firm. She scooted closer, wrapping her legs around him again as if she feared he might leave. The odds of that happening now were zero to zilch.

And then her hands were in his hair and stroking behind his ears and down his neck, going for the snaps on his shirt. He deepened the kiss and stroked his fingers in long sweeps across her midriff. She arched into his touch, grabbed the open halves of his shirt front in her fists and dragged him closer yet.

He pulled his wallet out of his hip pocket, flipped it open and dumped the contents onto the floor, then blindly ran his hand through the pile of stuff until he found the foil packet. Smiling against her mouth, he tossed the packet onto the dash.

She caressed the sides of his neck and face. "Thank you."

He kissed her palm. "My pleasure, darlin'. And I sure hope it's gonna be yours too."

When he slid his hands under the hem of her shirt this time, he skimmed them straight up her sides, taking the T-shirt with them. He wanted to see her, all of her, touch her and taste her and love her until neither of them could move. Her eyes widening as the T-shirt swept past her mid-riff, she jerked her elbows tight against her sides, trapping his hands under her arms.

He couldn't help groaning, or sweeping his thumbs over the peaks of her breasts. They were already standing up, begging for his attention. He was more than eager to give it to them.

"Don't be shy, sweetheart," he said. "We're both gonna be naked before this is over."

She chuckled and waggled her eyebrows at him. "You might want to put down that garage door first. Your neighbors will be shocked if they come through that alley and see you standing there in all your, um...manly glory."

"Shocked ain't the word for it," he said, laughing all the way to the garage door and back. "Now then, where were we?"

"We were getting to the part where you show *me* your manly glory," she said with a grin. "I, however, promise not to be shocked."

Ducking his head again, he leaned into the cab and kissed her thoroughly. He gathered the sides of her shirt in his fingers and lifted, hoping that this time she wouldn't stop him. Her elbows clamped against his hands again. "You really are shy, aren't you?"

She shut her eyes and shook her head. "No, it's not shyness, exactly."

"Then what's holding you back here, sweetheart?"

"My um, my...tattoo."

"What about it? You know I'm dyin' to see it."

"I'm afraid you'll laugh."

"Laugh? Hell no." He shook his head and smoothed her hair back out of her face. "That's not gonna happen. Besides, I might laugh *with* you, but never *at* you, Em."

"You're sure of that?"

"Sure as I'm breathin'."

Slowly she raised her arms, allowing him to finish peeling off her T-shirt. He tossed it aside and leaned over her, one hand propped on the side of the bench seat for balance. He should have known Emma Barnes wouldn't do anything ordinary. Her tattoo was no exception. No fire-breathing dragon here. No tiger's whiskers or lion's tail. He had to smile at it.

Curving around her left breast, it was a work of art, a whimsical, and vaguely familiar cartoon skunk. Obviously female from the long, curling eyelashes, she was lying in a bed of colorful flowers. The little gal's expression was amazingly sexy for a skunk. The swirly thing he'd glimpsed occasionally was the curling tip of her long fluffy tail.

"That's almost as adorable as you are," he drawled.

No longer interested in discussing much of anything, he covered the tattoo with kisses. Hot, wet, tasting kisses that circled all around her breast. Her back arched, offering a pouty nipple to his lips, and he knew, without a single doubt, that he held the most beautiful woman in the world in his arms.

Holding the back of his neck with one hand while he kissed her tattoo, she knew he was, without a single doubt, the most beautiful man in the world. While she loved the way he looked, his real beauty had little to do with the perfection of his features or his body. He was beautiful on the inside too, something she'd never seen so clearly in a man before.

From his big feet to his broad chest and shoulders, to his bushy mustache and thick black hair, he was all man. But he wasn't afraid to be gentle or give a compliment or show his appreciation for something. He'd been so careful and caring with her, before and after her accident.

She wanted him with a hunger she'd never experienced. She had trusted him with her tattoo and he hadn't made fun of it. Now she would trust him with her body. She wouldn't think about what she might trust him with next. It would scare the devil out of her, and she didn't want to be scared right now. She just wanted to love him and be loved by him, if only for a little while.

Sinking her fingertips into the springy triangle of hair on his chest, she felt the muscles flex beneath his hot skin. His lips closed around her nipple. She cried out at the pleasurable ache it caused, raised her hands to the sides of his head and buried them in his hair, giving him subtle signals of what she wanted. He followed those signals closely, lavishing even more attention on her breasts than she asked for.

His tongue traced fiery trails across her midriff, and swirled around and around her navel, his mustache tickling her unmercifully. While she was still laughing and trying to make him stop, his clever hands were unfastening the silver button at the waistband of her cutoffs, and tugging them down her legs and off over her cast boot.

Loving the sound of her sighs and moans, urging him on and telling him what she liked, he returned to her mouth. Kissing her deeply, preparing her for what would follow, using his palms to trace her narrow waist and the curve of her hips, caressing her soft skin, he felt drunk with the sensations. He peeled away her satiny panties and straightened as much as the cab would allow in order to feast his eyes on her nudity.

With a smile as tempting as Eve's must have been, she stretched out on the seat and raised her right knee, opening herself to him. His breath caught at the base of his throat. This was a woman who loved her own body and honestly wanted to share its delights with him.

What a humbling, mind-boggling, wonderful concept.

He hadn't known he could get any harder, but another rush of blood hit his groin, and he felt so heavy and tight, he couldn't drop his pants and briefs fast enough. Gripping the sides of her waist, he pulled her to the edge of the seat. Hands shaking, he rolled the condom onto his shaft, then slowly entered her.

Her body was tight and she tensed at his invasion. The resistance of her inner muscles created intense pleasure; waiting for those muscles to let go created equally intense discomfort. He held himself still, however, kissing her deeply, then dropping soft kisses all over her face, tickling her with his mustache and murmuring silly love words to her until she chuckled.

He pressed deeper again, waited again, pressed all the way inside her. Oh, man. This felt like heaven; it felt like home. Part of him wanted to cut loose and go for it until he reached the summit. Another part of him wanted to savor every moment, every nuance of making love with this woman. Whatever he did, he wanted her to be there with him at the end of the ride. Somehow, he doubted that would be any problem.

He pulled back and surged into her again, this time with more force and more ease, as well. She rose up to meet him on the third stroke, and then they found a hard, driving rhythm that tested his endurance and self-control to the limit. Only the pleasure he found in watching her face saved him from losing it completely.

She hid nothing, held back nothing. Everything she felt was right there in her expressions, in her moans and gasps, in her sighs, as easy to read as a traffic sign. Giving her pleasure increased his own, and he balanced precariously on the razor's edge between excitement and fulfillment.

Leaning down, he kissed her luscious mouth, mimicking the thrusts of his body with his tongue. She sank her fingers into his shoulder muscles and arched up against him. He reached one hand between them and caressed her most sensitive flesh. She arched again, cried out and finally relaxed onto the blanket.

Jaws clenching with the strain of maintaining control, he said, ''Again,'' and surged into her with renewed power. She gasped, but started climbing again. The climax gripped her faster this time, and the ecstasy in her eyes drove some wild part of him to push her up and up again.

Sweat dripped down the sides of his face and under his arms, and he felt the first twinges of his own release surging through him. With a hoarse shout, he found his own completion and collapsed into her welcoming arms, his heart racing like a freight train out of control on a steep grade. His muscles felt like deflated balloons. Emma's hands moved over his back in loving strokes, soothing strokes, guiding him back to sanity.

He breathed deeply, nuzzled her little skunk and figured he could happily die right here in her embrace. When he'd caught his breath and strength returned to his arms, he propped himself up on his elbows and gently tucked a wild strand of hair behind her ear. She smiled up at him, eyes misty, sweet mouth tremulous. He stole one last kiss for courage, then told her what he'd been hiding ever since she crashed.

"I love you, Em."

Chapter Twelve

Stunned by Cal's admission, Emma couldn't think of a thing to say. Oh, she knew what he *wanted* her to say—a part of her even wanted to say it—but the words stuck in her throat like a swallowed fish bone. She felt as if she would choke to death on them as the silence dragged on and his warm and loving expression became cool and distant.

"You don't feel the same way," he said, making it a statement, not a question. Then he smiled ruefully. "That's okay. I know it was a little sudden. Must've seemed like it came out of the blue to you. But I don't want anything from you that you don't want to give."

He kissed the tip of her nose, then pulled away from her, and set about finding and sorting the articles of clothing they'd flung around. She caught her shirt, cutoffs and panties, and struggled into them, refusing to so much as glance in Cal's direction. Suddenly, the most wonderful experience of her life felt tarnished.

The idea infuriated her. Their lovemaking had been real and honest and caring. Why had he had to spoil it by bringing up love? That four-letter word had been the beginning of the end for every important relationship in her life. She far preferred words such as *like* and *respect*, even *want* was better than the word *love*.

Cursing under her breath, she scrambled out of the truck, picked up the blanket and carried it back to the workbench. She might as well go pack her things and find a way to get out of Dodge. Everything got weird once that L-word had been spoken.

There you go again, Emma, running away.

"Oh, shut up," she grumbled at the voice of her conscience.

"Did you say something?" Cal asked.

"Just talking to myself."

He tilted his head to one side, his eyebrows drawing together in a frown. "You sure about that?"

"Of course, I'm sure," she snapped.

She left the garage by the side door, then hobbled across the lawn as fast as her cast boot would allow. Though she knew she should be grateful she wasn't sporting a real cast from her knee to her toes and using crutches besides, her lack of grace and speed only added to her irritation. Halfway up the deck stairs, she heard Cal coming behind her.

"Hold on," he called. "Where's the fire?"

Without bothering to answer, she finished climbing the stairs, went into the house and made a beeline for the bathroom.

She started a bath, grabbed some clean clothes from her room and returned to the bathroom, locking the door behind her. Avoiding the mirror, she stripped off her dirty clothes, sat on the side of the claw-footed tub and unfastened the velcro straps holding the cast boot together.

She carefully slipped it off and lowered herself into the hot water with a sigh of relief. Preferring the quickness and relative ease of a shower, she'd rarely used bathtubs before, and never one as old or as big as this one. Since staying here, she'd discovered the fine art of soaking, and had found the tub a productive place for thinking.

Not that she wanted to think right now. And why should she? She already knew how her relationship with Cal would end. She shut her eyes tight, but nothing could block out the vision of Cal's face, gazing down at her with such honesty, such tenderness, such intensity as his beautiful mouth said the words she would never be able to forget. "I love you, Em."

Why didn't he just rip out her heart with his bare hands and stomp on it with his big fat cowboy boots? Didn't he know how much she'd always longed to hear those words? How desperately she wanted to believe them? To believe that a man as dear and wonderful as Cal McBride really could love a nobody like her?

Her throat ached and tears burned the backs of her eyes, but she fought them back and breathed deeply to make sure she stayed in control. It wasn't that she thought he'd been lying to her. Heaven knew he'd already gotten what he wanted, so what would be the point of his lying?

No, she believed that *Cal* believed that he loved her. The part she didn't believe was anything that implied the future or forever. And while his mouth hadn't said any such thing, his gorgeous dark eyes had implied it, big time. She knew him well enough to know that at heart, he was a traditional man. He wouldn't say he loved her without wanting the traditional trappings that usually accompanied such declarations—marriage, kids, a mortgage.

But for her, there were no forevers. It was better that way. It sure beat getting her hopes dashed over and over and over. She just couldn't have a nice, modern, no-strings relationship with a guy like Cal. He'd build up all these expectations and when he learned the truth about her background, well...

Sighing, she set about scrubbing off the grease and grime she'd picked up while working on Cal's pickup. If a few tears did escape while she was in the tub, nobody else had to know about it.

Cursing himself for letting his big mouth get away from him, Cal watched Emma clump up the deck stairs and slowed his own pace to an amble. Right now, she was acting as skittish as a wild mare sniffing the wind. He wasn't going to crowd her into fleeing from him.

He knew how this was going to end. He knew Emma loved him, too; he'd seen it in her eyes, heard it in her ecstatic cries, felt it in the tender way she'd held him. Her sudden withdrawal now was only a minor setback.

She probably just needed more time to get used to the idea. He could give her that. Not a lot of time, but a few weeks wouldn't matter.

Now all he had to do was keep her in Sunshine Gap long enough to realize she couldn't live without him. He would find her something useful to do so she wouldn't dismantle his truck out of boredom. Then he'd give her plenty of space so she wouldn't have any excuse to accuse him of being too protective or too possessive of her.

Sunshine Gap would do the rest for him. She'd never admit it, but she was starting to love this little town, love the people in it and the way they had rallied around to help her after her accident. Shoot, she already knew half the folks in town by name and they all knew hers. He suspected it thrilled her every time someone stopped by to visit her, and he knew she'd get a real charge out of having people down on Main Street call out her name and wave. They'd do it, too.

He'd heard nothing but glowing reports from everyone who'd visited her. She was the sweetest little gal, and such a stitch. Why, she knew the most hilarious stories about Hollywood and making movies, you knew she couldn't possibly have made any of it up, and even if she did, who cared? Her stories were wonderful and she was a breath of fresh air. And on and on and on.

If he so much as voiced the idea that he was in love with Emma Barnes and wanted to marry her, she wouldn't stand a chance of getting away from him. But he didn't want to keep her under duress. He wanted her to stay more than anything in the world, but he wanted her to *want* to stay with him of her own free will.

Because she loved him. Dammit, she *did*. She just wasn't ready to admit it yet.

He heard water running in the bathroom when he stepped into the house. Glancing down at his clothes, he chuckled. They were smeared with the grease he'd picked up from Emma. His hands and face probably weren't much better. Well, he'd do a quick clean up and change his clothes. Then he'd see what the ladies had left in the fridge for their supper tonight. Like most women, Emma tended to be less cranky and more amenable when she'd been fed.

Emma dressed in her clean clothes, pulled her wet hair back into a ponytail and went out to the kitchen, hoping to find something to eat without bothering Cal. She'd half expected him to come pound on the bathroom door and demand to have a talk, but she hadn't heard a word out of him. With luck, he was already making his mayoral phone calls for the evening, and she could raid the fridge in peace.

It appeared that her luck already had run out. Her nose twitched at a delicious aroma just before she stepped into the kitchen. Her stomach growled like a big dog, and the poodles came running to see who had invaded their turf. She laughed at their ferocious little barks and leaned over to give them each a playful tussle.

"Hungry?" Cal asked, carrying a foil-covered pan from the oven to the breakfast bar. He'd already set out place mats, silverware and glasses of iced tea. How could she refuse to join him? She couldn't, of course, nor did she honestly want to. Jeez, she was so confused.

"Sure," she said, sliding onto the stool she'd come to think of as "hers." That kind of thinking would have to stop. This was strictly a temporary arrangement until she could ride Mama again, and she had to remember that. In fact, the sooner she made her intentions clear to him, the better. She waited until he brought a steaming casserole dish to the breakfast bar and sat on "his" stool.

Removing the lid with a flourish, he stuck a big spoon in the food, whatever it was, and said, "Dig in. This is Mrs. Miller's famous almond-chicken dish. People fight over it at potluck dinners at the Methodist Church."

Emma shot him a doubtful look.

"I'm not kidding," he said with a grin. "Try it."

She scooped a forkful into her mouth, then closed her eyes and savored the rich flavors bursting on her tongue. She swallowed, then took another bite. Lord it really *had* been that good. She wondered if Mrs. Miller was related to T.K. with the scrumptious cookies. "Amazing," she said. "I always thought casseroles were kind of yucky before I came here."

"Sometimes they are," Cal agreed. "The trick is in knowing who makes the good ones. It's the same way with all the gelatin salads we've been getting. You wouldn't believe some of the stuff the ladies around here put in them. Most of the time they taste pretty good, but when they don't, look out."

Emma smiled and the rest of the meal passed in a reasonably comfortable silence. She appreciated it at first, but the longer it went on, the more she realized it wasn't like Cal to be so quiet when he had something on his mind. So maybe he was waiting to finish eating before he brought up what he'd said to her in the truck.

But after they'd finished pieces of banana cream pie and drunk a last cup of coffee, he seemed more than content just to sit beside her, fiddling with his mug and occasionally staring off into space. When she couldn't stand it any longer, Emma cleared her throat. He glanced over at her, a raised eyebrow indicating his interest.

"I've been thinking," she said. "And I've decided it would be best for both of us if I, um...left."

Now both of his eyebrows climbed halfway up his forehead. "Leave? You can't do that, Emma."

Stacking her plate and silverware, she gave him a warning look. "Can't?"

As if recognizing a tactical error on his part, he hastily said, "I didn't mean that the way it sounded."

"Then how did you mean it?"

"I didn't mean *can't*, really. It's just...where would you go?"

"I don't know for sure." She carried her dishes to the sink, then turned back to pick up his. "Probably back to California. I can always stay with my friend Diana."

"The tattoo artist?"

"That's right. We've been best friends for years."

"How will you get there? Your bike needs some work, and you can't ride her until that cast boot comes off. You shouldn't, anyway."

"I'll figure it out." She came back around the peninsula and sat on the stool again. "Maybe I'll take a bus and ask Hope to haul Mama on the back of her motor home when she drives back to California."

"What are you going to do for money, Em? Do you have enough savings to live for a few months?"

She shrugged. "Not exactly, but I'll figure that out, too."

"How? Can you get another job when you're disabled like this? The doc said you have to wear that cast boot for another six weeks at least. Maybe eight, depending on how well it heals."

Nothing he said was anything she didn't already know, but his words managed to stir up plenty of fear and insecurity, nonetheless. She cleared her throat. "It's not your problem."

He paused before responding, as if he were conducting an intense inner debate, but he only smiled and said, "No, I guess it isn't."

Somehow, she'd expected a more forceful reply. Something along the lines of, *Like hell it's not my problem. I love you and your problems are my problems. And don't you forget it.* She would have known exactly how to handle an idiotic attitude like that. So why did he have to act so darned...reasonable?

Suspecting he was trying to tinker with *her* mind, she scrutinized him long and hard, but his expression didn't change. He was still up to something. She could smell it.

After several moments of silence, he stretched his arms over his head, then rested his forearms back on the counter, his fingers linked together. "I did have a suggestion to offer," he said. "That is, if you're interested."

"Sure," she said. "I'm always open to suggestions."

"I came home tonight planning to offer you a job. It's not much, really, but it sure would help me out of a bind."

She laughed at the absurdity of his last statement. "Oh, right. I'm so quick and graceful these days, I'd make a great waitress or a bar maid."

He looked perfectly serious now. "Em, I'm not kidding you. Will you just listen to the whole thing before you decide?"

"All right. What's the job?"

"It's so busy down at the café these days, I can't keep enough help in the kitchen. Everybody wants to work out front and have a shot at the great tips the movie folks and tourists are leaving," he said. "I'm not saying it would be an exciting job, but you'd get out of the house for a few hours a day, and you could do most of your work sitting down. If you stay here with me, you can save your whole paycheck for when you figure out what you want to do next."

"I'm pretty good at warming things up in a microwave, but I'm not much of a cook."

"You don't have to be. You'll just be doing stuff like chopping onions and green peppers, peeling hard-boiled eggs, slicing tomatoes for sandwiches and oranges for garnishing the plates, filling the salt and pepper shakers and the ketchup bottles. There's all kinds of annoying little jobs that need to be done for a restaurant to make a good impression, and nobody has time to do them right now.''

"This isn't just some charity thing you've dreamed up for my benefit?'' she asked.

"Charity? Hah! You'll wish. Cooks, waitresses, even dishwashers get incredibly cantankerous when they're this busy. You'll have your hands full just trying to do your job and get along with that bunch of yahoos. But it really would be a big help if you were willing to take this on. Will you do it?''

"What about…what happened tonight? In the garage.''

He nearly leveled her with his scowl. "I want you and you'll always be welcome in my bed, but making love with me will never be in your job description. As far as I'm concerned, that ball is in your court. Now, do you want the job or not?''

Smiling at his answer, she swivelled on her stool to face him directly. "The job's got to have a decent title for résumé purposes.''

He scrunched up one side of his face as if giving the problem serious consideration. "How about Veggie Technician?''

"Too cutsie.''

He made an even bigger show of thinking this time. Then he snapped his fingers. "I've got it. You can be the Chopper Queen. Get it? Motorcycles? Choppers? The Chopper Queen?''

Wishing for something unbreakable to throw at him, Emma laughed and nodded. She really didn't want to hear any more of his ideas at the moment. Crazy man. Still, she owed him a lot, and she would enjoy being able to repay a little of his kindness. Besides, she really didn't want to leave him yet. A few more weeks with him would be awfully nice.

"All right, McBride. You've got yourself a Chopper Queen."

"Terrific. You can start first thing in the morning."

Cal introduced Emma to the kitchen staff, then went back to his own duties. Within a week, she was joking along with the rest of the crew, and her worktable had become a new gathering place for people taking breaks. She not only got along with her co-workers, she appeared to be a positive influence toward convincing them to get along with each other. If she only did that much, he figured her paychecks would be money well spent.

But Emma Barnes was one of those rare individuals employers loved to find. She not only did the tasks assigned to her, she actively looked for other jobs that needed to be done, and did them with a positive attitude and a flair for creativity.

She was great in emergencies, too. When the dishwasher broke down in the middle of the lunch rush, she hobbled over to look at it, asked for a toolbox and calmly fixed it while everyone else was freaking out. When the toilet tank in the employees' bathroom wouldn't stop running, she fixed that too. Cal would have doubled her salary if he'd thought she would let him, but he knew the stubborn little wretch wouldn't. She was paranoid as hell about taking charity.

One afternoon Sylvia stormed into the kitchen, upset over her aging car's latest weird behavior. She didn't have money for a newer car, and the darn repairs were going to swallow the money she'd been saving all spring for a new TV. That John Murphy over at the filling station overcharged everybody in Sunshine Gap because nobody wanted to risk a breakdown out on the highway. Thieving varmint might as well wear a mask and carry a gun while he wrote out his bills.

Emma offered to look at the car and provide free labor if Sylvia would pay for any needed parts. After getting

Cal's permission to use his tools, she drove the car around, looked under the hood and stopped at the parts store before going home to see what she could do.

New spark plugs, a carburetor kit and a couple of other adjustments, and Sylvia's clunker no longer coughed and sputtered; it purred. Never one to do any job halfway, Emma washed the car, vacuumed the interior and cleaned all the windows, inside and out. Then she drove it back to Cal's Place in time for Sylvia's supper break.

Sylvia took it for a test drive and came back honking her horn. Everybody working the shift who could sneak away for a few minutes, including Cal himself, stepped outside to see what the all the fuss was about. Sylvia climbed out, stood there on the sidewalk, breathing deeply and looking at the car, her chubby hands covering the sides of her face.

"Well?" Emma said. "What do you think?"

Sylvia turned her face toward Emma and gulped loudly enough for everyone to hear. "It runs better than it did when I bought it, but I think you spent way too much money, hon."

Emma tilted her head to one side and studied Sylvia for a moment. "How much do you think I spent?"

"Well, honest to God, it's running a thousand times better. You must have spent at least three, maybe four hundred bucks."

"No," Emma said slowly, "not even close."

Cal could see the amused twinkle in Emma's eyes, but Sylvia obviously couldn't. She paled and gulped again before asking, "How much?"

Emma shrugged and handed over the receipt from the parts store. "Take a look."

Sylvia looked, glanced away, then her eyes bugged out and she did a double take. "F-f-f-fifty-two dollars and forty-eight cents? Are you pulling my leg, girl?"

"No, Sylvia," Emma said with a laugh. "There wasn't that much wrong with your car anyway."

For one of maybe three times in all the years he'd known

Sylvia, Cal saw her drop all of her jolly, wisecracking pretenses. With the receipt still in one hand, she approached Emma, her expression utterly serious.

"I don't know how to thank you. This is so much less that I expected to pay, won't you let me give you fifty for your time?"

Emma stepped back and glared at Sylvia as if she had intentionally insulted her. "No. That wasn't our deal. You're making way too much of this."

"But you washed it and cleaned it all up. You even emptied the ashtray."

"That was all a part of the job where I used to work. It's called customer service. Don't you get that out here?"

With her wisecracking self firmly back in place, Sylvia turned to the crowd of onlookers and rolled her eyes. "Oh, yeah, We get a load of customer service from John Murphy, don't we?"

The crowd's laughter quickly turned into grumbling.

"Murphy wouldn't know customer service if it bit him on the...nose."

"The old coot's hardly even civil most of the time."

"Yeah, and when he is civil, he's always got his hand in your wallet."

Emma raised both hands beside her head and held them palms out. "Hey, I don't even know the guy. I just did a favor for a friend. No big deal."

She turned and hobbled down the street. Cal sent everyone else back to work with a pointed look. Then he went after Emma, catching up near the corner.

"Want a ride home, lady?" he said, easily keeping pace with her. "Sounds like you've been on your feet a lot today."

She heaved an exasperated sigh, then stopped walking and gave him a wry smile. "I have been," she admitted. "And a ride sounds wonderful if you've got time."

"I've always got time for you, Ms. Barnes." He pointed toward the left. "I'm parked around here." He opened the door for her, helped her get settled and hurried around to the driver's side. "That was a nice thing you did."

"Not you, too," Emma said with a groan. "She's been nice to me since I came here. So have a lot of other people. Is there some reason I shouldn't have returned her kindness?"

He started the car and headed home. "No. But this kind of thing tends to set off a whole chain of amazing and unpredictable events."

She looked at him as if he'd just spoken to her in Russian or Arabic. "What do you mean?"

"I couldn't explain it if I wanted to," Cal said. "But give it time and you'll see."

"See what?"

Cal chuckled. "Who knows? In Sunshine Gap, it could be anything. But trust me, everybody in town and the ranching community in the outlying areas will know what you did within twenty-four hours. Sylvia will see to it."

"And you think something will happen because of that?"

"I don't just *think* it, honey, I *know* it."

"But what?"

"Ya got me. Like I said before, just give it time and you'll see."

She scrunched up her mouth and gave him the snake-eyed look some women were so good at. Made a man tremble in his boots unless he knew what a softie she really was. "McBride, I don't know what kind of bull you're trying to dish out, but I'm not buying it. Next you'll be telling me there's some old Indian legend involved, or a dead miner's gold, or you've got elves living in the sagebrush."

Cal laughed out loud. "Fine. Don't believe me. Just don't say I didn't try to warn ya."

Emma didn't believe Cal McBride. She wasn't superstitious and she wasn't gullible, either. He was just trying to poke at her the way he did everyone who worked for him. Besides, nothing the least bit odd happened for three days. By then there was a whole new topic of gossip when Cal's cousin Zack returned to the Flying M with his brand new fiancée, Lori Jones. Emma told herself that was the end of her fifteen minutes of fame in Sunshine Gap and forgot about it.

When Marvin Teague, a balding, middle-aged man who owned the bowling alley and was a member of the town council came back to the kitchen to see her two days later, she was curious about what he wanted, but that was all. He poured himself a cup of coffee and sat down at her worktable, chatting about this and that until most of the staff had cleared out and he had Emma's undivided attention.

Then he leaned forward, lowered his voice and got right to the point. "I'm in charge of the volunteer fire department in the Gap. We've got a forty-year-old engine that's actin' up, and no money to buy a new one. John Murphy's given up on it, and the mechanics in Cody tell me it ain't worth the cost of repairin' it, because the parts are so hard to come by."

"I'll bet they are," Emma said, wondering what this had to do with her.

Marvin gave her a crooked smile and sipped his coffee. "Well, we've got our congressman working on a grant for us, but until it comes through, which could be another six or eight months, we're pretty much stuck with Old Spew."

He grinned, momentarily reminding Emma of Diana's eight-year-old son Andy, who loved to tell incredibly dumb jokes.

"That must be the engine's name?" Emma guessed.

Marvin's grin widened. "That's right. We started callin' her that oh, about twenty years ago. And see, we're just comin' into fire season around here. The grass and forests are awful dry right now, and it doesn't take much to start a bad fire with these conditions. I don't mind tellin' you,

I'm real worried that Old Spew's gonna up and die on us when we need her most.''

''And you're telling me this because...''

''Well, I heard about what you did with Sylvia's old heap, and I got to wondering if maybe you'd be willing to take a look at that engine. We've got a couple thousand bucks put by for emergencies, and I consider this an emergency. The rest of the town council will too, except for John Murphy, of course. But we can vote him down, no sweat.''

Emma choked back a laugh. Poor John Murphy seemed to be on everybody's hate list. ''I'd be glad to do it, Mr. Teague, but as you can see, I've already committed to working for Cal until I go back to California. Maybe I could work on it after hours.''

''Don't worry your pretty little head about Cal, ma'am. If he can't find somebody else to fill in for you, I'll send my wife over to take your place. It's that important. And don't think we'd expect you to work for nothing. How does fifteen bucks an hour sound to you?''

''Not bad,'' Emma admitted. ''But I want to look at Old Spew before I agree to do anything, and I'll need to talk to Cal.''

''You do that.'' Marvin stood, the relief in his gray eyes palpable. ''Cal has keys to the engine and to the garage, and you can use any of the tools we've got stored there. If you need something else, just ask, and we'll track it down for you. Anything you can do to keep the old girl limpin' along for even a few more months will be much appreciated.''

He carried his coffee cup to the dishwasher and left. Cal came into the kitchen thirty seconds later, and the next thing Emma knew, she was elbows deep in Old Spew's guts.

Cal brought her a boom box to keep her company. Marvin brought her a jug of iced tea and a three-pound coffee can filled with his wife's chocolate chip cookies. He also found the engine's original service manuals. A lady named Bonnie Winston brought Emma a pair of coveralls and scrubbed the bathroom at the garage.

Nolan Larson, an attorney who also served as a council member, delivered his fourteen-year-old son, Rick, and Cal's thirteen-year-old niece, Tasha Talbot, to act as tool-fetchers. Nolan had recently become engaged to Cal's sister Alex, and the kids were practically bubbling over with excitement at the prospect of becoming a real family. Emma desperately envied them, and perversely enjoyed listening to them at the same time.

A week later, when Emma took her helpers for a ride around town in a freshly waxed engine that didn't even backfire anymore, most of the folks in Sunshine Gap swore she had performed a minor miracle. To her amazement, news of her success opened a veritable floodgate of job offers.

John Murphy complained about her giving him unfair competition and threatened to sue her for operating a business without a license. Nolan got her a business license and Cal gave her permission to use his garage until she could find an alternative site.

Then Murphy tried to hire her to work in his own shop, but Emma had discovered for herself what an old curmudgeon he was, and refused even to consider the idea. By the time the production company had wrapped the movie and started pulling out of town at the end of July, Emma had enough work orders to last her through half of September.

Through it all, a smiling Cal McBride simply stood back and watched her dig herself a little deeper and a little deeper and a little deeper into the community of Sunshine Gap. As one satisfied customer after another left her makeshift auto shop he couldn't resist murmuring an occasional, "Gotcha."

Chapter Thirteen

One afternoon at the beginning of August, Emma heard a deep rumbling sound and hurried out of the garage in time to see a motor home pulling to the curb in front of Cal's house. The engine shut down, and a moment later, Hope DuMaine opened the door and skipped down the steps.

"Emma, darling," she called, opening the gate and running across the lawn. "We just stopped in to say goodbye."

"We?" Emma asked, leaning to one side to see who was following Hope. There was no one there.

Hope waved a hand behind her, indicating the motor home. "Blair's in there. She'd come out to visit, but she's busy right now bawling her eyes out."

"What's wrong?"

"Oh, nothing, really." Hope linked her arm through Emma's and tugged her back toward the garage. "She's just in love with Dillon and now she's not going to see him for a long time."

"Why not?"

"Oh, they're trying terribly hard to be rational before they make any decisions about the future. They want to make sure it's not just a set romance, you know? But enough about them. As soon as this flick is in the can, believe me, the wedding bells will ring loud and long."

Emma had to smile at that. At least she wasn't the only woman from California who'd fallen in love with one of those, big, good-looking McBride men. Now that she thought about it, there were three of them if you counted Lori Jones. Not that Emma herself, was actually in love with Cal McBride, of course. She was only in lust with him. Well, she liked him, too, but it wasn't the same thing as the L-word.

Hope pulled Emma around to the back end of the garage, released her arm and stepped inside. Emma had just taken apart a tractor engine. Hope walked all the way around the mess, exclaiming over the framed business license Cal had hung beside the workbench. Turning around, she raised both arms raised like a television evangelist.

"Congratulations, Emma, you did it," she said.

"Did what?"

"You've made your big dream come true. You've got your own auto shop. Who would have thought you'd accomplish that in Sunshine Gap, Wyoming?"

Emma laughed and shook her head. "This is hardly the auto shop of my dreams."

"Well, it's a start," Hope said with a touch of indignation in her voice. "Most new businesses start small and gradually expand, don't they?"

"Yeah, but, come on, Hope. This is just temporary—"

"It doesn't have to be. From what I've been hearing, you've got a waiting list yards' long."

"Well, yeah. I've got a waiting list, but I don't really belong here."

"Tell that to your friend Sylvia down at Cal's Place. When I stopped in to ask if anyone knew where you were, she specifically warned me not to try to haul you back to California, because everybody in town wants you to stay.''

"But I don't have any real ties here, and—"

"Darling, outside of work you don't have any ties in L.A., either, do you? Besides, what about Cal?''

"What about him?''

"You're still living here with him, aren't you?''

"Yes.''

"You still want him, don't you?''

Unable to say the words out loud, but equally unable to deny them, Emma nodded. Hope smiled.

"And he still wants you?''

Emma shrugged. "Maybe. Well, I don't know. I doubt it.''

"You are absolutely the *worst* liar I've ever known. It's part of your charm, dear, but I don't believe you, and you shouldn't believe you, either.'' Hope laughed. "For your information, Cal was standing right there beside Sylvia, nodding with every word she said. And the look in his eyes...well, if he's not in love with you, he should be coming back to L.A. with us to start an acting career.''

Emma felt as if Hope had punched her in the head. Cal had been so careful not to put any sexual pressure on her since that one time in his truck, she'd started to believe he really wasn't interested in her anymore.

"You think?'' she asked.

Hope rolled her eyes. "Darling, I *know.* I just wanted to make sure *you* did. And now, I must be on the road.''

Emma walked her back out to the curb and returned the warm hug Hope gave her.

"You *will* stay in touch,'' Hope commanded.

"Yes, master,'' Emma retorted.

"Good,'' Hope said, as if she'd expected no other response. "Don't come back to California unless you have an extremely good reason. These McBride men are positively...prime.''

"Why aren't you getting one for yourself?" Emma asked.

Hope arched an eyebrow. "What makes you think I'm not?"

Before Emma could come up with a response beyond a dropped jaw, Hope trotted up the motor home's steps, closed the door and drove away, the big coach belching diesel smoke.

"You need a ring job!" Emma yelled, waving at the fumes.

She walked slowly back to the gate. If Hope considered Dillon, Zack and Cal to be "taken," she must be planning to go after Marsh or Jake. God only knew what went on in Hope's mind, and sometimes Emma wasn't too sure even He could keep up with the woman. But whichever man Hope had chosen, Emma could only wish him luck and stamina. He would need plenty of both.

Yip and Yap ran over to greet her when she stepped inside the fence. Realizing with no small jolt of guilt that lately she hadn't spent much time with her small pals, she led them over to the shade of an aspen tree and sat on the ground to play with them. They stomped all over her lap, licked her chin and lavished so much affection on her, she gathered a little dog in each arm and cuddled them close.

Suddenly, she felt lonely to her core, as if her last good friend had just left her. "And she did," Emma told the poodles. Their whole bodies trembled with the joy of her attention. She set them on the grass and sent them off to find a toy to play with. Then she laughed and swiped fingers across her suddenly damp eyelashes.

With Hope and Blair's departure, the entire cast and crew of *Against the Wind* had left Sunshine Gap. So why hadn't she asked some of the equipment haulers to take her bike with them? Why hadn't she asked Hope and Blair for a ride? What on earth was she still doing here? Had she lost her mind?

Or was she still harboring wishful dreams of a future

with Cal? Hope had hinted at it, and not very subtly, either. Well, maybe that blue-haired little witch was right. Emma had continually denied that she loved Cal, but when Hope had told her about seeing him at the café, Emma's heart had swelled with joy and longing.

What would she give to have him right here, right now, ready and willing to hold her until the loneliness passed? What wouldn't she give?

"Hey, Em," he said. "You look like you could use a friend."

"If I wasn't hallucinating you, I'd agree," she said.

His deep chuckle sounded real enough to make her look up.

"Well, if you're hallucinating me, I must be, too." He sat down beside her. "How about a hug?"

He held out an arm, inviting her to come closer. She accepted the offer without a trace of hesitation. He'd helped her with so many things since her accident, been there for advice and encouragement, she had no doubt that he truly was her friend. He wrapped his arm around her shoulders and leaned his back against the tree. The dogs came over to greet him. He scratched their ears, then picked up a ball and threw it for them.

Emma rested her head on his shoulder and closed her eyes, savoring the warmth of his body, the scent of his skin, the simple pleasure of being held by a strong, but gentle man.

"How did you know I was feeling low?" she asked.

"Just a guess. I know you and Hope are pretty good friends. Having her leave makes you the last of the Californians in the Gap. Must be a little weird for you."

She nodded. He rubbed the outside of her arm in a brotherly sort of gesture, and suddenly that wasn't enough anymore. She wasn't his sister and had no desire to be one, either.

Turning her head for a better view of his face, she said softly, "What if I tossed that ball back into your court?"

He went absolutely still. His eyes met hers, and she finally saw what Hope had seen. The same longing, the same loneliness, the same need for closeness to—not just another human being, but—to *her*. Oh, yes, he still wanted her. And there was something more. Maybe it was love. She didn't know. It didn't matter.

She wanted him. She'd been denying it for days and days—weeks, even—and now she realized she'd wasted that time. She could have been making love with him, enjoying his company, saving up memories to cherish when she finally did go back to California.

"Are you sure, Em? Really sure?"

"I don't know if it means what you want it to mean yet," she said, "but I do want to make love with you again."

The wariness in his eyes burned away in a surge of heat. The planes and angles of his face stood out in sharp relief, and instead of feeling brotherly, his touch suddenly felt possessive. His gaze traveled slowly over her, lingering in places that made her intensely aware of her femininity.

"That'll do," he drawled.

His wolfish smile of approval and the devilish gleam in his eyes contained a hint of danger that made the toes of her right foot curl against the sole of her work boot. She'd never seen this side of Cal McBride before, but she liked it. She liked it a lot. Venturing a smile in return, she scrambled to her feet and held out a grease-stained hand to him.

He took a firm grip on her hand and allowed her to pull him halfway up. Then he gave her hand a hard yank, tucked his shoulder into her midsection and wrapped his arms around her legs. Before she could even think about reacting, he straightened to his full height and draped her over his shoulder in a modified fireman's carry.

She shrieked with surprised laughter. The air rushed out of her lungs and blood rushed to her head as she tipped upside down, bouncing along with every stride he took on his way inside. He carried her straight back to his bedroom, and on into his private bathroom.

Carefully setting her on her feet, he held onto her for a moment, as if making sure she was steady. She reached for him, but he pushed her hands away. Without speaking a single word, he peeled off her clothes with the efficiency of an assembly line worker. Then he turned on the shower and, holding Emma's fascinated gaze, treated her to her very own personal strip show. She hoped the water in that shower was cool, or she was liable to melt and slide right down the drain.

"Are we, um..." She stopped and cleared her throat. "Are we in a hurry?"

"Yeah."

He removed her cast boot, grasped her waist and lifted her into the shower. Stepping in behind her, he grabbed the soap, worked up a lather on his hands and scrubbed her down as if she were a grubby little kid or perhaps a big dog. His urgency, which had seemed so exciting at first, began to lose its appeal. This was hardly romantic; it wasn't even in the same time zone as sexy. And now she'd had more than enough of it.

Turning around, she scowled up at him. "Cut it out, McBride. I may work as a mechanic, but I'm still a woman, and I have to tell you, this is a lousy excuse for foreplay. Is it possible that you could turn down the impatience a notch or ten?"

His eyes widened. His nostrils flared. His whole face turned red. He sucked in a deep, ragged breath, and his torso, arms and shoulders bulked up in what looked to her like some kind of powerful hormonal rush. Whether it was adrenaline or testosterone, she didn't think it mattered much at this moment. It brought out every instinctive, placating-the-beast skill she'd been blessed with, but it was too late for that.

"Impatient?" he said, his voice dangerously low, registering way down in the growling range. "You think I'm *impatient?*"

He was magnificent in a scary, but still exciting kind of way. She wasn't about to let him know she felt the least bit intimidated, however. "Yes. You're acting about as patient as a gorilla."

"After dealing with you, I'm about to be declared a saint and I'm not even a Catholic."

"Now, really, Cal—"

"Don't start," he said, his voice so loud now, it made a thunderous echo in the enclosed space of the shower. "You took me to paradise, dammit. I told you I *loved* you. You flipped out, so I backed off to let you get used to the idea and told you the ball was in your court. Do you have any clue how long you kept it?"

"A couple of weeks," she said.

"More than a couple. Try twenty-seven days. Twenty-seven days and twenty-six nights. That's almost four full weeks. In all that time, did you think I stopped wanting you so bad my guts ached with it? Did you even bother to think about me at all?"

"Of course I did. I've been living with you, Cal."

"Duh! And you traipse around half-naked sometimes and expect me to sit back like a trained dog. Like a trained, *neutered* dog, and pretend I don't notice. Trust me, honey, I *notice*. I don't know where your libido went, sweetheart, but mine's been right here wanting you, and loving you only makes it hurt more. And I've been more patient and restrained than—"

"You could have said something."

"Like what?"

"I don't know. Something. I wasn't trying to torture you."

Stepping back, he closed his eyes and rested the back of his head against the tile wall. After a long, moment of silence, during which she barely dared to breathe, she heard a low, rumbling chuckle. "I know you weren't trying, Em, but you succeeded anyway."

The hand he raised to caress her cheek trembled slightly, and when he opened his eyes and gave her a rueful smile, she felt humbled by the lines of strain she finally could see in his face. He'd been so unfailingly kind and helpful, and she'd repaid him by denying that anything important had happened between them. She did that sometimes, especially when she was confused about a situation and couldn't figure out the right thing to do. Better to ignore it than to do the wrong thing.

"I'm sorry, Cal."

"I'm sorry, too. You didn't need to hear all of that. I've been really frustrated, but it was my own doing."

She reached for the bar of soap, worked up a lather on her hands and went to work scrubbing him, slowly and sensuously—the way she would have enjoyed being scrubbed. He tensed when she first touched him, but she shushed him and told him to relax and enjoy himself. He groaned as if he didn't think he could stand it, but submitted himself to her attentions and turned around to let her wash his back.

His skin was smooth and sleek, and when he moved his shoulders, she felt hard muscles rippling underneath. She found great pleasure in sliding her soap-slicked hands over his broad shoulders, his tapering back, his narrow hips and tight buttocks. At that point she lost all sense of restraint.

Pressing herself against his back, she wrapped her arms around him and pretended to be scrubbing his chest, but the water had long ago rinsed all the soap from her hands. Cal didn't appear to notice. If he had noticed, she doubted he would have cared. He groaned again when her hands roamed lower, but it didn't sound like a protest.

His engorged shaft pulsed in her hand, and she could feel a matching, frantic beat under her other hand, which was splayed across his chest. She turned him around to face her and gazed into his eyes, dark with a fierce passion that would have scared her, had she been looking at anyone but him. Oh, he *did* want her. She'd known it. On some level, of course, she'd known it.

But no one had ever wanted her quite this way. She simply hadn't understood how strong his desire for her had been, or that it had been so much more than a physical desire. At this moment, she believed that he really *did* love her. How long it would last she couldn't guess. She intended to experience it and enjoy it until it ended.

No more wasting precious time with this man.

She turned off the shower and nudged him out onto the bath mat. He grabbed a towel, and made a cursory attempt to dry her, gave himself a couple of quick swipes, tossed it on the floor and carried her to his bed. Now she found his impatience exciting, and she reached up for him the instant he released her onto the bedspread.

He came into her arms, still damp, but wonderfully hot and aroused. He kissed her, delving deep with his tongue, as if he could never, ever get enough of kissing her. They rolled over and over on his big bed, devouring each other in an orgy of petting, tasting, exploring.

And now her own impatience grew into a writhing ball of nerve endings in the pit of her belly. She ached with a hungry emptiness that craved him, burned for him, made her crazy with wanting him. He reached out a long arm, snagged a condom from the nightstand and handed it to her.

"Put it on me, darlin'," he said, his voice a husky rasp.

He didn't need to ask twice. Though her hands were shaking, she opened the packet and rolled it onto his shaft with teasing, caressing movements that made him draw in a breath that hissed through his clenched teeth and jaws. Tendons and muscles corded in his neck and she quickly guided him into her body.

Heat, light, colors blossomed behind her closed eyelids when he entered her. He began to move, slowly at first, and then faster and faster, harder and harder. Oh yes, this was exactly what she'd wanted, what she'd needed, and for the life of her, she couldn't begin to understand why she'd denied herself and him this exquisite pleasure.

Whether or not her mind or her heart were ready to admit it, her body knew that this was *her* man, and he was loving her, encouraging her, enjoying her body as much as she was enjoying his. The feelings were intensely physical, but at the same time, they deeply affected her emotions, filled her lonely heart and revived her weary soul.

He touched her in so many different ways and on so many different levels, she wondered if she ever again would feel complete without him. This was the feeling she'd been searching for her whole life. She gazed up into his dear face, watching for signs that he might also be experiencing this happiness, this glorious sense of belonging.

Leaning down, he kissed her. She felt surrounded by his strength, seared by his heat, scorched by his intensity. His endurance amazed and delighted her. Still, she never wanted it to end.

She wanted to cling to his hard shoulders with her hands, press herself against his broad chest, feel the heavy pounding of his heart. On and on he drove her, sending her over the top of one shattering climax after another. All she could do was hang on for the ride and trust him to take her safely through to the end.

With a hoarse shout, he found his own completion, and they collapsed into each other's arms. Panting heavily, their hearts still beating to an identical frantic rhythm, they petted and stroked and kissed repeatedly, as if even now, they weren't close enough. Holding her tightly against him, he rolled onto his side and they settled onto a single pillow facing each other.

She raised one trembling hand and caressed the side of his face. "Oh, Cal," she murmured, "you're so wonderful and I'm so confused."

"About what, darlin'?"

"You. Me. Sunshine Gap." Her voice cracked.

"Everything."

He cuddled her against his chest and kissed her forehead. "I know. What confuses you the most?"

"It's this…love thing. I don't know what to do with it."

"Why do you have to do anything with it?"

"I don't know. That's the problem. I've never been around it that much, and I don't know the rules."

"It's just a feeling, Em. There aren't any rules."

She raised up on one elbow and gazed down into his troubled eyes. "That's why I'm so confused. I'm not even sure what it's supposed to feel like."

"It's different for everyone. You don't have to feel any certain way."

"Then how do I know if what I feel for you is love?"

He gave her a gentle smile that threatened what little control she had over the tears that kept wanting to fall. "I can tell you how it feels for me. Will that help?"

She nodded, then snuggled back into his arms and rested her head on the pillow again. He hugged her close for a moment, then started to speak.

"When I'm away from you, somewhere in the back of my mind, I'm still thinking about you. Missing you. When we've been apart even for an hour, and I see you again, I feel happy all over."

"Is that all?" she asked.

He hugged her tightly. "No, that's just the beginning. I love making you laugh. Seeing you smile puts this warm, fuzzy little feeling right about here." He pointed to a spot just below the exact center of his chest.

"That could be indigestion," she said dryly. He laughed, and she felt a warm, fuzzy sensation in exactly the same spot on her own body. Now *this* was getting interesting. "Go on."

"Well, the opposite is true, too. When you suffer, I suffer right along with you. I almost lost my mind that night we were looking for you and couldn't find you. And it was pure hell when we finally did find you, knowing you were hurting and I couldn't do a damn thing about it." His voice grew thick, as if he had a lump in his throat. "I never want to see you in pain again. Never."

"I'm not fond of it myself."

He gave her a crooked grin. "I just want what's really best for you. Your happiness is the most important thing in the world to me, and I'll do whatever I can to help you find it. Does any of this sound vaguely familiar?"

She nodded. "I don't like to see you unhappy, either. And I do love to make you laugh. I find myself wanting to share things with you that I've never shared with anyone else."

"Like what, Em?"

"Well, I haven't done it yet. I'm still too…scared."

"Of me?"

"Not of *you*, exactly. It's more…the way you might react."

"Is it about your background. Your family?"

She nodded. "It's not a pretty story."

"I figured that much out a long time ago," he said. "I just don't know the details. Whatever they are, they don't matter worth a damn."

"That's easy to say, but…"

"I'm dead serious. You don't ever have to tell me anything if it worries you. Whatever came before the day you hit Sunshine Gap is your business and I don't need to know a blessed thing about it. I love the Emma Barnes who's here in my bed, in my arms, right now."

"Okay. But what is it you want from me, Cal? And don't say it's nothing I don't want to give you. That doesn't help me understand anything. What do you want?"

To his credit, he took a moment to think before he answered. "I want you to love me back."

"I'm getting there," she said. "What else do you want?"

He gazed directly into her eyes, his expression so solemn, she felt as if he was looking into the confused, murky depths of her heart. "Hell, Em, I want it all with you. Love. Marriage. Babies. A lifetime."

His quiet, yet heartfelt declaration made her ache to say yes, to ignore her fears and throw herself headlong into whatever magical dreams he had for the two of them, but a deeply ingrained sense of caution proved stronger than temptation.

"That's what I was afraid of," she said. "That lifetime part scares me. I don't know how anyone does that."

"You don't have to do it all at once." Smiling, he stroked her cheek with the backs of his fingers. "You only have to do it one day at a time."

"But what if it ends? What if you have the babies and it still ends?"

"You want a guarantee that nothing bad will ever happen in a whole lifetime? Nobody gets that. You can only do the very best you can and hold on to your love with both hands. That's all anybody can do."

She snuggled closer, then pushed him onto his back and lay her head on his chest. His heart beat with a steady, reassuring rhythm, and he gently combed his fingers through her damp hair.

"What if I can't do it all though?" she asked.

"Then do what you can. All I really need from you right now is a promise that you'll think about it and give us a chance."

"I can do that." She tilted her head back and met his gaze. "If I can, um...sleep in your bed so I don't get too scared?"

His slow, sexy smile gave her that warm, fuzzy little feeling again. "Just try to get out of this bed. I dare you."

She snickered. "Oooo, I'm trembling. I love it when you get all manly. It gives me goose bumps."

His bellow of laughter gave her goose bumps, and another one of those warm, fuzzy feelings. He rolled her onto her back and proceeded to show her just how manly he could be. When they collapsed an hour later, supremely satiated, their limbs tangled, she finally faced the truth.

She was in love with Cal McBride. As Hope had said, everything she'd ever wanted lay within her grasp. Her own auto shop. A wonderful man who loved her and wanted to marry her. The possibility of having children and a huge family of relatives—if Cal's family would accept her.

The question she had to answer now was, did she have, or could she find the nerve to reach out for what he was offering her? She didn't know the answer. She only knew that she had to try.

Chapter Fourteen

When the last members of the movie crew cleared out, so did the tourists who had flocked to Cal's Place in hope of seeing a movie star. He'd expected the slowdown, of course, but it made him more determined than ever to find a way to bring some new life and new jobs to Sunshine Gap. Still, it was tough going from working full-out sixteen to eighteen hours a day, seven days a week for two solid months, back to business as usual.

Thank heaven he had Emma to soften the blow. She'd moved into his bedroom six days ago, and ever since he'd felt as if he'd been on an adventure in Honeymoon Land. Though he'd never admit it out loud, he actually felt happy that his business had quit booming. Now he could spend more time with her.

In that ironic way life often had, however, Emma didn't have a whole lot of time to spend with him. It had been years since they'd had a crackerjack mechanic in the area. With the insane prices for new machinery these days, every farmer and rancher in a fifty-mile radius wanted her to revive old pickups, combines, tractors, balers, well pumps, and any other mechanical thing they thought she might be able to fix.

The school district had a couple of school buses for her to work on. She even had a couple of jobs lined up for snowmobiles and snowplows. As news of her abilities spread, Cal had no doubt that fifty-mile radius would expand. She'd probably get job offers from Cody, Powell, Thermopolis, wherever. It was hard for small towns to attract and keep doctors any more. The same thing applied to other skilled people like Emma, who could earn a lot more money in bigger cities.

Well, she was one skilled worker he intended to keep around. He took every opportunity he could find to support her and help her new business grow. He drove her out to meet new customers so she wouldn't get lost on the back roads, many of which had no signs. He picked up new parts in Cody, helped her set up a bookkeeping system and started looking around for a building she could lease that would give her more room than his garage.

Not two miles from his house, he found a steel building Orville Purdy had put up behind his small house when he'd decided to raise ostriches for their meat. Unfortunately for Orville and the ostriches, a wily old mountain lion had developed a taste for the big birds. Within a year, Orville was out of business and living in Idaho.

Cal wasn't sure what the building's intended purpose had been, but it was big, and it had a nice concrete slab under it. They could put in a lift, build her a workbench and lots of shelves, rig up some decent lighting, and she'd really have something here. Fingering the penny in his vest pocket, he wondered if the property came with enough acreage to build a bigger house and a fenced yard for poodles. Maybe some kids.

It took a little digging, to locate the owner, but Cal found him and went to see him within the hour. He came back out of the man's house whistling, then set off to find Emma, jangling a new set of keys in his pocket.

Emma straightened up from working on Slim Hanson's pickup, wiped her forehead with the back of one forearm and stretched out her lower back.

"Hey, there, pretty lady. You look like you're ready for a break," Cal said, coming into the garage through the side door.

"Hi, handsome." She turned to him with a smile. It was probably a tired smile, but having him pop in like this was always a bright spot in her day. "What's up?"

He stuck his hands deep into his front jeans pockets. "Business has been pretty good, hasn't it?"

"Yes," she said cautiously, knowing a sales pitch when she heard one starting.

Twisting his torso this way and that, he looked around his own garage as if he'd never seen it before. "Kinda cramped in here, though, isn't it? Dark too."

She couldn't help laughing. "Cut the act, Mr. Mayor. You want your garage back?"

"Oh, no, it's not that," he said with a grin. "But I found you one heck of a deal on a building that'd make an ideal shop. Interested?"

"Of course, I'm interested, but I don't have much money."

"Aw, don't worry about that now. We'll figure out something." He pulled a set of keys out of his pocket and waved it back and forth. "Come look at it with me."

She stepped down from the pickup's bumper and set her wrench on the workbench. "Are you sure you weren't a Pied Piper in a former life?"

"You got me. Know any channelers back in California?"

"A few," she said dryly. "But not lately."

He grinned. "What do ya say the next time we go down there, we'll look one of 'em up and find out?"

"Oh, for sure, man. Like, I mean, no problemo, dude."

"You're making fun of me again, aren't you, Barnes?"

"It's my favorite form of entertainment, McBride."

They harassed each other all the way to what Cal kept referring to as "the place." His enthusiasm was so infectious, Emma had to keep reminding herself that she probably couldn't afford whatever it was he'd found. He pulled to the side of the gravel road and pointed out a fenced field just ahead.

"Now imagine this, honey."

He'd started calling her all sorts of affectionate names lately, and it never failed to give her a little thrill. He held up his hands as if framing a picture. "There's a nice new sign right on that corner and it says Emma's Engines. What do you think so far?"

"Catchy," she said. "Real catchy."

Giving her a droll look that made her laugh, he turned into the lane and they bounced from one rut to the other for two hundred yards. Then they rounded a curve and she became entranced with the panoramic view in front of her. A typical, blue Wyoming sky arched over a huge red steel building on the left, and a funky little white clapboard house which was surrounded on three sides by towering cottonwood trees on the right.

A low, winding line of willows indicated the presence of water, a creek perhaps, or an irrigation ditch. The yard was weedy and overgrown. There were patches of peeling paint and a sagging porch on the front of the house. Emma saw nothing but possibilities. It looked like…home. And she wanted it.

She started when Cal opened the door for her. "Sorry. I didn't see you coming around."

"It's all right." He lifted her to the ground and slung his arm around her shoulders. "You were busy. Want the grand tour?"

"Yes. Yes, please."

He led her through the steel building, pointing out likely

spots for various pieces of equipment she might want. It was more than adequate for her needs in every way. Though the house needed work on the outside, the interior didn't need much more than a good cleaning. It would provide a comfortable place to take a break, meet with customers or handle paperwork.

"So, what do you think now?" Cal asked.

She turned to him with a smile. "I think you're a wretched, horrible man."

"Excuse me? How can you say that when I've found you this...palace?"

"Easy. Now that I've seen it, I want it. And there's no way I can afford it."

"It'd be a stretch," he admitted. "But this is one time you'll be real glad you're not in California. Real estate prices in Sunshine Gap are a lot lower than you would expect."

"How much?"

"When I talked to the owner, I asked what he'd want for a lease with an option to buy."

Her mouth went as dry as the tumbleweeds mashed up against the fence by the winds that rarely seemed to stop blowing in Wyoming. "What did he say?"

"It's really not that bad—"

"Cal, just tell me. How much?"

He named a ridiculously low figure. But in her business, cash flow was always a problem, and he was right that it would be a stretch for her budget. She sighed with discouragement and turned toward the front door.

"Now, wait a second," he said, laying a hand on her arm.

She turned back to face him and felt warmed by the sympathy she saw in his eyes. "Okay, it was sweet of you to find this place, but—"

"But nothing, sweetheart. Let's go home and put a pencil to paper. You may be surprised."

Two hours later, he'd reduced her business to a bunch

of numbers. He tapped the tip of his pencil beside the figure that filled her with exhilaration and despair at the same time.

"That's all you need to move your business to the next level. With the orders you've already got scheduled, it's obviously time to do that," he said. "Some of this stuff can wait, but you have to get a better setup if you want to keep growing."

"I know that," she said, "and I'm not questioning your math or your business judgment. I just don't have that kind of money, or any legal way to get it."

He set down his pencil and covered her hand with his. "Hell, Em, I'll loan it to you. I made a lot of money this summer."

"And you spent a lot of money on extra help, your taxes are going to go up, your building needs a new roof and you're heading into leaner times, so forget it. I'm not taking your money. I don't like to be in debt, anyway."

"Nobody does, but it's a fact of life for most of us. At the rate you've been going, you could have this paid off in under a year. Or, if you won't take it from me, I can find you a silent partner. My brother Jake would jump at the chance to invest in a business like yours."

"Let me think about it."

He opened his mouth as if he would argue, then shook his head and clamped his lips together. A moment later, he said, "All right, honey. Just don't forget that a lot of people in your position borrow money from family, friends and anyone else they can talk into it. You can do this if you want to, Em. I know you can make it work."

Knowing he'd never shut up and let her think unless she distracted him, she got up and walked around to his side of the table. He watched her approach, his head tilted a little to the left, one eyebrow riding higher than the other. Standing close to him, she took the pencil from his hand, scooped together the papers that had been ripped from his legal pad and pushed them across the table.

She nudged one leg of his chair with her foot. When he shifted the chair away from the table, she straddled his lap and slid her fingers into his hair, just behind his ears. Massaging his scalp, she smiled when his eyelids closed and he gave a soft grunt of pleasure.

"What are you doing, Emma?"

"Distracting you." She planted quick, nibbling kisses across his eyebrows, his cheekbones, his eyelids. "Is it working?"

"Mm-hmm." His lips curved into a slow, sexy smile and he put his hands on her hips. She kissed her way back across his cheekbone and then down across his tickly mustache and over to his right earlobe. "Oh, yeah, it's workin', all right," he murmured. "What are you distracting me from, darlin'?"

"All this money talk. It makes me nervous."

He chuckled and smoothed his big hands over her back. "You think *this* is gonna calm either one of us down?"

"Not right away." Feeling her temperature rise at the delights that particular tone in his voice brought to mind, she rubbed her nose against his. "But I'll bet you five bucks we'll get there eventually."

"I'm not dumb enough to take that bet, sugar. I'd be too busy helpin' you win it."

Tightening his arms around her, he stood up, waited for her to wrap her legs around his waist and carried her into the bedroom. They loved each other long and hard, and several hours later, she lay on her side, watching him sleep. Cal had such a charming grin and expressive eyes, she'd expected him to look younger, even a little boyish, when he slept.

Nothing could be farther from the truth. Awake, asleep, Cal was all man, with a man's burdens and responsibilities. For all his easygoing ways, he took his part-time job as the mayor of Sunshine Gap seriously, and he had a long list of residents he kept an eye on, in case they ever needed help and were too proud to ask for it.

The employees down at Cal's Place even joked among themselves about being Cal McBride's strays. Given the way he had taken her in after her accident, and given her a job, Emma could hardly classify herself as anything else. She appreciated his help to the depths of her heart, but she didn't want to go on being someone he had to look out for.

If she was going to have her own garage, she wanted it to be *hers,* something she had earned for herself, not something Cal had needed to help her with. Oh, she wouldn't mind getting his advice and using him as a sounding board for business decisions. She loved listening to him share his expertise and watch his eyes glow with enthusiasm for his subject.

She also wouldn't flinch at letting him help her make important contacts and introduce her to prospective customers. It seemed to her that the man must know half the people in the state. Not that there were all that many people living here, she thought with a grin. Who ever would have thought she would one day be seriously considering becoming one of them?

Wyoming was such a funny combination of things. Scenery so beautiful in some places, you almost couldn't believe it was real. Ten minutes later, you might be driving through barren, windswept land with jagged rock formations that actually looked deformed, with little vegetation other than weeds, sagebrush and a few gnarled and twisted pine trees. There would be no water or other people in sight for a hundred miles or more. You had to wonder how on earth the original settlers in this state had found the fortitude to stay and try to make a living here.

And yet, everything about Wyoming seemed big, open and unspoiled, especially when compared to Los Angeles. There simply was something here that called out to her. Whether it was the land itself or the spirit and character of the people she had met and begun to call her friends, she didn't know. It had been there, at least in part, even on that first day she'd arrived in Sunshine Gap and ridden out to the Flying M. And now, in her heart of hearts, she knew Wyoming had its hooks so deeply imbedded in her soul, she didn't want to leave it, any more than she wanted to leave Cal.

So what are you going to do about it, Emma? her conscience asked. *Cal's right. How are you going to find that money to get your business off the ground, if you won't borrow it from him?*

There was a way. The idea had been lurking in the back of her mind ever since Cal had shown her the property. She just didn't want to consider it. A month ago doing even that much would have seemed obscene. But now?

She wished Cal would wake up and distract her this time. As if he'd heard her thinking about him, he reached out a hand and patted the bed until he found her. Eyes still closed, he smiled, then wrapped his arm around her and pulled her closer to the warmth and shelter of his big body. When he had her all tucked in against him to his satisfaction, he heaved a contented sigh and drifted back to a deeper level of sleep.

The sheer sweetness of that action made the decision for her. She was going to have her new business, and she was going to finance it herself. If life got rough...well, this time she wasn't going to run away. There was a way to accomplish all of those goals, and there was no reason to procrastinate. She was going to sell Mama.

When Emma told him the news, Cal was flabbergasted. He even tried to talk her out of selling Mama. Though he didn't completely understand why, he knew that motorcycle meant more to Emma than anything else she owned, and he hated to see her have to give it up. At the same time, he was absolutely thrilled at what her decision obviously meant.

Emma was going to stay in Sunshine Gap.

Relief hit him so hard, it was a good thing he was sitting down or he probably would have fallen. As soon as the

giddiness passed, however, he made a quick call and drove
Emma to the ranch. She was quieter than usual, and Cal
decided not to bother her with chitchat. If he ever had to
give up his '51 Ford pickup, he'd need time to get over the
loss. Emma deserved no less.

Jake met them in the drive, and accompanied them to an
old machine shed. Cal opened the door wide to let in some
sunlight. Jake stepped inside and pulled a tarp off the motorcycle and rolled it into the open. Emma inhaled one deep
breath, and then got on with the business of checking Mama
out to see how much work she needed to get her ready for
sale.

Amazingly enough, the bike itself had sustained very little damage in the accident. A few dings and scratches on
that sexy red paint job, a broken headlight, a bent mirror,
and that was it. The working parts had come through just
fine.

Jake offered her the use of a ranch truck to haul Mama
to Cody or Billings, or wherever she wanted to sell it. To
Jake's surprise and Cal's delighted amusement, Emma accepted his offer and came back with an offer of her own.

"That's great," she said. "And I really appreciate that,
Jake. But since I'm selling my only means of transportation, I wonder if you might have an old pickup around the
ranch somewhere that nobody uses anymore."

Eyeing her warily, Jake rubbed the back of his neck, then
slowly nodded. "Yeah, we do. You want it?"

"Maybe. I'd have to see it first. But if I do, would you
be interested in a little bartering for it?"

Jake looked at Cal. "You put her up to this?"

"No, but I wish I'd thought of it," Cal said, winking at
Emma.

She winked back at him, then made a shooing motion
with one hand. "I'll handle this. Okay?"

"You bet. I'll just mosey on up to the house and see if
Grace has any fresh cinnamon rolls this morning."

Grace did have fresh cinnamon rolls and a pot of coffee

brewing. Sniffing appreciatively. Cal stepped into the kitchen. Grace glanced up from a pile of dough she was kneading and smiled at him.

"Hi, there, stranger," she said. "Haven't seen you in a while."

Cal crossed the room and kissed her cheek, then tweaked her long braid the way he had done ever since they were little kids. He helped himself to a cup of coffee and dug a roll out of a still-warm pan. "I've been busy, Gracie."

"So I hear." Grace covered the dough with a damp cloth, then washed her hand at the sink. "You and Emma have been keepin' the ol' grapevine hummin'."

"Well, good. Those old bats need something to do, and I'm always glad to be of service to the community. And I think we're about to give 'em a whole new round of phone calls."

"Really?"

"Yeah. I'm in love with her, and I'm gonna marry her just as soon as I can get her to say yes."

Grace clutched one hand to her chest. "Oh, my. Did somebody put a love potion down the well, or what? First Dillon. Then Alex and Zack. Now you? I'd better get up to Billings and buy a going-to-a-wedding dress."

"That's not a bad idea," he said with a chuckle. He filled her in on the important events of his life during the past month. "Everything about her is just so right for me, but she's still pretty skittish."

"Well, she'll come around." Grace leaned closer and gave one end of his mustache a playful tug. "Just keep focusin' all your charm on her, and she won't be able to resist you for long."

"That's what I'm countin' on. You like her, don't you?"

"What's not to like about Emma? I don't know her very well, but I'd sure like to. And when I see a smile like that one on your crabby old face, I figure she's got to be good for you."

"It means a lot to know you'd welcome her into the family."

"Of course, I will. But speaking of family, there's something I want to discuss with you."

"What's that?"

"When are you and Marsh gonna make up?" she asked.

Cal took a sip of coffee to buy himself a little time to think before responding. "Well, I guess that's up to Marsh."

"Oh, come on. Do you really expect him to apologize again?"

"Yeah," Cal said. "He didn't mean it the first time, and he embarrassed the hell out of me right in front of Emma."

"He shouldn't have hit you," Grace conceded. "But how would you feel if you saw Emma out with some other guy? Wouldn't you be angry? Especially if you knew she'd slept with him?"

Cal took a huge bite of cinnamon roll and chewed it slowly, imagining the scenario Grace had laid out for him. "I'd probably want to kill the SOB. But Marsh and Sandy broke up years ago. I don't get why he's still acting like I seduced her away from him. Furthermore, and not that I'm in the habit of kissing and telling mind you, Sandy and I never did the big deed."

"You *didn't?*"

Cal and Grace both started, then turned toward the doorway leading from the kitchen to the living room. Marsh stood there, his eyes wide with what appeared to be shock, his whole body rigid. The guy showed obvious signs of suffering. His face looked pale and thinner, and there were deep, bluish crescents under his eyes. His eyes looked so haunted, Cal almost felt sorry for him.

Almost, but not quite.

"You make a habit out of eavesdropping on other people's conversations?" he asked.

Marsh blinked, then shook his head with an air of distraction and crossed the room to stand beside Grace. "Why not? You were engaged to her. How could you not..."

"I don't think we should talk about this," Cal said. "It's not respectful to Sandy."

"It's not idle curiosity," Marsh said, his eyes glittering with a quiet intensity that left no doubt about his sincerity. "Please, Cal. I'll apologize again. I'll beg, if you want. But I need to know the truth. How could you not..."

"Want her?" Cal asked, feeling a little sorry for his cousin, after all.

"Yeah."

Cal shrugged. "She's a beautiful woman and a genuinely nice person, and I loved her. But it just never felt right to put any real moves on her. After I met Emma, I finally realized I love Sandy sort of like I love Alex and Grace. Truth is, I don't think she ever felt any more than that for me. Does that answer your questions?"

Marsh shut his eyes for a moment and exhaled a ragged sigh. Looking back at Cal again, he offered a crooked smile. "Thanks, Cal." He held out his hand. "Truce?"

Cal hesitated for all of thirty seconds, then he knocked Marsh's hand aside and gave him a quick, hard hug. "Truce. Just remember, you owe me big time."

Marsh grinned. "Well, I might know a few things about California women that could come in handy. Just a little friendly advice now and then. Interested?"

"Probably."

"Not in front of me," Grace said with a laugh. She shooed them both out the back door. "I don't need to know this kind of stuff about you guys. It's almost as bad as hearin' your parents talk about sex. Yuck."

At the bottom of the porch steps, Cal and Marsh saw Emma and Jake walking across the barnyard.

"She's a hell of a woman," Marsh murmured.

"I know," Cal murmured back. "I just hope I don't screw this up somehow."

"Give her lots of rope, and don't be in any rush to get

your brand on her," Marsh said. "She's as independent as they come."

"No kidding." Cal chuckled. "But what a gal."

Emma and Jake arrived, both of them grinning as if they'd made a great deal. Emma came over to stand beside Cal and slid her arm around the back of his waist. He hugged her against his side and winked at her.

Propping his hands on his hips, Jake studied Cal and Marsh for a moment.

"You two finally make up?"

Marsh looked at Cal. "Is it just me, or is he really starting to look and sound just like your old man?"

Cal snorted. "Hell, that's been goin' on for years. Get a load of all that gray hair he's gettin'. Pathetic, isn't it?"

Jake scowled at the two of them, then looked at Emma and rolled his eyes toward heaven. "That's just how they used to be when they were little brats. I liked it better when they weren't talkin' to each other."

Cal and Marsh cracked up and gave each other a high five. Jake went into the house, grumbling under his breath.

"What was that all about?" Emma asked.

Cal and Marsh grinned at each other. Then Cal said, "When you grow up in a litter, that's how the middle ones survive."

"Right," Marsh said. "The middle kids have to gang up on the others or get ignored. We never did like being ignored."

"Doesn't that rivalry thing ever end?" she asked.

"Only when somebody's in trouble," Cal admitted. "Then we circle the wagons and stand together. Nobody with half a brain wants to mess with all seven of us."

Chuckling, Marsh shook his head. "Yeah, but the minute the trouble's over, the old rivalry starts right up again. It's the law of a big family."

Jake stepped back outside, held up a set of keys and called to Emma, "Here you go, Em. I'll get the paperwork taken care of and bring it over to you."

Emma caught the keys when Jake tossed them. Smiling with satisfaction, she held them in her palm, then tossed them into the air and caught them again before elbowing Cal in the ribs. "It's fine if you want to stay and visit, but I've got to go now, and I've got my own wheels to drive."

"Oh, yeah?" Cal said. "How'd you do that?"

"I just pointed out everything going wrong with that old truck and made Jake an offer he couldn't refuse."

"What was the offer?" Marsh asked.

"And why would that be any of your business?" Cal asked.

"It's not," Marsh admitted. "But I'm a writer, and we make our living by being nosy. So shut up, and let her tell me."

"Who said I was going to tell either one of you?" Emma said with a laugh. Gripping her keys, she hobbled across the barnyard, climbed into the driver's seat of a twenty-year-old, three-quarter-ton Ford pickup with her bike already loaded in the back, and fired up the engine. Well, fired up was stretching the truth, since the truck did an awful lot of coughing and sputtering and backfiring.

"Aw jeez," Marsh said. "Whatever Jake got out of her for that piece of junk, he robbed her blind."

"Don't worry about Emma. Next time Jake sees that old heap, he's gonna be sorry he ever let go of it," Cal said. He shook hands with Marsh and headed for his vehicle, calling back over his shoulder. "Come into Cal's Place for a visit and your first drink'll be on the house."

Marsh gave him a thumbs-up and went back into the ranch house. Cal drove away, feeling happier than he'd been in a long time. He doubted that he and Marsh would ever be as close as they'd been as kids, but it sure was a relief to be friends with his cousin again.

And if Emma went through with selling Mama, Cal figured he had her pretty much where he wanted her. Marsh might be right about not rushing to put his brand on her, but then Marsh didn't know everything there was to know about women, now did he? Well, he'd help Emma set up her new shop, and then he'd see where they were.

But he sure didn't plan to let his woman run around the county for long without some visible sign that she was taken. He'd just go ahead and pick out an engagement ring for her. When the right opportunity came along, he'd be ready for it.

Chapter Fifteen

Free at last from the bulky cast boot, Emma practically boogied out of the orthopedic surgeon's office. She'd grown so used to dragging the thing around during the past six weeks, she'd forgotten what it felt like to walk without it. She would have to do exercises and stretches to strengthen the muscles in her calf and ankle, but her new freedom felt great.

She climbed into her truck, reached for the ignition, then changed her mind and settled back against the seat. She'd worked so hard during the past two weeks, she hadn't had a moment's peace to think about anything. To an extent, that had been intentional on her part.

The only way she'd been able to get through selling Mama, had been to focus all of her time and energy toward the future. Cal had been right there beside her every day. She didn't know who was running Cal's Place these days, but it wasn't him.

After she'd restored Mama to her former glory, he had

been the one to haul the motorcycle up to the dealership in Billings and work out the terms of the sale. While Emma had continued to finish as many jobs as possible out of his garage, he had been out locating equipment and tools she needed, and arranging for a small inventory of parts and excellent terms for replacing them. Their individual talents meshed surprisingly well when it came to setting up her new shop.

While he wasn't a professional mechanic, Cal knew a lot about engines. When it came to getting the best possible price, either selling or buying, he was a master negotiator. He continually amazed her with the "deals" he made on her behalf.

She loved him for his concern. She sincerely appreciated all of his help. She knew she never could have accomplished half as much in such a short time without him. But she wished he would back off and give her just a little space to develop her own ideas and procedures.

That sounded so petty and ungrateful, she was ashamed of herself for thinking that way. She knew he didn't mean to be bossy or pushy. She knew his only intention was to help her get off to a fast start. And she knew she was going to go completely nuts, if he didn't tend to his business soon, and let her muddle along as best she could with her own.

Maybe they were just spending too much time together. She wasn't used to getting so much help. She wasn't used to living with someone else, not for weeks at a time, anyway. She certainly wasn't used to sharing a bed with anyone else. It was all becoming far too intense and intimate.

On the other hand, she would rather die than hurt Cal's feelings. She had no clue how a person went about diplomatically bringing these things up for discussion. In truth, she felt confused and nervous, and that old, familiar urge to flee grew stronger every day.

She rested her head back against the seat, closed her eyes and sighed heavily. Being alone felt so good. Thank God she'd managed to convince Cal to stay in Sunshine Gap this morning, but her relief at having a few hours to herself made her feel guilty, too. Was she becoming a guilt magnet or what?

"And sitting here worrying about it isn't solving anything," she muttered.

She sat up, started the engine and headed for Sunshine Gap. Cal wasn't at home when she arrived, but Yip and Yap gave her their usual greetings. She scooped them up for a cuddle, then set them back on the floor when the phone rang a moment later. Barry Jacobson's voice boomed in her ear.

"Emma, how are you?" he asked.

"I'm fine," she said.

"Glad to hear it," he said. "Still in the cast boot?"

"Just got it off this morning," she said.

"What did the doctor say about your ankle?"

"It healed great. I'll be back to normal in a few weeks."

"Excellent. When are you coming home?"

The word *home* gave her heart a sharp pang. She'd never really thought of L.A. as being home, exactly, but she'd spent her whole life there. Suddenly she missed it. Missed her old haunts and the familiarity of always knowing where she was going. She even missed the smog and the traffic and the heat.

"Emma? Are you still there?"

"Sorry, I was just…thinking about something."

"I'll repeat the question then. When are you coming home?"

"I don't know," she said. "Does it matter?"

"Only if you're interested in a job," he said.

"What kind of a job?" She didn't really want one, but she could satisfy her curiosity, couldn't she?

"How would you like to be the emcee for the stunt show at one of the studio tours? You, know, telling the audience about the stunts and how they're done. Answering questions."

"I'm not a public speaker," she said. "I wouldn't be comfortable doing that."

"You'd only have to do it until you're a hundred percent again," Barry said. "It'll keep your foot in the door, and you'll know what's happening in the business."

"I don't think so, Barry."

He was silent for a moment, then asked, "What's going on, Emma?"

"It's…complicated."

"Does it involve Cal McBride?"

"In a way. I'm, uh…thinking about staying here. Cal's helping me start a business."

"A *what?*"

The tone of Barry's shout told Emma he thought she'd lost all of her marbles. She gave him the abbreviated version of her life during the weeks since she'd last seen him. When she finished, she held her breath, waiting for the inevitable explosion.

"Oh, Emma. This isn't like you."

"Maybe I'm discovering a new me," she said. "I'm good at this, Barry. I like these people, and I love being my own boss."

"I understand that, but Sunshine Gap? Can you honestly see yourself spending the rest of your life there?"

"That's what I'm trying to figure out," she said.

"Get real," Barry snapped. "You don't belong in a dinky burg like that. It's a dead end. They don't even have a movie theater, for God's sake."

"Well, impossible as it may be for you to believe, there are millions of people who live quite happily without movie theaters. The entire world does not revolve around Hollywood."

"Did McBride drug you, or—"

"No. It's something I've figured out all by myself."

"I'm sorry, Emma," he said. "Really, I am. I know I didn't pay as much attention to you after your accident as I should have. But you know how nuts it is when we finally start shooting. I had my hands full trying to find a replacement for you, and—''

Emma closed her eyes and willed her temper back under control. ''I know, Barry. I'm not blaming you for anything. You've been a wonderful friend for a long time, and nothing will ever change that. But I think I've got a real chance for happiness here, and I don't want to give it up.''

''You're in love with Cal, aren't you?''

''I think so. It's…difficult for me. You know?''

''Yes, I do,'' he said softly. ''Just don't lose touch, okay? If you ever do want to come back, remember the door's open.''

''Thanks, Barry. I'll do that.''

She hung up the phone, then turned away, shaking her head. She hadn't completely burned her bridges, but she certainly had scorched them. Old insecurities rose up to haunt her. Maybe she really didn't belong here. Maybe she never would fit in here. Maybe she wasn't capable of maintaining a long-term relationship with anyone. Not even Cal.

''Yeah, and maybe the world's going to end in five minutes,'' she grumbled, heading for the bedroom to change into work clothes. That calmed the panicky little voices in her mind for the moment. She didn't know how long that would last, but she didn't intend to give in to them. All of a sudden, she wished Cal would come home.

Hurrying home late that afternoon, Cal mentally ticked off his plans for the evening. He was taking Emma out to celebrate, and he wanted everything to be perfect for her. If all went well, this was going to be a big night for both of them.

He found her working on yet another tractor, and he smiled to himself, unable to believe his good fortune. Feeling no remorse, whatsoever, he dragged her away from the job, bullied her into the house and on into the shower. She grumbled a little about pushy men, but he figured that was just Emma.

As he expected, she relaxed during the drive to Cody. They had another delightful dinner at the Irma Hotel and shared a good laugh over the manager's wary smile when he walked by their table, obviously recognizing them from their last visit. By the time they'd finished thick wedges of apple pie à la mode for dessert, Cal couldn't wait any longer.

"Emma," he said, reaching across the table to take her hand between his palms. "You're the most fascinating, sexy, wonderful woman I've ever met."

She raised her eyebrows at him for an instant, then grinned slightly. "Gee, thank you, but what brought that on?"

"A lot of things. Watching you work. Living with you. Learning about you."

A soft pink flush swept over her face. "I like you too."

"Like? You still only *like* me?"

"There's more to it than that," she muttered, darting a glance over her shoulder as if she feared someone else might be listening. She was getting the small-town gossip thing down fast.

"How much more?"

She grinned at him, then said dryly, "Well, I want your body."

"That's a given. Come on, Emma. You know what I mean."

"Yes, I do. But I've learned it pays to know what you're up to before committing myself to anything. What is it you really want, Mayor McBride?"

Inhaling a deep breath for courage, Cal stuck a finger into his vest pocket and carefully peeled off the tape he'd used to anchor the ring he'd hidden there. "All I really want is you, darlin'. Will you marry me?"

Her eyes widened. Her teasing grin vanished. Her warm fingers turned icy in a heartbeat. She yanked her hand back and looked away from him. Her whole body looked so rigid, he was afraid she might shatter at the slightest touch.

Cal suddenly wished he'd listened more carefully to Marsh's advice. A lot more carefully. He'd thought everything had been going so well, but...hell, he hadn't thought about anything but his own need to feel secure about Emma. And Emma was looking at him the way an animal might look at the trapper who's come to collect his catch. Two more seconds and she'd be out the door.

"Emma, it's all right," he said, struggling to keep his voice steady. "You can say no, darlin'. You don't have to freak out. We can talk about this later."

Her nostrils flared and her chest expanded. The panic faded from her eyes. She cleared her throat and shifted around in her chair, avoiding his gaze as if seeing his eyes might poison her. Her reaction ripped a gaping hole in his heart, hurting and angering him at the same time.

Damn. If only he could get his hands on whoever had made it so hard for her to deal with the idea of someone loving her...

"No. We can't," she said, her voice so soft he had to lean closer to hear it. "I don't want to keep hurting you."

"I'm okay, Em."

"No," she said again, slowly raising her anguished gaze to meet his. "I'm hurting you, and you don't deserve it."

"If I just understood a little more, it would help," he admitted. "But you don't have to explain anything, either. I shouldn't have surprised you like this. Let's just pretend I never said anything."

"What's in your pocket, Cal? You've got a ring in there, don't you?"

He looked down at his vest and saw his fingers tucked into the pocket. And, yes, they were clamped around an engagement ring, but there was something else in there, too. He wasn't going to lie to her, but he didn't have to tell her everything. Not right now, he didn't. Pulling out his "Emma penny," he held it up and let her see it.

"Just my lucky penny," he said with a rueful smile.

Well, he hoped it looked rueful. Anything but guilty would be good.

She looked at him for a long moment, her concentration so fierce he feared she wouldn't believe him. Then her shoulders relaxed slightly and she sat back, clasping her hands together in her lap. "All right. Could we go back now?"

He wondered if she'd wanted to say *home* instead of *back*, but he didn't ask her. He signed the credit card slip for the waiter, and in five short minutes, they were on the road to Sunshine Gap. Emma remained silent for the first couple of miles, and then, as if the gathering darkness somehow made it easier for her, she began to talk.

"Since you're obviously not going to give up this marriage idea on you own, I think I should tell you the truth about my background. The only thing I ask from you is that you hear me out before you start asking questions. Will you do that for me?"

"Sure, Em, if that's what you want."

Her laugh carried a note of despair. "I don't want to do any of this, but it's not fair to let you go on thinking…what you're thinking, when there's a good chance I'll never be able to marry you." She gulped in a deep breath. "My mother died when I was two or three. I don't know for sure. I just know I was so young I don't remember her at all."

She paused to take another breath, and Cal wanted nothing more than to pull over to the side of the road and hold her, but he feared she would stop, and he desperately needed to hear this.

"Sometimes, I dream about being held very close to a soft breast. That's what I think it is in the dream, anyway. And I'm wrapped in a fluffy blanket, and there's a sweet, gentle voice talking to me, but I don't know if that was really my mother, or if it's just something I made up to convince myself it really happened. The only reason I know she died, is that I remember my father telling me that Mommy had gone to heaven.''

He drove on for another mile before she spoke again. "My father is also vague in my memory. I don't know what he did for a living. I just remember traveling around a lot and jumping on motel room beds. And being told to shut up a lot.''

Cal muttered a curse. Emma shot him such a quelling look, he clamped his mouth shut.

"My father wasn't mean to me," Emma said. "I don't remember that he was, anyway. I think he was really...sad a lot of the time. I don't know why. He just was, and I suppose caring for me by himself was pretty hard. One day when I was about four, he took me to a bus terminal in L.A., and he...left me there.''

Her voice had become very soft and very high, like that of a small child, and he could imagine what terror she must have felt. He wondered if her old man had had the decency to hang around and make sure some creep didn't get her.

"I remember running all over that big building, crying for my daddy, but I couldn't find him anywhere. A policeman finally found me and tried to help me find my dad, but I never saw him again.''

They passed the sign announcing the turnoff to Sunshine Gap. Emma asked him to drive on, and Cal grudgingly agreed. He'd much rather go home where he could see her face better and comfort her, but he respected her need to do this in her own way.

After taking another moment to collect herself, Emma continued. "The policeman turned me over to social services. I went into foster care, and stayed there until I turned eighteen. It wasn't terrible and nobody ever abused me. But nobody ever wanted to keep me, either.''

"Aw, Em," Cal whispered, aching for her.

"Shut up. I'm almost done. Then you can say whatever you want to say.''

"I'm sorry, darlin'.''

"I don't know what my real last name is," she said in a rush. "No one had ever bothered to teach it to me, and the authorities never found a birth certificate for me. I told you I was born in Texas, but I really don't have a clue about that, either. I chose Barnes because that was the name of the policeman who helped me at the bus terminal. I used to pretend he was my real daddy, and the other man who left me there was just a stranger who didn't mean anything to me."

They passed the sign announcing the turnoff for Meeteetse. She signaled him to turn around, and when he'd completed the maneuver, she went on.

"I made up a lot of wild, romantic stories about my family. You know, my parents were like Romeo and Juliet, and they were thrown out by their families. She died of some tragic disease and he left me at the depot because he knew he was dying of a broken heart. My imagination came up with other variations, too. My favorite was the one where I had really rich grandparents who were desperately looking for me."

"You never know, Em. There might've been—"

"No. I stopped the fantasies a long time ago, because ultimately, they hurt more than they helped. As far as the State of California was concerned, I was a baby Jane Doe, and that hasn't changed. I don't know when my birthday is. I don't know who I am or where I came from, and I have no hope that I'll ever know any of those things. In case you haven't figured this out, I am *not* the kind of woman a man like you is supposed to bring home to meet the folks."

Neither of them spoke until he parked behind his garage, and they walked into his kitchen. Tamping down his own churning emotions, Cal went to the refrigerator and took out a pitcher of iced tea, more to give himself a minute to calm down than because he really wanted a cold drink. He poured one for himself and one for Emma, shoving hers across the work peninsula with a more force than was strictly necessary.

"Are you done now?" he asked.

She extended one hand, palm up, and said, "Go ahead."

"All right." Taking a sip, he leaned back against the sink and crossed one foot over the other. "You got a raw deal from your dad and your childhood stunk to high heaven. It breaks my heart to think of you being a little girl, all alone and scared like that, when somebody should've been cuddling you and loving you. But I am *not* feeling sorry for you now, Emma."

"Good," she said, clearly not believing him.

He refused to let her sucker him into a fight. It would be the perfect excuse for her to run away again, and he would be damned if he would give her that.

"I mean it," he said. "You're an incredibly strong person. You've survived in spite of terrible odds, which is more than a lot of kids would have done. Shoot you've not only survived, you've grown into a wonderful, talented, beautiful woman who is kind and compassionate and perfectly capable of taking care of herself."

"Oh, please—"

"No, dammit. You've had your turn. Now it's mine. I'm not the only one in Sunshine Gap who loves you, Emma. You've made a lot of other friends here, and once your shop really gets off the ground, you'll make more money than I do."

"What's your point?"

"My point is that, none of what you told me tonight changed my feelings for you one bit. You can make me and my family out to be snobs if you want, but we're not that shallow. We judge some animals on their bloodlines for breeding purposes, but we judge people by their integrity and the skills they can contribute to the community. You've got more than your share of both. And if my crazy parents ever come home from their grand trip around the world, I will be damn proud to introduce you to them as my wife.''

"Cal, don't.''

"No, Emma, *you* don't. You've got it all laid out so nice and neat in your head. Because other people didn't love you the way you needed to be loved, you've decided that nobody ever will. That's bull. I *love* you, dammit.''

"You'll get over it.''

"That's bull, too.''

"Even if you and I could make this work, I would never fit in with your family. I've met them. I've been around them. And I know it's such a perfect family...your relationships are so tightly interwoven, I'd only mess everything up—''

"My family's not perfect, Em. Didn't you read Marsh's whole script?'' She shook her head and he pushed on. "Ol' Riley McBride, our great founder, was nothing but a gunslinger who was probably wanted in three or four states. His wife Elizabeth grew up being dragged from one mining camp to the next. She was hardly a great role model for being a lady, if you know what I mean. There's not a McBride alive who would judge you. In fact, half of 'em already love you, and they already told me so.''

All this time, she hadn't shed one tear. While she stood there, staring at him from eyes with no hope, tears welled up and trickled down her face. When she finally spoke, her voice cracked. "Sometimes people like me at first. I try really hard to do what I'm supposed to do. But there always comes a time when somebody has to say, 'It's over, now. It's time for Emma to move on.'''

"That won't happen here,'' he said.

"Oh, yeah? Well, I happen to think that's bull, McBride. The only thing that's ever been permanent in my life is losing all the people I love. And I won't go through that again.''

She swiped roughly at her eyes with the backs of her hands. "Now I'm the one who decides when it's time for me to move on. I'm the one who leaves, not the one who gets left behind. And I wish to hell that I'd never sold Mama because I can't stay here, and I can't marry you.''

Cal couldn't take any more of not holding her while she wept. He crossed the room and gathered her into his arms, ignoring her weak attempts to shove him away. ''It's okay, darlin'. Everything's gonna be okay.''

With a gut-wrenching sigh, she lay her head against his shoulder and allowed him to rock her and stroke her back. He lost track of time and everything else but Emma. She reminded him of a wounded robin he'd found when he was a kid.

He could still feel the frantic beat of that little bird's heart against his palm. He'd doctored it up the best he could, and somehow, the bird had survived. He'd become so attached to it, he'd wanted to keep it forever. But it had been so sad and dejected, he'd realized he had to let it go or watch it die.

He was very much afraid that the same principle applied to Emma. Set her free or watch her die inside.

''What do you want to do now, Emma?''

''I have to leave.''

''All right, darlin'.''

She went on as if he hadn't spoken. ''What we've had has been the most intense, wonderful and exciting thing that's ever happened to me. You're the dearest man I've ever known, and I thought that with you, I could try this one more time. And I do love you, Cal, but I'm so afraid I'll disappoint you somehow, and I think I would die if you ever turned away from me, too.''

''I know,'' he murmured.

''So I'm going to move in to the house at the shop. I'll fulfill the commitments I've made, but then I'll be moving on.''

''All right. We'll get started on that in the morning.''

She raised tear-filled eyes to meet his. ''I'm so sorry,

Cal. I never meant to hurt you. I just wanted a little time with you.''

"It's not your fault, sweetheart. You tried to tell me how you felt, and I didn't listen. I've put us both through a lot of pain, and I'm sorry for that. I'll do whatever I can, to help you get things straightened out.''

"No thanks," she said. "I can do it myself.''

Pulling away, she gave him the saddest smile he'd ever seen. Then her chin came up and her shoulders went back and he saw a hint of the biker attitude flicker across her face. Watching her reminded him of putting on football pads when he'd played tight end for the high school team.

What part of Emma did that don't-mess-with-me attitude protect? The terrified, abandoned four-year-old? The little girl who dreamed of rich grandparents who would give her the home her parents should have provided for her? Or the lonely, isolated woman who saw herself as unwanted and unlovable? Or maybe all three?

Over the next week Cal spent a lot of time thinking about that question. There was another question that nagged at him when the first one gave him a moment's rest. What would it take to convince Emma that her heart was safe with him? That his feelings really wouldn't change and he would never tell her it was time to move on.

He'd tried words, but they hadn't worked. He didn't blame Emma for that. Talk was always cheap, and some people promised kids all kinds of things in order to make them behave. So what could he do to *show* Emma he really was willing to commit himself to her for a lifetime?

She moved into the little house beside her shop the next day. Her friends opened their attics to her, providing her with the essentials she needed to live on her own. Days passed, but she never set foot in Cal's Place, or called him. He kept track of her by eavesdropping on Sylvia's loud conversations with customers and other employees.

All reports said Emma was okay and working real hard, but he also noticed an occasional hesitation in a speaker's voice that told him something wasn't quite right. When he finally swallowed his pride and asked Sylvia straight out, she gave him a long, hard look. Her strident voice practically vibrated with accusation.

"What do *you* care?" she asked. "You haven't lifted a finger to help her since—"

"She told me to butt out," Cal said. "She doesn't want me to help her."

Her expression softened. "Oh. Like that is it?"

"Yeah. So what's wrong? She's not taking care of herself, is she?"

"Aw, she's fine, Cal. That little gal's tougher than whang leather. She's just workin' awful hard is all. It's like she's driven, you know?"

"Yeah, I do. Thanks, Syl."

Cal walked back to his office, sat in his chair and propped the heels of his boots on top of his desk. He knew Emma was driven, all right, and he knew what was driving her. The need to get away from him. And he'd made it practically impossible for her to do it.

He'd encouraged her to get into this new business from the day she'd fixed Sylvia's old heap. He'd helped her sell the motorcycle and spend a big chunk of the resulting cash on inventory and tools she would never want or need for any other purpose than to work on engines. None of that would have mattered if she still wanted to stay in the Gap, or if she wanted to marry him.

But now? The poor woman probably felt like some kind of an indentured servant. She'd have to work here for a long time to make enough money to provide her with a stake to get back to California. Without ever intending to cause her more pain and trouble, he'd trapped her in Wyoming, just like he'd trapped his little wounded robin. And like that little robin, wouldn't she beat herself half to death, trying to get back her freedom?

Swearing under his breath, he swung his feet to the floor, gathered up his financial papers and told Sylvia she was in

charge again until further notice. Then he went home, borrowed a pickup from a neighbor who could actually keep
his mouth shut and headed for Cody.

After two hours with a banker who would never breathe
a word of what he had done to anyone from Sunshine Gap
or anywhere else, Cal had a new mortgage on his building
and a letter of credit that would get him what he wanted.
Grabbing a hamburger at a fast-food joint, he set off for
Billings.

The Harley-Davidson dealership still had her bike, thank
God for small favors. After an hour's worth of wrangling,
Cal bought her back and added on the new leather gear
Emma would need, as well as a new helmet. Thousands of
dollars poorer, he stepped outside, exhaled a deep sigh and
looked around for a moment so his heart would stop dou-
ble-clutching over what he was doing to his own financial
future.

Hell, it didn't matter. He still had Cal's Place, his house
and his share of the Flying M, so he was hardly destitute.
If Emma wouldn't have him, he wouldn't have to put any
kids through college or pay for any fancy weddings or an-
niversary parties. Damn, if only he could figure out a way
to get through to her.

A car horn honked somewhere down the street to the
west. He glanced in that direction and, for the first time
since Emma had left him, he smiled and meant it. Tipping
his Stetson hat farther back on his head, he climbed into
the pickup with the bike already loaded into the back and
made a left turn toward the flashing, neon sign that advertised the answer he'd been wracking his brain so hard to
find.

Tattoos. No Waiting.

Chapter Sixteen

Emma climbed back onto the step stool, wiped the back of one wrist across her sweaty forehead and leaned down into the open hood of George Pierson's ancient Packard automobile. She could hardly believe he was still driving it as his primary form of transportation. This was no lovingly restored classic car; it was just an old heap that hadn't seen much tender loving care in its life.

Kind of like George himself, she suspected. But his problems were none of her business. As cranky as he was, he'd undoubtedly brought most of them down on himself, and she was going to leave here as soon as she could. It was not her job to take care of him.

She shouldn't even like the wacky old geezer, but she did. He was so gruff, half the people in town were scared of him, but she had his number and he darn well knew it. They were two of a kind, both lonely as hell and putting up the best fronts they could manage. Fooled most of the people, most of the time.

But it hadn't fooled Cal.

Unbidden and unwanted, her conscience had been talking to her for over a week now. Why it had to dwell on Cal McBride, she couldn't begin to imagine, but that was all the little voice wanted to discuss. If it didn't let up soon, she wasn't sure what she would do.

Still, now that she'd had enough time and distance to put the last awful evening they'd spent together into perspective, she couldn't deny that the little voice in her head might have said a few things she should think about.

Such as, she was still madly in love with Cal. Considering the amount of emotional baggage she'd dumped on him all at once, he'd been amazingly supportive and understanding. And every time she thought about him now, she had a sinking sensation in the pit of her stomach that she'd made a terrible mistake in refusing his proposal with such finality.

He'd rushed her. He'd overwhelmed her. But he'd loved her, too. Far more than anyone else ever had done.

Finally getting all of that stuff out into the open had left her drained of energy and emotion, but after a few days, she'd started to feel better, lighter and stronger. Unbelievably stronger. Sometimes, she even felt almost peaceful about her background now. The urge to pick up the phone or drop by Cal's Place to say hi was a continual battle she fought with herself.

At this point, the only thing holding her back was sheer cowardice. She didn't know how to ask him for another chance. After the way she'd shoved him out of her life, she wasn't entirely certain she deserved another chance.

But oh, how she missed him.

For a second, she heard a low, throaty rumble that sounded like…no, she was only imagining it. It must be an airplane or maybe she was hallucinating. No, darn it. She did hear it, it was coming closer and it sounded exactly like Mama.

Straightening, she tossed her wrench onto the workbench

behind her and grabbed the rag she tucked into her back pocket to wipe the grease off her hands. She could see a dust cloud coming up her lane now, and hear other engines, and her heart kicked into a higher gear. It couldn't be Cal. But who else would be crazy enough to—

Oh, Lord. It *was* Cal and he *was* riding Mama and he looked absolutely wonderful. And unless she was sadly mistaken, those pickups rolling in behind him were the rest of the McBrides circling their damn wagons. She wondered if that meant they thought Cal was in trouble, or if she was. She felt a little silly standing up here on her step stool, but for the life of her, she couldn't make her feet go anywhere.

Cal stopped Mama barely ten feet away from her. The members of his family climbed out of their rigs and lined up in a semicircle behind him. They all grinned or winked at her behind Cal's back. She thought that meant she wasn't the one in trouble, and seeing them all standing there behind Cal, she hoped she was right. They were an impressive group of people.

Cal pulled Mama back onto her kickstand, then turned to face her. "Hello, Emma."

"Cal," she said with a nod. "What are you doing here?"

He came forward a couple of steps, then stopped with his feet spread apart and his hands propped on his narrow hips. "I've come to make amends with you and set you straight about a couple of things."

"All right."

He hesitated, as if he hadn't expected her to listen to him, and now he didn't know where to start. She felt sad about that, and sad that he looked so unhappy and so tired.

"Okay," he said. "First off, I have to admit that I intentionally set you up to meet lots of people and put down roots in Sunshine Gap. I wanted you to stay here for the community's sake as well as my own. This whole town needs you, Emma, and not just for your mechanical skills."

"I don't understand what you're saying."

He shoved his hands down into his front jeans pockets

and gave her half-hearted shrug. "We need your fresh ideas and your enthusiasm and your drive to get things done. Your incredible drive and energy in pulling this shop together has set a fire under a lot of folks to spiff things up and fix things and make the Gap a nicer place to live."

"I didn't have anything to do with that."

"Yeah, you really did."

"Get on with it, Cal," Jake called.

"Shut up, Jake," Cal called back, seeming unruffled by the interruption. His gaze remained focused on her face with that unnerving intensity she'd dreamed about, night after night.

"Truth is, Em, I helped you get into this situation because I wanted you to stay here for me. But I never meant to take away your freedom to leave. So, I got your bike back for you. Somebody here has all the leather gear you used to wear, and I've got a couple hundred bucks set aside for you to buy some new boots. If you want to go back to California, I'll help you return your excess parts, clean out the shop and settle up with any customers you haven't been able to get to yet."

"I don't know what to say," Emma said.

"Come on, Cal," Alex said with a smirk. "Hurry up and get to the good part."

This time he turned around and jabbed his index finger at the snickering crowd behind him, "You can all be uninvited, you know. When I need your help, I'll ask. Until then, zip your dang lips."

Emma desperately wanted to laugh, but he clearly was doing the best he could under difficult circumstances, and she didn't want to add to his stress. He turned back to face her, squaring his shoulders like a gunslinger getting ready to draw his six-shooter.

"Here's the deal. You can leave any time you want, or you can stay for as long as you want without any hassle from me. But, for the record, I want you to know I'm still in love with you. My proposal still stands.'' He pointed at his vest pocket and grinned a little. ''And I've still got your ring right here in my pocket.''

''Oh, Cal,'' Emma murmured.

''Of course, we can take our time about putting it on your finger, sweetheart. I know the idea of marrying me scares you to death, so I brought the family along to let them try to ease some of your fears.''

He was so earnest, she wanted to grab him and kiss him until he said ''uncle.'' Then he glanced back over his shoulder and called, ''You guys willing to accept her as a McBride?''

Their thundering chorus of ''Hell, yes!'' indicated a certain amount of rehearsal must have gone into it.

Smiling at her, Jake stepped forward. ''We'd love to have you join us, Emma, unless you don't like *us* all that much. Some folks don't, you know.''

''What're you talkin' about?'' Dillon demanded. ''We're not too ugly or too loud for Emma, are we hon?''

''Well, maybe we're just a little too country,'' Grace suggested. ''Not quite civilized enough?''

''It's not any of that,'' Alex said with laugh. ''I'll bet she doesn't like cops. Will you marry Cal if we get rid of Zack?''

''She likes me,'' Zack said indignantly. ''If she marries Cal, and keeps him under control, I'll even let her ride my horses.'' He gave her a broad wink and added, ''We'll do whatever we can to make you feel at home with us, Emma.''

Marsh stuck his hands into his back pockets and grinned wickedly. ''In my humble opinion, Emma, you would bring a huge dose of class to this bunch of renegades. I say we get rid of Cal and keep you.''

"Oh, thanks a chunk, Marsh. I knew I could count on you for support," Cal grumbled.

Emma felt tears leaking down her face, and feared that if these crazy McBrides didn't stop, she might cause a flash flood. Turning on Cal, she said, "How could you involve all of them?"

"How could I not?" he said with a laugh. "Darlin', they're part of the package. You marry one McBride, the rest of them will be your sisters and brothers, too. Whether you like it or not, you'll get adopted right into the litter, and you can make up any rules you want as you go along. That's what we all do."

"We can always use another sister," Alex called.

Nolan Larson put his arm around Alex. "They're really not as bad as they seem sometimes, Emma. And Lori and I have started a support group for new in-laws. We'd be happy if you'd join."

"All right, all right," Cal said, holding up his hands in a referee's time-out sign. "You've helped about all I can stand for now. Pipe down back there."

Turning back to Emma, he let out a sigh. "I *love* you, Emma Barnes. I know we've still got a lot to learn about each other, but we've already been through some bad times together and it hasn't changed the way I feel about you. Nothing ever will."

"How do you know that?" she asked, hating herself for needing more reassurance after all of this, but needing it, anyway.

"Well if they do change, I've sure made one hell of a big mistake."

There was a reckless glitter in his eyes that made her nervous. "What do you mean?"

He reached inside the neck of his shirt and pulled out a chain with a coin hanging on it. "Guys out here don't usually wear necklaces, do we fellas?" His brothers and male cousins heartily agreed with his statement. Cal continued, "But here I am wearing one, and you know what it is? It's that lucky penny I always carried around in my vest pocket. You know where I got it?"

Emma shook her head. It looked like any other penny to her.

"This is the tip you left me the day I threw you out of my bar. Remember that?"

She grinned and nodded.

He grinned back at her. "Yeah, I thought so. Well, I've kept it ever since, because even then, I knew you were going to change my life. You've made it a hundred times better."

"Oh, Cal."

"Oh, Emma." His grin stretched clear across his face. "That's just the beginning."

Noting the intensified glitter in his eyes, she said, "Cal, what have you done?"

"This." He grabbed the front of his shirt with both hands and popped the snaps so hard they sounded like firecrackers in the sudden silence. And there, right in the middle of his gorgeous chest, the insane man had a tattoo the size of baseball.

The design was an adorable, musclebound male skunk with a decidedly lustful gleam in his eyes and a long, fluffy striped tail. In his front paws, he held a bright red heart with "Emma" written across the front of it. Emma was so stunned by what he'd done, she didn't know whether to laugh or cry. He turned around and showed his family.

"Holy Moses, would you get a load of that?" Dillon said.

"Why would he pick a skunk?" Grace asked.

Cal turned back around and walked closer to Emma. "It's real, darlin', and it's permanent. I'm branded like a bull calf, and it's your brand I'm wearing. I'll never find another woman who'll want me now, but I don't care. The only woman I'm ever gonna want is you."

Biting her lower lips to keep from sobbing uncontrollably, Emma could only shake her head at him.

"Well?" he said. "Don't you have anything you want to say?"

She looked deeply into those luscious dark eyes of his and suddenly, her tears dried themselves and her heart simply opened up. Smiling, she climbed off the step stool and walked right up to him. "Yeah, I've got something to say. Let's see that ring."

He let out an explosive sigh, as if he'd been holding his breath. Then he scooped her into a bear hug and kissed her, and kissed her, and kissed her some more. Her heartbeat boomed in her ears, but somewhere in the background she heard the others talking.

"Isn't she just a kick?"

"Yeah. I still don't get what that skunk's all about, but she'll sure keep Cal on his toes."

"She's gonna be real good for him."

"Oh, she's gonna fit in just fine. Maybe she was one of us in another life. Ever think about stuff like that?"

If he didn't stop kissing her soon, she was going to pass out. She kicked her feet and pounded on his shoulder until he finally set her back down. She could see his fingers trembling as he fumbled for his vest pocket. At last he found it, poked around inside it with two fingers and came up with an engagement ring, sporting a beautiful, clear, burgundy-colored stone.

The other McBrides laughed and cheered, whistled and stomped and generally made nuisances of themselves. Fearing she would miss some tender word or gesture from Cal with all the noise they were making, Emma glared over her shoulder at them.

"What're *you* bozos looking at? Haven't you ever seen a couple get engaged before?"

Cal's laughter boomed off the rafters of her shop. He swept her into another embrace, then turned her to face his family with obvious pride. "That's *my* gal," he said. "Thanks for your help, gang, but now if you don't mind, we could use a little privacy."

* * * * *

Don't miss the next exciting story in the
HEARTS OF WYOMING *miniseries.*

In December 1999,
WYOMING WILDCAT *features Grace McBride—and the mesmerizing man who steals her heart...*

coming to you only from
Silhouette Special Edition.

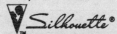

If you enjoyed what you just read,
then we've got an offer you can't resist!

Take 2 bestselling love stories FREE!
Plus get a FREE surprise gift!

Clip this page and mail it to Silhouette Reader Service™

IN U.S.A.	IN CANADA
3010 Walden Ave.	P.O. Box 609
P.O. Box 1867	Fort Erie, Ontario
Buffalo, N.Y. 14240-1867	L2A 5X3

YES! Please send me 2 free Silhouette Special Edition® novels and my free surprise gift. Then send me 6 brand-new novels every month, which I will receive months before they're available in stores. In the U.S.A., bill me at the bargain price of $3.57 plus 25¢ delivery per book and applicable sales tax, if any*. In Canada, bill me at the bargain price of $3.96 plus 25¢ delivery per book and applicable taxes**. That's the complete price and a savings of over 10% off the cover prices—what a great deal! I understand that accepting the 2 free books and gift places me under no obligation ever to buy any books. I can always return a shipment and cancel at any time. Even if I never buy another book from Silhouette, the 2 free books and gift are mine to keep forever. So why not take us up on our invitation. You'll be glad you did!

235 SEN CNFD
335 SEN CNFE

Name	(PLEASE PRINT)	
Address	Apt.#	
City	State/Prov.	Zip/Postal Code

* Terms and prices subject to change without notice. Sales tax applicable in N.Y.
** Canadian residents will be charged applicable provincial taxes and GST.
   All orders subject to approval. Offer limited to one per household.
   ® are registered trademarks of Harlequin Enterprises Limited.

*In bestselling author **Joan Elliott Pickart's** engaging
new series, three bachelor friends have bet that
marriage and family will never be a part of their lives.
But they'll learn* never *to bet against love....*

TAMING TALL, DARK BRANDON
Desire #1223, June 1999
Brandon Hamilton had long ago given up on the idea of
home, hearth and babies. But when he meets stubborn beauty
Andrea Cunningham, he finds himself in danger of being
thoroughly and irrevocably tamed....

THE IRRESISTIBLE MR. SINCLAIR
Special Edition #1256, July 1999
Taylor Sinclair believes marriage is for fools, but he
reconsiders when he falls for Janice Jennings—a secretly
stunning woman who hides behind a frumpy disguise. A
barrier Taylor vows to breach...

THE MOST ELIGIBLE M.D.
Special Edition #1262, August 1999
She's a woman without a past. He's a man without a future.
Still, **Dr. Ben Rizzoli** cannot quell his passion for the delicate
amnesiac who's made him live and love—and long for the
family he believes he can never have....

*Don't miss **Joan Elliott Pickart's** newest series,
The Bachelor Bet— in Silhouette Desire
and Silhouette Special Edition!*
Available at your favorite retail outlet.

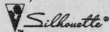

The combination of physical attraction and danger can be explosive!

Coming in July 1999
three steamy romances together in one book

HOT PURSUIT

by bestselling authors
JOAN JOHNSTON
ANNE STUART
MALLORY RUSH

Joan Johnston—A WOLF IN SHEEP'S CLOTHING
The Hazards and the Alistairs had been feuding for generations, so when Harriet Alistair laid claim to her great-uncle's ranch, Nathan Hazard was at his ornery worst. But then he saw her and figured it was time to turn on the charm, forgive, forget…and seduce?

Anne Stuart—THE SOLDIER & THE BABY
What could possibly bring together a hard-living, bare-chested soldier and a devout novice? At first, it was an innocent baby…and then it was a passion hotter than the simmering jungle they had to escape from.

Mallory Rush—LOVE SLAVE
Rand Slick hired Rachel Tinsdale to infiltrate the dark business of white slavery. It was a risky assignment, Rachel knew. But even more dangerous was her aching desire for her sexy, shadowy client….

Available at your favorite retail outlet.

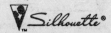

Look us up on-line at: http://www.romance.net

PSBR799

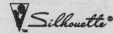

This August 1999, the legend continues in Jacobsville

DIANA PALMER

LOVE WITH A LONG, TALL TEXAN

A trio of brand-new short stories featuring three irresistible Long, Tall Texans

GUY FENTON, LUKE CRAIG and CHRISTOPHER DEVERELL...

This August 1999, Silhouette brings readers an extra-special collection for Diana Palmer's legions of fans. Diana spins three unforgettable stories of love—Texas-style! Featuring the men you can't get enough of from the wonderful town of Jacobsville, this collection is a treasure for all fans!

They grow 'em tall in the saddle in Jacobsville—and they're the best-looking, sweetest-talking men to be found in the entire Lone Star state. They are proud, hardworking men of steel and it will take the perfect woman to melt their hearts!

Don't miss this collection of original Long, Tall Texans stories...available in August 1999 at your favorite retail outlet.